REGENCY GLAD TIDINGS

Carla Kelly

CAMEL PRESS

Kenmore, WA

CAMEL PRESS

Camel Press books published by Epicenter Press

Epicenter Press
6524 NE 181st St. Suite 2
Kenmore, WA 98028.
www.Epicenterpress.com
www.Coffeetownpress.com
www.Camelpress.com

For more information go to: www.Epicenterpress.com
Author's website: www.carlakellyauthor.com

First published by Signet, an imprint of New American Library, a division of Penguin Putnam Inc.

ISBN: 9781684922222 (trade paper)
ISBN: 9781684922239 (ebook)

LOC: Applied

Dedication

To my friend, Crescent Wells. Wishing you all things merry!

Books by Carla Kelly

Fiction

Daughter of Fortune

Summer Campaign

Miss Chartley's Guided Tour

Marian's Christmas Wish

Mrs. McVinnie's London Season

Libby's London Merchant

Miss Grimsley's Oxford Career

Miss Billings Treads the Boards

Miss Milton Speaks Her Mind

Miss Wittier Makes a List

Mrs. Drew Plays Her Hand

Reforming Lord Ragsdale

The Lady's Companion

With This Ring

One Good Turn

The Wedding Journey

Here's to the Ladies: Stories of the
    Frontier Army

Beau Crusoe

Marrying the Captain

The Surgeon's Lady

Marrying the Royal Marine

The Admiral's Penniless Bride

Borrowed Light

Enduring Light

Coming Home for Christmas: The
    Holiday Stories

Regency Christmas Gifts

Season's Regency Greetings

Marriage of Mercy

My Loving Vigil Keeping

Double Cross

Marco and the Devil's Bargain

Paloma and the Horse Traders

Star in the Meadow

Unlikely Master Genius

Unlikely Spy Catchers

Safe Passage

Softly Falling

One Step Enough

Courting Carrie in Wonderland

A Regency Royal Navy Christmas

Unlikely Heroes

A Hopeful Christmas

The Necklace

Her Smile

When We Meet Again

The Unlikely Gunwharf Rats

A Naval Surgeon to Fight For

HOLLY AND IVY

Chapter One

Question of the year for Mr. Jacob Frost, surgeon in the British Army: When does a war end? The guns had been silent since July of the Year of Our Lord 1815, but that wasn't the conclusion of Jake's war, oh no. Others could pack up with their regiments that had seen hard warfare in the Peninsula since 1809 and return to parades, honors and families.

This was not war's end for the Medical Corps...never the Medical Corps. Maybe earlier in the war Jake might have felt sorry for himself to miss out on returning with the regiment, but he had matured since then, forced into maturity by constant, noisy warfare. If he had learned anything from Napoleon beyond hatred, it was endurance.

The best thing about this November in peaceful Belgium? Silence. There was the usual hospital ward noise, but the guns that filled those hospitals were still now, as peace covered Europe for the first time in a generation. Napoleon's "lovely daughters" had been spiked and sent to foundries to be melted down. Napoleon himself was on his way to an exile much farther away than mere Elba. At least that was the rumor.

Jake counted his blessings. One was the satisfying sight of more empty beds, not because men were dying now, or even that over-eager commanders had sent the slightly better ones back to their companies to die there before they were well enough to die in battle. Many of these slightly better lads were on their way home to Yorkshire, or Dorset, or any number of villages and shires that despaired of ever seeing them again.

Some remained. Many of these warriors would never leave Belgium, some to be tended in loving silence by nuns devoting their own lives to patients wandering in that shadowland between life and death. It pained Jake mightily to write "comatose" on those charts. He was already inured to the fact that for the rest of his life, he would wonder if there was something more he could have done for those nearly dead/not quite alive soldiers.

Others – professional soldiers – waited more or less impatiently for their own orders to come through. "Maybe we'll be posted to Canada," was a common wish. Jake used to wonder why Canada. He decided Canada was a choice destination because it was far away from noisy Europe. No one ever heard much about it, beyond freezing winters.

Surgeons and physicians, Jake Frost among them, waited for signatures on their letters requesting release from the British Army that had owned them until war's end. They were not commissioned officers as such, but they were in the Medical Corps until the end, no matter how long. For years, Europe had danced to Napoleon's tune, but now the dance was over.

The British Army physicians still in Belgium months after Waterloo had trotted to that gavotte. Their dance cards had been full to overflowing, and now they wanted to leave the party. One surgeon broke down and cried in the ward when his release letter came back to him approved and signed. The other doctors cheered. Waiting for that release letter became something not to speak about, as if it would cast an evil spell on the ones who waited.

Jake had formerly been the philosophical sort, happy for those on whom Dame Fortune smiled. The son of a vicar in a small Yorkshire parish, he knew it was some sort of sin to wish ill on those lucky "early-outers," as they came to be known. In truth, what was his hurry? His father had died mid-sermon six years ago, when the British Army was experiencing its own peril of retreat towards the Spanish coast at Corunna. When Jake got the news, he was too busy to mourn, which Papa probably would have considered a sin, anyway. It was hard to tell with Papa.

Gentle Mama had survived until last year, during the triumph that was Toulouse and the Corsican Beast's first exile to Elba. Jake missed her letters most of all, and their hearty good cheer that buoyed him up as men died around him. Jake's older brother was a minor official in the East India Tea Company and living in Benares. Jake never felt the loss. There was no sorrow that he never got a letter from remote India. Truth to tell, Abner Frost had always bullied his younger brothers. Jake's sister Amelia had followed her ambitious husband to Massachusetts, America. Little Ben died of a wasting disease at home.

Jake Frost was alone, but that never meant he had no plans. He had always been too busy to spend much of his salary, so there was enough and to spare to start a practice in some small Yorkshire village, because he did love and miss the Dales.

Now it was mid-November. He was almost alone in this convent/hospital; his former cheerful attitude hardened now into something he didn't like, but could abolish if he tried. His letter had not been endorsed and countersigned, releasing him from medical bondage to the British Army. Even the nuns were starting to regard him with pity. He thought he knew the problem, but was unsure of a remedy. He could ask the nuns to pray for his exit, but all those years of fighting and dying had made him wary of the Lord Almighty, who obviously played favorites. Better the nuns didn't know that.

Like too many problems, Dame Experience nudged his shoulder to remind him his current dilemma began with the less competent officers who bought their commissions. General Sir David Baldwin, a minor baronet with a modest amount of wealth, was one. In actual fact, Sir David had proved to be a reasonably good commander of the Yorkshire Fifth Foot. His blind side, and what rendered him a threat to Jake, was his son and ADC Captain George Baldwin, who still lay injured…well, sort of injured.

To refer to George Baldwin as injured would be an exaggeration. Hypochondria was his disease of choice. He had endured a minor flesh wound at Mont St. Jean, generally known now as Waterloo. A French ball had entered and quickly exited his right calf when

Captain Baldwin was running away to hide in the center of the square formed to ward off approaching French cavalry.

When the battle finally ended, Baldwin was dropped at Surgeon Frost's aid station, literally dropped there by Fifth Foot soldiers who had endured that fool as long as they could bear it. There were seriously wounded men in the overloaded aid station who needed Frost's ministrations. Sadly, but true to form, General Baldwin ordered him to treat his son first, making George Baldwin Jake Frost's problem. This also put a period to Jake's ordinary good will.

After years of dealing with both father and son, Jake knew which side his hard bread was buttered on. He treated Captain Baldwin promptly and efficiently, then quickly returned to the serious business of dealing with the truly injured, which were literally piled up at the forward station. He forgot Captain Baldwin.

That was his mistake. Captain Baldwin became Jake's cross to bear. Here it was, months and months later, and still Captain Baldwin languished and moaned in the best room in the Convent of the Sacred Heart, where Jake and others of his profession continued their medical care among those who really needed it.

Knowing full well that George Baldwin could leave anytime he wanted––as Jake had gently reminded him several times––Jake knew better than to appeal to the captain's better nature, because he had none. He tried the route of Cupid next. "Sir, haven't I heard that you have a fiancée back in Yorkshire?" he asked one morning, when he had been called upon yet again to clean the captain's now non-existent wound. "Surely she is eager to see you." *Far more than I,* was his personal opinion, wisely left unsaid.

George Baldwin tossed his head from side to side. "She wouldn't be able to bear the strain of seeing me in this low state," he managed to gasp out, before faking a faint. He opened his eyes quickly enough and glared at the physician, when Jake held an ammonia pad under his nose.

"I am certain she would be delighted to see you, Captain Baldwin," Jake said. "I mean, who wouldn't? You're a war hero." *I will have to wash my mouth out for saying such a lie,* Jake thought, *but I am desperate.*

There the matter stood, until Jake's own desperation to be rid of this useless human baggage shouldered aside his typical reluctance to rock a boat too hard. He knew General Sir David Baldwin liked to make his own stately way amongst his troops, and waylaid him one morning.

"Sir David, I have been wondering when you will sign my release from my commission," he said, after an inspection that had included a number of Yorkshire Fifth Foot who were preparing to leave Belgium in a rumored troop transport waiting in Antwerp. "The wars are over and Napoleon has been defeated. I have fulfilled all that is required of me, except for your endorsement and signature."

"My own son is still your patient," the general reminded him.

"He has had my permission to rejoin his regiment and return to England for more than a month now, sir," Jake replied, trying to be as obsequious as possible without actually kissing the man's hairy bum. "I believe it has been longer, sir. I am certain he can accompany *you* home to Yorkshire with no ill effects."

"A bit premature, wouldn't you say?"

"Actually, he's been ready for months, Sir David," Jake repeated, already feeling desperation sweat on his back.

"He is still suffering," General Baldwin said with some serenity. "So he tells me. As you were, Mr. Frost."

So that's how he was, until even the calmest of natures rebelled and the worm turned. That was when Jake knew it was time to sidle around his immediate commander. He fired off a letter to Lord Wellington himself, requesting his service be abrogated, which it was promptly, accompanied by a scrawled note of congratulations from the great man himself. "'My ADC reminds me that you were ever faithful all across Spain and up to Mont St. Jean,'" he wrote, which pleased Jake and almost made up for General Sir David's serene denial of his release.

Still General Baldwin refused to agree to Jake's release. "How can he hold up my release?" Jake fumed to a fellow physician who was even now packing, the traitor. "The wars are over, but I'm a hostage."

"And a little over-dramatic, Jake?"

Perhaps, perhaps. "I suppose," he admitted, "but Whittaker, have you ever had that patient who simply wouldn't go away?"

"Aye, laddie. You'll survive."

He did. He minded his mouth, knowing better than to swear fluently in several languages around the nuns. *Merde*, uttered softly, became his current password, in a world where passwords had become unnecessary.

He had nearly resigned himself to taking Orders and becoming a Dominican--he hadn't found the time to bed a woman in ages-- when some evidence of glacial movement became apparent. It came in the form of the Bishop of Brussels, who visited the convent then issued an ultimatum to General Baldwin, a lapsed member of the Anglican Church, whose only god was money and acclaim, he being short on both.

Jake only learned of it when the general paid his daily visit to his son, who still languished in a bed--long gone were the iron cots--even though only the faintest scar remained of his wound. The general stood over his son and shook his head. "Poor, poor boy," he said, "I fear we must chance a trip across the channel with you."

Jake could have fallen down in gratitude, except that years in the thrall of this general and his prissy offspring had shown the uselessness of drama among the self-centered. He merely crossed his fingers under the chart in his hands.

The general turned to him. "You, Surgeon Frost, will of course accompany him to my manor in Brierton, near Kirkby."

Captain Hypochondria is perfectly capable of finding his way home, Jake wanted to say, but this was the closest he had come to escape so he merely nodded. "I'll be happy to take him home," even came from Jake's mouth.

"And remain there with him through the end of the year," the general added. "I will arrive at my estate before Christmas."

In a pig's eye, Jake thought. "Certainly, Sir David."

Chapter Two

They embarked from Antwerp on November 5, sailing down the majestic River Scheldt to its salty, wide mouth that emptied them into the North Sea, and then across the English Channel.

It was a stormy crossing, with Surgeon Frost, two other surgeons and assorted stewards in charge of the remaining soldiers from the Brussels hospitals who were probably as fit as they were going to be, considering. It chafed him to also escort Captain Baldwin, who was more robust than nearly anyone on board, including the doctors. The only thing that made Baldwin's stifling presence endurable was that the medical crew knew his complaints and groans were fictitious.

"Sir, if he says, 'When you get a moment, please bring me a headache powder,' one more time, I swear I will carry him across the deck and toss him overboard," Jake's favorite hospital steward said. The man wasn't many inches beyond five feet, but Jake understood the desperation in his voice, and thought perhaps he could do it.

"Patience, Douglas," was his only comment. "Remember that you are heading soon to Canada with fellow hospital stewards. I still have to lug this…this boat anchor home to Yorkshire. I must admit I envy your destination."

"I thank you for your endorsement, sir," Douglas said. "I wish you could come along."

You have no idea, Jake thought. "Someone has to get Captain Baldwin to Brierton," he said, striving for serenity.

Thanks to a strong stomach, Jake had no *mal de mer*. Neither did Captain Baldwin, except that the man moaned and tossed his head when anyone came within earshot, stretching out a feeble hand and weakly asking for a basin. "You have deserted me," he managed to gasp when Jake came near. "I am sinking."

If only, Jake thought, tired of the man. "It's no desertion. There is a more sick man than you are on board, a corporal in your own Fifth Foot."

"You mean you are truly abandoning me?" the captain asked, nothing in his voice sounding weak now. His eyes narrowed into mean little slits. "For a corporal?"

Deep breath, Jake, he told himself. *Deep breath*. "No, sir. I am merely assisting someone far more ill than you are. Look around you. There is a basin to puke in. Over there is water, wine, and crackers suitable for someone troubled with sea sickness."

"But I require beef roast with drippings and potatoes," Captain Baldwin tried again. "You know how I like it, lightly seared, then allowed to stew in its juice."

"Excuse me, please. There is someone actually sick," Jake said and left the captain to stew in *his* juice.

He spent most of the short crossing with the corporal, who never complained of his festering leg wound that never healed, then had never complained when Jake was forced to amputate higher up a month ago. During the crossing, Jake stayed at his side, sleep a distant goal never reached. With the help of his steward, the two of them carried the corporal on deck as the white cliffs of Dover came into sharp relief at last. The railing was lined with ambulatory patients eager for that look at home.

"I wanted to see it one last time," the soldier told him. "Thank you." It was his final conversation as he looked, shuddered, then died as quietly and bravely as he had lived.

Jake had thought he was immune to death. The corporal's quiet request for one glimpse of home touched something deep inside, that war and tumult and Waterloo had not been able to extinguish. He didn't close the dead man's eyes until some moments had passed, preferring to hold him, slightly raised, for whatever view remained in those now-peaceful eyes.

"I am so tired," he whispered to his last actual patient of Waterloo. He knew the others would make it to hospitals in England, and ultimate discharge. "I have done my duty by you, corporal. You were worth ten thousand Captain Baldwins."

It still remained to get the captain to Brierton. Baldwin sulked through disembarkation in Plymouth, and a brief stay in Stonehouse Naval Hospital, where other medical men shook their heads over him and out of his hearing gave their condolences to Jake Frost, tasked with getting this useless hunk of carbon to Yorkshire.

Then at last—at last! The matter became magic. Like the sorriest nag who raises his head and sniffs water and the stables, Captain Baldwin roused himself from his self-induced stupor to engage a post chaise. Insisting on crutches—he didn't need even a cane—the captain made his fictionally painful way to a popular counting house and fortified himself with money. He managed a graceful collapse in the foyer of Carter and Brustein's firm which gave him the sympathy and adulation for a wounded warrior that the man craved.

When he was carried by some of the staff to the waiting post chaise, Captain Baldwin glared at Jake. "You are a miserable disgrace of a surgeon," he said.

How much can one man take? Jake managed a serene smile. He had his letter of release from Wellington himself, grudgingly also signed by General Sir David Baldwin. He was on English soil now and no longer connected to the British Army Medical Corps, except that he was bound now by honor, since he had given his word to the general. Still...

"Au contraire, Captain Baldwin," he said. "I prevented your death on so many occasions in Brussels."

"That's impossible," his boat anchor and millstone sputtered. "There was no enemy in Brussels!"

"I can name you any number of physicians, surgeons, and stewards—maybe even a few nuns—who would happily have killed you," he replied, his voice even, his mind clear because he had to get this man to Yorkshire. "You demanded services for an almost non-existent wound and robbed our time to work among the truly suffering."

"I could have died at Waterloo," Captain Baldwin insisted.

"Unlikely, since you were either hiding in the center when the regiment formed squares, or seeing how fast you could get there."

They stared at each other. The captain looked away first and silence reigned. The act continued when they stopped that first night, with Baldwin bamboozling the innkeep and his wife, who probably didn't know the difference between a hangnail and sepsis, and cosseted this self-proclaimed Waterloo hero.

Jake took a long walk that night. He argued with himself that he could abandon Captain Baldwin the moment they arrived at the family estate, and yet he couldn't, because in a weak moment he had, indeed, promised General Sir David Baldwin that he would stay by his son's side until the general arrived before Christmas.

As he crunched through snow, Jake reminded himself that anyone could get through a month, and then a year, then several years, until it all jumbled together: battles, aid stations, grievous wounds, and recuperation. That had been his life from 1809 to 1815, and he was no more special than other doctors who had done the same.

"Less than a month," he told a Jersey in a nearby field, placidly nosing through the snow for a little more roughage. "I know I have been saying it for six years, but I can stand anything for that long. See here, Bossy? I am living proof."

Only hours from their arrival at the Baldwin estate, something cheerfully called Summer's Edge, Captain Baldwin deigned to speak to Jake again. "There is a chamber next to mine where you will be installed, so no worries about staying belowstairs."

And that is supposed to placate me? Jake thought, wondering when he had ever been lumped in with the hired help. "Why, thank you, sir," he said, well aware that Captain Baldwin had no comprehension of sarcasm.

"You're welcome," the man said serenely. "I will even let you accompany me to the neighboring estate, where my fiancée resides."

"Such an honor," Jake murmured. His head began to ache.

"As soon as I am comfortable in bed and reasonably out of pain, I will send her a note," Baldwin continued. He sounded less petulant than usual, because he really didn't understand sarcasm. Ah, here it came: "*She* will at least take some pity on me."

"You have a fiancée?" Jake couched it in conversational terms, and not in hair pulling, Good-God-there-is-someone-on-this-planet-who-can-tolerate-you terms. *It's only a month more, it's only a month more,* he repeated in his tired brain.

"Yes, of course," Baldwin replied, continuing in that irritating complacency that made Jake want to shake him. "I will admit she isn't much to look at, but her family is wealthy, and that can make the oddest woman beautiful, don't you think?"

There was no answer required beyond, "Most certainly," to remain in the gentrified world Jake inhabited, considering that his father was a vicar. Jake knew he could have entered that tepid, vicarish world, too, except that he was a hands-on sort of chap who had always wanted to know how things worked, in his case, the human body. The Frosts had eventually resigned themselves to *his* eccentricity. Who was he to complain about odd-looking?

Still, odd-looking? Gad, what a callous man.

Chapter Three

Ivy Pritchard came back from a morning of tramping through the trees and bushes, intent upon capturing the elusive holly and ivy. Mostly she enjoyed getting outside with an excuse to prowl about, pay attention to winter birds perhaps contemplating a flight south, because their warm autumn had fooled them into longer residence in Yorkshire. No one ever objected to her feeding the birds. Larch, the under footman, had even created a wooden platform low enough for her to reach, and yet high enough to keep cats eternally frustrated.

"The servants coddle you," Mama had told her on numerous occasions. "Ivy, they are only the staff and we pay them. Don't be so...so..."

That was where it usually ended. Vain Mama, shallow Mama, never could bring herself to admit that she looked down on those patient souls who provided her with comfort and ease. All Ivy had to do was nod wisely, and go about her own business of kindness to her belowstairs friends, because they *were* her friends.

There was another reason for a good walk in the woods, holly and ivy on her mind, but consternation in her heart. Her own eyes sparkling, Mama had presented her with note from Captain George Baldwin, who had returned to Summer's Edge three nights ago. In the note, the captain stated that after three days at home, he finally had the strength to write to her. Mama had never minded looking over her daughter's correspondence first. "I am a careful mother," she had announced when Ivy offered a weak protest years ago. "I want to keep you safe from encroachers." And that was that...Mama read everything first.

"Your own Waterloo hero has returned," Mama announced, giving each word more weight and bearing than anything perhaps up to and including the Second Coming.

Oh goody, Ivy thought. "Thank you, Mama," she said dutifully, even sweetly, though she did not resist the urge to add, "Did you answer this note already?" she asked.

Mama gave her a wounded look. "I would never…" she began, then added with considerable dignity, "You see that he wants to visit here tomorrow afternoon, provided he has the strength."

"Very well," Ivy said. "Provided he has the strength. I'll write to him."

The whole exchange was worthy of more time outside, so she seized the moment, putting off answering the note a little longer.

But how long could she avoid duty? *My hero*, she thought as she returned home, shaking the snow off her cloak and handing it to the footman. She went downstairs and put the basket of holly and ivy on the table in the servants' dining room. Molly the 'tween stairs maid was there, Molly who had a knack for decorating. "Do you think this will work, Molly?" she asked.

Molly nodded. "We'll add it to the other pile and have t'upstairs looking like Christmas soon enough."

Ivy trudged upstairs and into the library that no one frequented. It was her solitary pleasure, and contained a writing desk. Soon a note was on its way across the fields to Summer's Edge. She rested her chin on her palm, slouching at the desk in a way Mama would have disliked, remembering the two letters she had received after Waterloo, months ago now. The first was obviously in another man's handwriting, firm but a little hard to read, stating that yes, her fiancé was wounded, but the wound was relatively superficial and would heal promptly. The next letter a month later was a spidery scrawl that meandered over the page, looking as pitiful as the words that penetrated her somewhat skeptical mind.

The most memorable sentence was something like '…knocking on death's door, but doing my duty in the face of terrible danger.' H'mm. Which letter to believe?

"I wish I didn't know you so well, George," she told the paper in front of her. She closed her eyes, imagining life with George Baldwin. Mama and Papa had both assured her as kindly as possible that she probably wouldn't get a better offer, but *this*?

The wishful thinking side of her brain wanted to believe he was a wonderful man who had been wounded nobly in the service of his country. She liked to believe that side. Who wouldn't? The skeptical but more rational side told her that nothing had changed and she was engaged to someone concerned more with the size of her marriage portion.

"I don't like my choices, which amount to no choices," she said, raising her voice because the library had only books and no one to shush her. She was stuck and she knew it.

She had to chuckle then. Stuck to the hem of her dress was an ivy leaf, prickly and forever green. She noticed the pinch when she crossed her ankles, and bent down to remove it. She held off the pretty thing for a good look, thinking of the Christmas story, of the red holly berries representing the blood Jesus shed on the cross. Somehow it was couple with ivy, perennially green and fresh. Fancy Mama and Papa having enough flight of fancy to name her Ivy. True, her favorite name was in third place, tucked away after Augusta Frances. It was the afterthought, because she was born on Christmas. No wonder she favored ivy. She was also the afterthought.

The note to her fiancé was answered promptly, with that firm signature she remembered from the Brussels letter. "Captain Baldwin wanted me to tell you that he and I will see you tomorrow afternoon around two of the clock." She looked closer at the smaller print and had to suppress a laugh. "Provided he is not languishing upon death's door. It's hard to tell, sometimes." It was signed Surg. Jake Frost....Or was that Jack Frost, which made her laugh out loud this time, considering the proximity of Christmas.

It was silly; it was a laugh. She needed a laugh. The thought, unbidden, came to her that the tone of the note suggested the Surg. needed a laugh, too.

She told Mama about tomorrow's visit, which sent her parent into transports resembling, if not delight, then relief, a more or less silent reminder that her daughter Ivy was twenty-four years old, not getting younger, and her obvious defect remained.

Trust Mama…"Good! Perhaps when Captain Baldwin's health is no longer precarious, he and Papa can sit down at last and draw up the details of your marriage portion. After all, you're twenty-four."

"I know, Mama, and you know, I look about as I did at twenty, twenty-one and twenty-two through twenty-three," she added on impulse. It sounded a bit brazen to her, but that little missive with Surgeon Frost's commentary still gave her the giggles.

Mama managed a smile, followed by her quiet admonition. "Daughter, he hasn't seen you in a while. You remember how to sit, don't you?"

Ivy felt her face grow rosy. Did she need a reminder?

"Yes, Mama."

Ivy heard the crunch of gravel in the driveway punctually at two of the clock. The estates were close enough together and within easy walking distance, but as she thought about it, Captain Baldwin never walked.

She arranged herself on the sofa in the sitting room, sitting with her left side away from view, as she had been taught since early childhood, and a neighbor child had gasped, stared and pointed. Come to think of it, Captain Baldwin didn't seem to know which eye to look at. Hopefully that would change, once they were married.

Lansing announced the two men and she looked up from her book. She had thought the captain might look worn and finedrawn from his medical ordeal, but no, he looked healthy and even plump, and not someone wracked with pain and suffering. To her surprise, it was the other man, obviously the surgeon, who looked exhausted.

If Captain Baldwin had been wounded, she observed no such evidence until he saw her, and began what she could only call a performance. She tried not to stare as he limped into the room, leaning heavily on his cane. He didn't stifle his groan, which worried her at first. A glance at his companion told a different story: fleeting scorn, eyes heavenward briefly, then a small sigh.

"George, do seat yourself," she said and rose from her perch. "How nice to see you again." She held out her hand.

Poor George. He groaned and sat down in the closest chair, the one facing her right side. "How I have suffered in the service of my country," he said, with a shake of his head.

"Poor dear," was all she could manage, mainly because she glanced at what must be his surgeon, who seemed to be chewing on the inside of his cheek, perhaps so he would not say what he wanted to.

There was apparently to be no introduction from George, which embarrassed her. Her fiancé was treating this man of medicine as though he were a servant and unworthy of comment. Something in Ivy's active brain seemed to whisper to her heart, as if she should take note that this was an important moment in her life.

The choice was clear to her. She could ignore the surgeon, or she could introduce herself, since George Baldwin wasn't going to, and engage him in conversation, too. She knew she wanted to do precisely that. He was a tall and handsome man in a remarkably plain uniform that was clean but well worn.

What did it matter if he saw the other side of her face? That same little something in her brain had told her for years that the issue was a simple anomaly unworthy of comment, except among people to whom looks were everything and meant the difference between a good marriage alliance and none at all. Stupid.

She came directly to the surgeon, faced him, and bobbed a curtsy. He smiled and bowed.

"I am Ivy Pritchard, Captain Baldwin's fiancée," she said. "You must be the kind man who sent me that letter after Waterloo."

He inclined his head. "I am Surgeon Frost and pleased to make your acquaintance," he said. "I don't know about kind, but yes, I notified a number of people after Waterloo, when we were established in Brussels and had a moment."

"I can't even imagine how busy you must have been," she replied. "Wherever did the medical corps find space for all the wounded?"

"Everywhere, Miss Pritchard, from regular hospitals to convents and monasteries, and even to tents in the city squares. We were...."

"Surgeon Frost must have considered himself the only surgeon in the British Army," George interrupted. To Ivy's ears, he sounded remarkably petulant, as if he knew everyone should focus on him and his suffering, and not carry on a conversation, as if he were not present.

"Thank God I was not," the surgeon replied firmly. "I've never seen such suffering. Waterloo might go down in the history books."

She wanted to know more, but George shifted himself, sucked in his breath, and let out a low moan, the pitiful kind. "Ivy dear," he managed to gasp out. "Please put that footstool under my leg. Frost, help her."

"Allow me."

The surgeon picked up the footstool and set it before the captain, whose face contorted in...something. Pain, perhaps? "There you are, George," he said, as he picked up her fiancé's left leg and settled it on the footstool. He put the back of his hand against his patient's forehead. "Perfectly normal. You'll be fine."

"I don't feel fine," the captain snapped.

Surgeon Frost seated himself on the sofa close by. "You'll feel better soon, and look, you can admire your fiancée and tell her about your exploits."

That was all it took. After the maid brought in tea and cakes, George proceeded to bore Ivy with the minutia of his duties as a captain and leader of men in the Yorkshire Fifth Foot. She had not expected him to be interested in anything but himself, so she steeled herself for the ordeal, knowing it would eventually lead to Waterloo and what he had already referred to as his grievous wound. He asked nothing about her life and how she did. He did not ask after her parents, or solicit her advice or comment.

Is this to be my life? Ivy asked herself in silent desperation. *I can't. I just can't.*

The surgeon remained silent through all the boring commentary. She noticed he was observing her. A glance in his direction meant a smile and a nod. He tapped his foot a time or two, which suggested, perhaps as nothing else could, how much he wanted to be away and doing something useful. This was not a man to sit idly by.

At least, until he was. After her fiancé's lengthy, self-serving, boring tale that Ivy suspected was leading up to Waterloo, she glanced at the surgeon again.

To her surprise, then amusement, then deep sympathy, she saw that he was sound asleep. *This man is exhausted*, she thought. *Simply exhausted.*

Chapter Four

God knows Jake tried to fight off slumber. He had fallen asleep before when Captain Baldwin was droning on and on about his gallantry, which was a total hum and lie. If Jake was honest with himself (and he sometimes was), the past few days of travel by post chaise from Plymouth to near Leeds had been somewhat beneficial, in that he could snatch little naps while the captain nattered away.

He wanted to stay awake, because Miss Pritchard was interesting. Like everything else about his detestable patient, Baldwin's rude comments about his fiancée's odd appearance were simply not true. Her "defect" was *ptosis*, a drooping eyelid. It drooped more than some, but that was all. He'd seen it before, and Miss Pritchard's was typical. Jack thought it rather charming, as though she was half-winking at him, which only made him want to wink back.

There he was, though, sinking into a really comfortable sofa. The fire in the grate had warmed the sitting room to the perfect temperature for a snooze. To compound the felony, Miss Pritchard's voice – when George Baldwin shut up long enough for her to comment – was low and soothing, with that little lilt so pleasant in Yorkshire women.

She was easy on the eyes, too. He had seen too many woman in Spain skinny to the point of emaciation to never want to see such again, because it meant hunger and deprivation. Miss Pritchard was round in all the right places, with a smallish waist. Her skin was rosy in hue and he admired her dark hair neatly braided at the

21

back of her neck, suggesting to him a wondrous fall of wavy locks when it was unfettered.

All he wanted to do was sleep. He fought it, swallowing down yawns and blinking his eyes, but in vain. He was so tired. If some villain had held a dirk to his neck and demanded to know when he had last slept soundly or he would slit his throat, it wouldn't have made a difference, because he could not remember.

Talavera, Ciudad Rodrigo in a siege or two, Badajoz the same, Bussaco, Salamanca, Burgos, Vittoria, retreat, retreat, then finally Toulouse. It was all noise and dust and stink and terror, and too few resources, and too many needing too much. Exile to Elba promised some relief from the Tyrant of Corsica, but it proved to be only a recess from conflict.

Worst of all was Waterloo, even though it was the last clash of two mighty armies that had been slugging it out for years. In some way, the final victory was worse, with the victors returning to frenzied, welcoming throngs. How easy it was for the fickle public, also war weary, to forget the wounded and near-dead languishing in Belgium and the Low Countries. The wars of a generation were over, except they weren't over for the surgeons and physicians who still fought against inadequate supplies and a government quite happy to forget about those convalescing in foreign places.

All those emotions seemed to come together as Surgeon Jacob Frost sank lower into a comfortable sofa that seemed determined to finally wrestle him into submission, but gently. As he sat there, nearly paralyzed with exhaustion, he felt his brain turning into butter. His shoulders seemed to relax and lower for the first time since 1810.

He thought Miss Pritchard said something to him, but he had no words to reply. He tried to open his eyes, but it was hopeless. He thought Captain Baldwin shook him and tried to rouse him from the comforting arms of Morpheus, but it must have been Miss Pritchard who demanded that he stop. Her voice wasn't loud, but it was firm. "Leave this poor man alone," he heard most distinctly, before everything went dark and he slept.

He struggled to open his eyes when he heard what sounded like a low-volume quarrel. He winced to recognize Captain Baldwin's whiny voice, but more impressive was the woman's voice, calm and measured--he had no idea what she said--but indominable. He winced again when the door banged shut, and tried to sit up, but it was as though some supernatural power had trapped him in the most comfortable sofa in the universe. He could not resist it and did not.

Time had no meaning. He had a vague notion of someone raising his legs so he could stretch out on the sofa, and someone removing his shoes, loosening his belt and unbuttoning his trousers. He hoped it wasn't Miss Pritchard, then, oddly enough, he hoped it was. Someone arranged a softer pillow behind his head, and covered him with a blanket. He heard a door close, and then, nothing.

Morning came, and with it, the immediate concern for his patients above and beyond those of the final campaign. With considerable speed, his mind worked its way through a series of battles and surgical results before he opened his eyes.

When he did, there was Miss Pritchard, embroidering. The sun was up. She sat close to the fire. Somehow, someway, it touched his heart that her half-open eye was his view. *She knows I don't think it odd*, was his only thought, before he returned to sleep, strangely comforted, as though someone watched over him.

His bladder woke him an hour later and could not be ignored. What to ask this serene miss still embroidering? "Um, I..."

"Larch will help you," she said, gesturing to the door, where an attentive fellow in domestic livery stood. "Then he will direct you to the breakfast room. You *do* like breakfast don't you?"

"Best meal of the day, Miss Pritchard." What a woman.

He knew it had to be long past the hour of breakfast. His timepiece had stopped at some point, but there were bacon and eggs on the sideboard, plus toast. He filled his plate, loading on the bacon until he should have been embarrassed, but wasn't, since Miss Pritchard seemed to like bacon, too.

"My word, this is good," he said, as he munched.

"Our cook loves pig," was all she said, which was so funny he laughed.

He filled up eventually, and pushed his plate back, which he knew was bad manners, but oh well. Miss Pritchard was sipping tea by now. He knew he needed to apologize for his gigantic lack of manners, but where to begin?

"Miss Pritchard, please excuse my inexcusable breach of decorum," he said, which didn't begin to convey his mortification. She didn't seem too appalled, so he took the light touch. "I blame your sofa. It grabbed hold of me and refused to let go."

"When did you last have a good night's sleep, sir?" she inquired, but kindly.

He thought back. "P'raps four years ago. Yes, that was it. Before we left the lines of Torres Vedras and returned to Spain to fight again. 1811."

Her cup came down with a noticeable click on the saucer. "Surgeon Frost, if you ever hear me whine and complain, just... just stop me, please."

Her comment seemed to imply that this wouldn't be his last encounter with Miss Pritchard. He wondered if she meant more by it, or was merely engaging in routine small talk. Whatever it was, he appreciated plain speaking.

"It was a hard slog through Spain." That was enough. She would probably think him remiss if he didn't ask about his current responsibility, considering that Captain Baldwin, not present now thank the Lord, was her fiancé. "I was derelict last night. How did Captain Baldwin get home?"

"I sent George home with Larch, the under footman."

"Poor Larch," escaped him before he could stop it. His comment brought out her dimple below that half-open eye. God, she was charming, but he didn't know what to say. "Well, I..." was the best he could do.

Maybe the less he said... He put lemon curd on the last piece of toast and stared at it, hating to think he had squashed her conversation with his rudeness. He got brave enough to look at her, and noticed her hesitation. "Um, is this where I say, 'Shoot me now?'" he asked, hoping to turn the conversation to something lighter until he could escape and leave her alone.

She smiled at that, then waited a measured moment, before glancing around and leaning closer. "Tell me, Surgeon, was he even wounded?"

"A miniscule piece of shrapnel passed through his right calf, striking nothing important. Two stitches on the points of entry and exit were enough to close the wound," he said, trying to maintain a detached air. "I turned him over to my assistant to patch him up."

"He winced and gasped when Larch helped him to his feet," she said. "I'm surprised he didn't wake you up. It seems he wanted to. It took Larch and our butler to get him to the carriage for the ride to Summer's Edge." She sat back and looked at him. "Why is he doing this?"

She seemed not to mind words with no bark on them. Besides that, he doubted he would be invited back for another breakfast before he quitted these environs. "He is a coward and a malingerer." Should he? Yea or nay? Yea. "Miss Pritchard, you can do better than George Baldwin."

Chapter Five

*O**h dear. This nice man is going to think I am humiliated by his plain speaking*, Ivy thought. She watched his face redden and found herself charmed that someone with such a fraught life in a time of war could blush. She did what she knew might help and raised the teapot. "More tea, sir?"

Somehow, that tickled his funny bone. He laughed again, even leaning back in his chair. She couldn't help smiling, because his merriment diffused the situation remarkably. "See here, Captain, you have been too long from England if you have forgotten that more tea is good at warding off upstarts and people with no imagination."

"Neither of which I am, Miss Pritchard," he assured her. "Still, it was unkind of me to say he was a ...well, I shan't repeat it."

"Coward and malingerer?" she said, her own face warm. She set down the pot and stared at her hands. "I don't doubt you."

He visibly started at her comment, recovered himself and persisted. "I should not have maligned your fiancé. That was inexcusable. Perhaps I should leave before my big mouth gets me in more trouble. Thank you for the wonderful breakfast, and a sound night's sleep."

When he rose, Ivy raised her hand and lowered it, knowing he would either sit or he wouldn't. She had no control over him. She didn't know what to say. To her relief, he sat and held out his teacup. She filled it and they sipped in silence.

When he said nothing for a lengthy time, she decided he would probably apologize for saying that she could do better, and then take his leave. Any other consideration was outside the realm of probability, considering how life usually went for women (This based on observation, which she was good at). *The onus is on you, sir*, she thought. She decided it was worth the wait, until she realized that no, the onus was on her. He had told her she could do better. He deserved a response. It was unlikely she would ever see him again after this encounter. This required a deep breath before she began.

"Sir, it must be obvious to you that I have a facial defect," she said, chin up, shoulders squared, as she remembered children teasing her when she was little. That stung a bit, even now. She hoped it didn't show on her face.

"A very small defect," he said. "D'ye mind?" He leaned closer and raised her eyelid. "No strabismus; you're not cross-eyed. It's ptosis. Many call it 'lazy eye.' Can you see clearly?"

"I can."

"No problem then."

"Not unless you're the only unmarried lady in the district with a lazy eye," she said. "My parents assured me that a comeout of any sort, even here in Yorkshire, would be pointless."

She could tell that startled him. "You never argued the matter?"

Oh, these men! They think women have a choice in anything. "I obeyed," she said quietly. "It's what ladies do." She needn't add that her mother was vain and shallow and had never reconciled herself to a daughter with a flaw. That wasn't his business. "I obeyed," she repeated, more for herself than him probably, because she was beginning to think she had been treated unfairly by her parents.

"Seems unfair. As I said, it's a small matter. Some might think it a charming defect. It has certainly never bothered me."

She blushed at that. "It bothers my mother. She has always made me sit facing sideways, so no one will notice it." *Did I actually say that out loud?* she thought, appalled at herself. "I…mean…"

"I wouldn't do that to a child of mine." He touched her hand, just a touch. "Doctor's orders: We never repeat a confidence." His smile relieved her heart. "I think Hippocrates himself said that first. We in the trade of medicine all live by it. No fears."

His frankness surprised her; so did his evident sympathy. She wondered if she had ever known anyone who said what he thought. Perhaps it was a peculiarity of doctors. "I cannot change that now," she told him. "Please don't think my parents were unkind. They settled a good marriage portion on me, and the Baldwins next door agreed. I have been engaged to Captain Baldwin for four years."

His frown deepened, but he said nothing. What was there to say? She decided on a change of subject. "You mentioned last night that you were leaving as soon as the general returns."

"I am. Your fiancé won't believe me, but he is perfectly fine and doesn't need my help. I am leaving as soon as I can."

"What are your plans?" she asked. "I don't mean to pry, but it must be nice to be able to do whatever you want."

His expression turned bleak. She put down her cup and grasped his arms. It was horribly forward of her, but she had an idea—only an idea—how terrible his war had been. Last night she had looked in on him and even sat by him briefly, when he started to mutter and thrash around. A hand on his arm had quieted him then. Might as well tell him.

"I was sitting by you last night when you started moving and talking in your sleep," she said.

She must have touched a nerve, which wasn't her intention. He started, then shook his head. "It's a foolish thing. It seems I am doomed to think over all those men I could not save, and rehearse what I should have done better."

Where was her nerve coming from? Poor, poor man. She gave him a little shake, just a gentle one, because this was far from appropriate. "Perhaps instead you could lull yourself to sleep by thinking of all the men you saved."

She realized she still gripped his arms, and let him go, embarrassed. "My apologies, sir," she murmured.

"No, no. Thank you," he told her. "I have often wished I had a choice in the matter. Maybe I have a choice in how I remember it. Thank you again," he repeated.

She knew it was time for a monumental change of subject. "I hope you have a wonderful place in mind where you can start a medical practice. Of your choosing," she added, sounding droll enough that he laughed, clearing the air.

"I had thought maybe Yorkshire," he said hesitantly, then seemed to forget himself. "What would you do, if you could choose?"

So much for clearing the air. No one had ever asked her that. "I'd probably run away," she said with a smile, hoping he would think it was a joke, even if it wasn't.

To her relief, he must have thought she was teasing because he asked, "Where would you run away to?"

"P'raps Baltimore, in Maryland," she said, striving for a light tone. "I have a cousin there and he says the air is balmy and never really cold." No need to tell him that she thought about Baltimore all the time, dreaming she could somehow buy a house there and raise chickens and not wear wool stockings in the winter that made her legs itch. She knew it was wishful thinking. "See here, sir, I am going to give up wishful thinking in a New Year's Resolution."

He fell for it, to her relief, and laughed. "I hope you get to Baltimore soon, Miss Pritchard! I had better return to Summer's Edge. I made no such resolution, so I shall wishfully think myself somewhere else, too."

"You'll be leaving soon, though, won't you?" she asked, hoping she didn't sound wistful.

"As soon as ever I can, Miss Pritchard," he replied.

She could tell he meant it.

Jake politely declined her offer of a conveyance, and footed it across the meadow between the two estates. Thanks to a good sleep, he felt alert and positive that he could weather two more weeks here, more or less, and then bid farewell to the most useless patient he had the misfortune to deal with.

His good cheer vanished as soon as he arrived at Summer's Edge. Practically plucking at his sleeve, the butler urged him to hurry upstairs to the captain's room.

"Sir, he declares he is in the verge of a relapse, and we do not know how to placate him," Chickering said. "His mother has gone into strong hysterics. I believe you gave her some sort of draught the last time this happened."

"I'll see her first," Jack said. "Bring a glass of warm water to my room. I'll add those special powders."

While he waited for the water to arrive, he dug into his medical satchel and took out a packet of alum and sugar. He stirred that into the water, and added a drop of oil of cloves. The result smelled vaguely medicinal, with the alum making it bitter enough to convince the worst hypochondriac that it would do some good.

Lady Prudence Baldwin seemed well enough when he tapped on her door and opened it. When she saw who it was, she began to weep and carry on, claiming heart palpitations and dizziness and blaming him.

"How could you leave my poor son for so long?" she demanded, between wiping dry eyes with a lace handkerchief.

"He'll be fine, Lady Prudence," he soothed, wanting to strangle her, along with her equally useless son. He couldn't help but think that any children belonging to Ivy Pritchard would be practical and useful, at least as long as she didn't marry George Baldwin. "Here you are. That's better. You'll feel fine soon. Just lie down. Ah, that's good. I'll see to George now."

Out of morbid curiosity, he opened Captain Baldwin's door without knocking. He peered in to see his patient admiring himself in his full-length mirror, turning this way and that to preen. As soon as he saw Jake's reflection in the mirror, he collapsed by lowering himself gently enough to the floor. "I am in such agony," he gasped. "Don't think I won't complain to the Medical Department! You abandoned me."

"I did no such thing. Complain all you wish," Jake said. "I have signed letters releasing me from service. The minute your father crosses the threshold at Summer's Edge, I will be gone. What is bothering you now?"

"Your neglect," George snapped. "Anything could have happened to me last night or this morning, and where were you, but slumbering away at my fiancée's house. Have you no shame?"

"None whatever. Here drink this."

It was another useless potion. George was asleep in minutes. Jake went to the window and stared across the field to the Pritchard manor. *Ivy, you deserve someone much better than George Baldwin*, he thought.

Another thought sidled into his brain and stood there, waiting: *Me, perhaps.* That was all. He shrugged and put it down to holly and ivy and other Christmas nonsense.

Chapter Six

One day passed, and then another. Jake found himself looking out the window often, wondering how Miss Pritchard fared, and thinking about her wish to run away. As much as he might complain about the hand fate had dealt him and so many men of his generation, he had all his faculties, all his hair, and money enough from unspent salaries and a little inherited money to truly do what he wanted, within reason.

What did he want? He was thirty and well-trained. It was time to think about a wife, and children, and somewhere to enjoy both. On a whim, he went to the library at Summer's Edge, which boasted a librarian, even. It was a magnificent room, with books lining all the walls, and shelves rising ten feet toward the ceiling, with a clever ladder on wheels to access the higher shelves.

He decided quickly that no one came to the library often, because the librarian was overjoyed almost to the point of tears to see someone, anyone. Jake knew the man would probably collapse and die if he told him that he had picked up a Bible printed by J. Guttenberg, just lying on the floor in a ruined manor in Badajoz after that final siege. It was a massive thing, but he quickly stowed it with his medical kit and it trundled along in the baggage cart from battle to battle. Even now, carefully wrapped in brown paper, the Bible occupied a safe spot in his campaign trunk.

His conscience only bothered him briefly after he took it. He had seen pages torn from other rare books and used in privies. A Guttenberg Bible deserved a better fate. It was his little secret.

He had another errand in this library. He told the librarian what—or rather, who—he was looking for. The man produced the book of English rulers, after clambering up the ladder on wheels and whizzing along at breakneck speed. In mere moments, he turned to the requested page and handed it to Jake with a flourish.

Precisely. He hadn't been wrong. He knew he was observant. "Would you let me show this page to Miss Pritchard after dinner this evening?" he asked. "The Pritchards are coming here tonight. Could I leave it here on the table?"

"Certainly, sir," the librarian said, after a loving, almost reverent, look at the book. "I don't think anyone has opened this in a hundred years. Are you, er, of Plantagenet origins?"

"Not I," Jake declared. "I hope to become a simple country doctor as soon as my duty to Captain Baldwin is discharged."

Perhaps the librarian sensed a kindred spirit. Who knows what a chap thought when no one ever came into his library? Jake could probably have wagered a fortune that George Baldwin had never crossed the threshold. Or maybe the librarian liked to gossip.

"I believe the plan tonight is for the Pritchards and the Baldwins to settle up those marriage papers." He shook his head. "I hear she is a mousy thing with a facial defect of some sort."

"Actually, she's quite lovely," Jake heard himself saying, and meaning every syllable, because it was true. "She has an eyelid that droops a little, but what is that to anyone?" He tapped the page with its two kings. "She is obviously in august company."

The librarian frowned. "*I* heard she was missing an eye." He giggled. "Sort of like Cyclops."

You, sir, are an idiot, Jake thought, angered. His heart broke a little around the edges as he wondered how many rumors had come Ivy's way. "It's nothing like that," he said, then, "Don't spread such nonsense about."

"It's what people in the district say," the librarian said.

"They are wrong!"

Jake stewed about the matter all afternoon, when he wasn't tending to Captain Baldwin's imaginary ailments, which now included a weak heart, perhaps in imitation of his mother. He tossed his head from side to side and moaned when Jake assured him that his heart rhythm was steady and he was sound as a roast.

When Baldwin was finally sound asleep, convinced that Jake's useless potion had done its job, the doctor went to the window again, wanting to cross that meadow, knock on Ivy's door, and sit down with someone possessed of sense and wit.

"Why the hell not?" he said finally and wrapped his surgeon's cloak around him. "Going for a walk," he told the butler. "If Captain Baldwin wakes up before I return, assure him that I will return before he shuffles off his mortal coil. No, no. Tell him to practice deep breathing and have a glass of sherry."

As it turned, he didn't need to knock on Ivy's door, because she was outside said door, trying to figure out how to hang a monster wreath.

"You're a little short for that," he said as he came up the walk.

She turned around in surprise, smiled at him, and Jake—exhausted, weary, cynical Surg. – knew he was a no-hoper. He remembered a drunken session years ago with other single officers, when the topic turned to how a man knew he was in love. There was one attempt, something along the lines of, "You'll know when it happens, m'boy." Too much whisky had put some to sleep, and the others were too fuddled to even attempt a partial answer. He had his answer today. For the first time in his fraught, harried, busy life, he understood love. It stood before him trying to wrestle with a Christmas wreath.

He was still some distance off. "I never want to leave you," he said softly. "Never."

She leaned forward and put her hand to her ear.

"This is a job for someone taller," he said, too shy to repeat it. "Just tell me precisely where you want it."

She did, and stepped aside as he stood beside her and hung the wreath. He took a deep breath of the pine boughs and holly and ivy twined inside. How many Christmases had found him laboring away in hospitals or tents, or God help him, a blanket held over him and a wounded soldier in the rain? This Christmas was different.

No artillery shells rained down, no desperately poor Spanish women held out their hands for whatever food he could toss from the baggage cart before an officer stopped him. Here was a doorstep on a quiet estate in North Yorkshire, and a pretty lady stood beside him.

"This was just what I needed, Miss Pritchard," he said, when he wanted to say much more, then, "It's nice to be useful."

A man of science, he was not a fellow to indulge in fantasy of any shape or variety and yet he did precisely that, imagining that Ivy Pritchard was really Ivy Frost, and he could open that door to their house, usher her inside, and shut the world out.

This would never do. He had only vague plans. Captain Baldwin, damn the man, had firm plans and a prior claim. He frowned. "I was just out for a walk," he said. "I get tired of silly people next door. Glad to be of service." He tipped his hat to her and stepped down. "I'd better get back. I believe you and your parents are coming to Summer's Edge this evening."

He could have sworn a little of her sparkle dimmed. "Yes, we are. Papa wants to sign some papers, and Mama is determined to set a wedding date."

Dash it all. Even though he had not one single claim on events between these two families, this wasn't what he wanted. He was a surgeon, yes, but a man currently without employment, and someone certainly not of the same rank and prestige.

"I'll...I'll see you this evening?" Ivy asked. She sounded uncertain, perhaps even a little afraid, as if what to come was going to be an ordeal. What was he thinking?

"I never miss a meal, Miss Pritchard."

Coward.

Chapter Seven

Jake dressed with care that evening, wishing he had a uniform less worn. At least he had a uniform. Years of war had produced a regulation uniform at last, in the army's case, a plain red tunic with bluish trousers with no insignia beyond Yorkshire Fifth Foot in plain embroidery. He confessed to envying the Royal Navy's deep blue and even plainer uniform. At least they did not show bloodstains.

It took a force of iron will to help George Baldwin dress in his best uniform, ignoring the man's ridiculous groans and assuring him that downing Jake's latest harmless but evil-smelling potion would set to him rights for the ordeal ahead. If this was part of the practice of medicine, he didn't admire himself.

Jake didn't think his odious patient could surprise him, but surprise him Baldwin did. Was there something in that concoction of olive oil, alum, a few grains of pepper and rum he was unaware of? Jake knew it wouldn't do any good. In George's case, it also loosened his tongue.

"I did this once before, you know," the captain confided.

"Did what?"

"Got married. Well, nearly."

Jake stared at him. "You did *what*?" He sat down with a thump beside his odious patient.

"Not to put too fine a point on it, the only way I had access to her…person was to propose, then forge a license," George said. He rubbed his hands together, apparently still delighted with the whole, sordid matter. "She thought it was a license, but her

36

reading skills are rudimentary, at best. We were garrisoned near Portsmouth. The promise of marriage was the only way I could get her to, uh, unbend a little." George giggled, a most unpleasant sound. Jake edged away from him. "I still laugh about it. I sent her a little money now and then, but not lately." He resumed his sorrowful expression. "I am too ill now to bother. Elsie Baldwin she calls herself now, of Mack's Inn, Portsmouth, the last I heard. Perhaps I should send her something."

"It would be the kind thing to do," Jakes said, when he could manage speech. *And here I supposed you couldn't be more wretched,* he thought.

The captain rubbed his hands together. "It's a small matter and no one knows. There'll be papers to sign tonight. The Pritchards are eager to have Ivy off their hands." He rubbed two fingers together. "Money." He sighed the sigh of a martyr. "Too bad she is strange to look at."

The only thing that saved George Baldwin from a great pounding by his surgeon was Jake remembering Hippocrates and his Oath, *Do no harm.* But he wanted to, oh, he wanted to.

To keep his hands off Captain Baldwin's throat, Jake made himself scarce as everyone else waited for the Pritchards and their solicitor to arrive. *I am going to pack my bags and get out of here tomorrow,* he told himself, his anger unabated at Captain Baldwin's casual cruelty. He reconsidered. *Not unless Ivy Pritchard is with me.* How that might happen, he had no idea.

He stayed in the library until he heard the arrival of the Pritchards, and went up the backstairs. Numb with disgust over this latest revelation from his "patient," he helped Captain Baldwin down the grand staircase in silence.

Dinner was served promptly. In his position, seated well below the Baldwins and Pritchards, he ate with his eyes on Ivy. She sat closer to Captain Baldwin and his mother, a wispy-looking woman. As much as Jake detested the Baldwins, the surgeon in him wanted to check Lady Olive's heart and lungs. She appeared to be the real patient here, but no one ever asked him.

This was the first time he had eaten a formal meal at Summer's Edge, George Baldwin confining himself to meals in his room. Jake's father, a mere vicar, was no landed gentry, not like the Pritchards and Baldwins. An invisible line separated him from them. He thought about Ivy's remarks concerning Baltimore, and wondered if life in America was somehow more equal.

After dinner, the Pritchards and Baldwins made their way to the book room. When Ivy hung back, he asked, "Are you supposed to be in there, too?"

She shook her head. "No, at least, not yet."

"Come to the library with me. I want to show you something."

She walked beside him. Their shoulders touched once or twice, telling him worlds about her fears of what was going on in the book room.

The volume of England's kings still lay on the table. As Ivy edged nearer, interested, he turned to the bookmarked page with its illustrations. "Look there," he said, pointing to a portrait of King Henry the Third, and his son, Edward the First, two remarkable and powerful rulers. "Look closely."

Ivy bent over the book and looked at the little portraits. She smiled. "I had no idea. Kindred spirits!"

"You're in rarefied company," he told her. "I came across this in medical school. I believe some of the Howards also had this same lazy eye. We'll agree they're distinguished, too."

She touched his arm. "I doubt their mothers made them sit with the sleepy eye turned away."

"And you needn't either, dear heart."

He hadn't meant to say that. It slipped out. She took his breath away when she turned to face him, making no effort to hide her eye. "Thank you," she said simply.

Her mother opened the library door, frowned at him, and gestured to the hall. "You're wanted now, Ivy," she said. "Goodnight, sir."

He knew a dismissal when he heard one and went upstairs to his room, wanting to protect Ivy Pritchard from these people who should have been concerned for her best interests, and not theirs. He stared out at winter in Yorkshire, unsure of his next move.

At least he was a man with the potential to earn a respectable living. He had tucked the signed endorsements from both the Duke of Wellington himself, and General Sir Harvey Baldwin in his wallet, which he carried in his medical satchel, where his medical credentials already resided. He had enough money to establish himself somewhere. Familiar Yorkshire was his first choice, but as he sat there, he knew he wanted to broaden his horizons. It was a large shire, to be sure, but would likely house George and Ivy Baldwin, too.

His frame of mind suffered when the footman summoned him to the foyer as the Pritchards were taking their leave. "Captain Baldwin requires your assistance to get him up the stairs," the man said, eyes forward. Jake had seen him roll his eyes a few times over Captain Baldwin's exhausted and feeble poses, but the family was assembled, and this was no time to risk censure.

Jake's heart sank to see the distress on Ivy's pretty face. She had again turned away from the others, the lifetime habit ingrained in her. He saw the paleness of her complexion and somehow felt the distress the others ignored. *I will see her tomorrow somehow,* he told himself. It was feeble and he knew it, but here was Captain Baldwin demanding his help, even as he turned away from his fiancée without a word or a smile.

Jake slept lightly that night, if at all. As usual, he thought through the questionable cases where he knew he should have done better. Maybe it was a blessing of the season that he reached out for Ivy's little lifeline, considering instead all the soldiers he had saved. He admitted he had his own method of wishful thinking, now willing to replace it with the knowledge that he had done his best, no matter how feeble. He had Ivy to thank for that. He would tell her in the morning. What else could he do?

He woke up before dawn to the persistent tinkle of little pebbles against the window. He thought at first it was ice pellets, certainly not unknown in wintry Yorkshire. As he lay there with his hands behind his head, listening, the fog of sleep lifted.

He leaped out of bed and opened the window. Looking down he saw Larch, the Pritchard's under footman, about to toss another handful of pebbles at the window. What in the world? He leaned out.

"Surgeon Frost, she's run away! Hurry down!"

Chapter Eight

Jake Frost needed no more encouragement. After a splash of cold water, he dressed and packed his bag rapidly. Hang Captain Baldwin anyway. He could ring his stupid bell until someone came, but it wouldn't be Surgeon Frost.

He scribbled a note for the captain, assuring him that he didn't need the services of a physician or surgeon. He pushed it under Baldwin's door and vowed never to waste another moment of his life thinking about him.

Satchel in hand, his surgical kit slung over his shoulder, he crept quietly down the stairs in his stockinged feet, then put on his shoes in the foyer. He had one irrational moment when he feared that if he opened the door, all manner of alarms and booby-traps would activate themselves and trap him here forever. Nonsense.

Larch took his grip from him and they hurried across the sleeping meadow. He looked back at their obvious tracks in the snow and shrugged. The Baldwins could think what they liked.

"She was so quiet-like last night after they came back. She usually is, after a visit to the captain, but this time was different," Larch said as they hurried. "It was worse."

"Did she say where she was going?"

"Oh, no. She asked me where to meet the mail coach in Brierton." He sighed. "She was pretty offhand about it, like someone might ask about the weather, but I should have told someone."

"You told me," Jake said. "That was enough."

"She told me she stole some money from the bookroom."

41

Good girl, he thought, *but you probably didn't take enough*.

They parted company at the crossroads, Larch to hurry home before he was missed. Jake moved at a trot now, the kind of quick step reminiscent of his army days across Spain, when even the surgical teams did their share of skulking and dodging on foot.

Brierton was stirring to life as the sun rose. In the two miles from the estate to the crossroads, Jake formed a plan. It was a small plan and hopefully not subject to much scrutiny. Maybe it was stupid. Time would tell. He asked for pen and paper in the public house where others waited for the mail coach. The innkeep was helpful and asked no questions. Jake thanked his lucky stars that he had wrapped the man's sprained ankle only a week ago, when he saw him wincing in pain on one of Jake's visits to Brierton and the apothecary.

He wrote carefully and in block letters, and stuffed in a few bills that he knew would suffice. He addressed it and gave significantly more money to the innkeep, directing him to give it to the post rider for a fast delivery.

Now came the important task, where failure or success meant everything. When it was his turn, Jake asked the agent, "Do you remember a pretty little lady late last night? She probably kept her head down."

To Jake's relief, the agent nodded. "I remember her because I doubt she had ever been on a mail coach. Soft voice? Something sweet about her?"

"The very one," Jake said. "Where did she go?"

The agent fixed a stern look on him. "You're not an irate husband, are you?"

"I'm an army surgeon. She needs me."

Whether that was true or not, time would also tell, but it was enough for the ticket agent. Jakes reckoned that if anything good came from nearly six years of hard slogging, it was an air of command.

"She had enough to get her to Carlisle, so that was that." The agent leaned on the counter. "I hope she had someone waiting there for her, because it took her last farthing."

Ivy, what were you thinking? he asked himself as he bought a ticket to Carlisle. Jake could picture her running from her probable fate like a frightened animal. *How will I find her?* was his next thought.

That matter became simple, too. He wondered for a small moment if there really was some truth to myths about extra goodness during the Christmas season. How did he know? War had burned away all of his expectations…maybe. He took a deep breath, right there in the smoke-filled public room and sensed something else. What, he couldn't have said, but it felt, oddly enough, like a gift.

This was no time to moon about. "I hope I can find her," he said as he took the chit from the innkeep who managed the mail coach stop, too.

"Might be easier than you think, sir. A rider came through not long ago. There's even more snow north of the border. As of a few hours ago anyway, everyone is stuck in Carlisle."

Carlisle was hours away. "Oh, please God," he asked the cold air outside the inn. "Keep her stuck there." He shook his head at his own folly. What a stupid prayer. He followed it with another one even more idiotic. "See here, Lord, sir, I am not a time waster. Let's do this for Ivy Pritchard."

They started off at a spanking pace, changing horses in the usual places, under the control of an experienced coachman. His stomach tied into knots, his head aching, Jake maintained his silence, keeping his eyes resolutely shut so no one would bother him.

It didn't work. Before they changed horses again and stopped for a late afternoon meal, he held a restless child on his lap to relieve a tired mother who nursed a newborn. He surprised himself by remembering and retelling stories his nanny had told him about trolls under bridges, and princesses in distress, who had probably never considered running away to Carlisle, but were waiting complacently for a knight to save them. The little one finally settled back against him with a contented sigh, which made him wonder if he actually would make a good father someday.

More food for thought, which seemed to be all he was snacking on, these days.

Let it snow, let it snow, let it snow, Jake thought as they pushed on, only to stop ten miles short of Carlisle in Penrith. Wasn't the Lord *listening*? Well, of course not. Jake was an amateur at entreating the Almighty, and the Lord must know it.

The young mother burst into tears, which meant Jake had to hold her young daughter tight when she started to cry, too.

It came out that she was to meet her parents in Carlisle. "My man died at Mount Sinjin," she said, after Jake handed her his last handkerchief for a good nose blow and eye wipe. "I'm going to me parents in Dumfries."

Mont St. Jean. Jake thought of the squares forming and reforming to drive off the French finally, thanks to British grit, Wellington, and the timely arrival of the Prussians. Carrying the young girl, he led the widow with her baby inside the inn and paid too much money for a room and board for them for the night. She protested until he shushed her gently. "I was at Sinjin, too, and saw the bravest men. Rest here. Your folks will see you in Carlisle tomorrow. Don't argue with me."

She didn't and he felt better about his own disappointment at reaching Carlisle. Maybe it was time to talk to the coachman.

He found him in the public room, exhausted and nursing a tankard of ale. Jake sat beside him and wasted not a minute. "Do you think anyone will try to get through tonight?" he asked, after ordering the man another pint.

"Aye, lad, I do. It'll be a slow trot, but there is a laird in a post chaise as impatient as you are. Over there."

Jake nodded and looked across the noisy room full of complainers. *God, since you've been so charitable so far, let it be someone in need of my professional services,* he thought. What would it hurt?

There were several possible lairds, but it became obvious who the likely man was. An overstuffed fellow sat with his leg elevated on the next chair. To dither, or not to dither? Army experience had taught him that Scots liked their conversation plain, with no bark on it. He cleared his throat and plunged in.

"Sir, the coachman over there tells me that you are eager to continue to Carlisle," he said.

"I am, laddie. And?"

Well, that was stringent. Before Jake could reply, his companion jostled the chair and the laird let out a bellow, then unleased a pithy string of impenetrable curse words. My, but the Scots had a knack.

Jake knew an opening when he heard one. "Sir, I am a surgeon recently released from army duty." He looked at the leg, as if examining it, even though an examination wasn't necessary. "It appears you are suffering from the gout. A recent flair up?"

"Aye, laddie. I want to get home to me own bed, and not potter about here in Penrith."

"Understandable. You know, I could wrap that tighter. If we could procure a hot water bottle of some sort…It wouldn't stop the pain, but it would alleviate it."

"Anything, anything," the laird said.

Jake worked fast, the only way he knew how to practice medicine. In minutes, the leg was bound tight. On his command, the innkeeper produced an iron pig wrapped in a towel.

The traveler sighed in immediate relief. "How can I pay ye?"

"Let me travel with you, if you're going on ahead," Jake said promptly. "I can adjust the wrapping if needs be."

"It'll be slow-going," the laird warned.

"At least it'll be going."

Now that his pain was slightly minimized, the laird proved to be a canny fellow. "Laddie, you're either on the run from the law or an irate woman."

Jake laughed. His mum had told him years ago that Christmas was a magic time. She hadn't mentioned that could also be humorous. "Neither, sir. I'm looking for a lady who ran away from an unfortunate situation."

The laird eyed him with a penetrating glance that reminded him forcefully of his bones professor at the University of Edinburgh. "Will she be glad to see ye or nae?"

"Glad, I hope."

He held his breath while the scrutiny continued. He wondered briefly whether his brains had dribbled out of his head after meeting Ivy Pritchard, or if, after all his unending labors of the past years, fortune decided to smile, should he choose to shed a layer of cynicism.

He so chose. "I'm in love."

The laird let out a shout of laughter this time, and not a bellow of pain. He clapped Jake's shoulder with a hard blow that threatened his wind.

"Let's go!"

Chapter Nine

They went – Laird Cowan, Surgeon Frost, and the laird's dour servant, who had the look of one who had never suffered a fool gladly, and didn't intend to begin now. By the time they arrived in Carlisle, the sun was up, the servant asleep, the laird yawning, and the surgeon ready to bite his nails down to his wrists.

Once in Carlisle, that last bastion of England before the rough and tumble of Scotland, Jake admitted to no idea how to play this next hand. Maybe Ivy had resources in Scotland that neither he nor Larch the under footman were aware of. Maybe she wanted nothing to do with men in general or him in particular. Maybe she wanted to find a household that needed a nanny or a governess and be left alone. He didn't know her well, but Ivy Pritchard seemed to be a resourceful lady.

Was she even in Carlisle? "Time's a'wasting, laddie," Cowan said. "It appears some of the Scotland-bound coaches have been getting through, now that the snow has stopped."

Jake hesitated at the open door of the post chaise. The laird gave him a little push with his good foot. "All she can do is say no," he said. "I'll follow."

Is that where I am? Jake asked himself as he shouldered his medical pouch and picked up his bag again. *I barely know her.*

His closed off, calloused, infinitely weary heart suggested–– just suggested, mind you – that maybe the test would be a glimpse of her. He girded his loins, squared his shoulders, and went into the public room where mail coach riders waited.

He didn't see Ivy at first. He saw irate, exhausted travelers milling around. Then his shuttered, calloused heart knew precisely where to look, and there she was.

She sat in a corner, her face averted from the others. The room seemed to bulge with people in all stages of irritation and desperation, but Ivy's corner looked quiet, simply because she was there, exerting no influence, making no scene, just creating calm. As he watched her, he felt his shoulders lowering again, and his too-busy mind slowing down. It was then he realized that Ivy was a sea of serenity and he an exhausted mariner. He probably needed her more than she needed him, even if she was destitute at the moment and out of ideas.

I have ideas, he thought. *Quite a few.* He lost all fear as a beguiling idea propelled him to her quiet corner. He sat down beside her. She started, turned to see who had invaded her space, and to his tired heart's delight, melted against him, wordless. His arm went around her as though it belonged there.

Neither of them said anything for a long moment. Then, "All I knew to do was run."

He could tell Ivy had more to say before he thrust in his oar, so he squeezed her shoulder gently. That was all the encouragement she needed. "They sat me down and told me I was going to marry Captain Baldwin when his father returned."

"I gather you weren't too impressed," he ventured finally, after another silence, followed by the agent announcing another mail coach leaving for all towns west along Solway Firth.

"Papa told me once that the Baldwins lived beyond their means and would need resuscitation. Such a marriage had been everyone's plan for four years." She turned in his grip to look him in the eyes. "George Baldwin was even less impressed. He wouldn't look at me. I…I think he felt sorry for himself."

"You have described my least favorite patient. Ever."

"I don't know that I ever met a full-blown hypochondriac before." She said it so candidly that he couldn't help smiling. "He acts like he's in constant pain, but *he* is a constant pain."

"The more fool he," Jake said, and kissed her, pretty certain that no one would notice, even though there were travelers all around them. Her lips were so soft. She ended the kiss first, as if wanting to look at him and assure herself that he really meant it.

He really meant it. He kissed her again. Her hand went to his neck this time and he was in heaven. He looked around eventually, noticing that the room was clearing out and they were now obvious. Two older ladies smiled at them.

"Oh, dear, we're making a scene," Ivy whispered.

"I know. It's grand," he replied, which made her rosy up and laugh. "What made you…"

"I panicked." She looked down at her hands, the quiet woman again, but only for a moment this time. "No matter what happened to me in Scotland, I knew I didn't want a life of humiliation. Twenty-four years was enough."

Her quiet words struck something deep inside Jake Frost that he didn't know existed until that moment in a posting house in frozen-solid Carlisle. He had forgotten that people who weren't at war fought their own battles, too. Here was this kind and quiet woman with the least-important defect imaginable, waylaid from childhood by shallow people who should have known better. Wonder of wonders––maybe it was the season––she saw something in him. She saw a better man than he knew he was, and she was going to make him even better.

"Ivy Pritchard, I haven't known you long, to be sure, but I am pretty certain that I love you," he said, matching the softness of her voice with his own. "You're kind; you're lovely. I was so consumed with disliking George Baldwin – I still can't stand him – that I had decided that nothing in Yorkshire was going to please me. What a sorry specimen I am."

"Kindly don't be so hard on yourself."

"It's nothing that can't be remedied," he said, his forehead against hers now. "It might not be the smartest thing you ever do, but it will be the smartest thing *I* ever do, if you consent to marry an unemployed surgeon of no particular background who hasn't the foggiest notion what to do, now that peace has broken out." He took her by the shoulders for a better look. "And look, this ill-mannered lout proposed to you in a posting house."

She looked at him expectantly. "When was that?"

Sheesh, what an idiot this poor woman was hoping to marry. "Ah! I should formally propose, eh? Will you marry me, Ivy Pritchard? I love you and I will always take care of you and our children."

Maybe a hopeful husband wasn't supposed to be so brazen as to speak of the baser side of the bargain, but he was a surgeon and he understood the visceral side of life. Yes, children. He knew how they started and arrived. From her blush, he suspected she did, too.

"I will marry you because I love you," she told him. "I doubt my father will settle any money on you, though."

"I can bear up under the strain," he teased, convinced right down to his stockinged feet that he had just made the best decision of his life.

"Well, laddie, there you are and isn't she a pretty lass!"

Jake looked up from contemplation of his future bride to see Laird Cowan leaning on his servant and a cane. "Laird Cowan, this is Miss Ivy Pritchard, who had just consented to marry me. Ivy, Laird Cowan kindly let me ride to Carlisle with him. I believe the roads are still blocked to the south."

"Aye, they are." Cowan looked them over. "What would you say to continuing the journey a little longer to Lockerbie? My holdings are there. You'll both have time to think things through. *My* bonny lassie will make a fuss over you both, and you can doctor my foot again, if you please."

"My pleasure. If Lockerbie has an apothecary, I will concoct a nasty-tasting brew that might help, as well." Did he dare? Certainly. "I might also suggest a plain diet that will alleviate some of your suffering."

"Och, laddie, belt-tightening waits until after Christmas!"

Ivy's hand on his shoulder, Jake tightened the bandage again. He and the coachman helped the laird back into the post chaise, Ivy following with her bandbox. They sat close together, Ivy's head against his shoulder, as the driver picked his way through darkening Carlisle and soon to the border.

When they passed through Gretna Green, equally dark, Laird Cowan hollered for the coachman to pause. He gestured with his cane and tapped on the window. "If ye have mind, we can return in a day or two and the blacksmith can marry you across the anvil. Interested?"

So it happened that two days later, Christmas Eve, Jacob Frost and Ivy Pritchard, accompanied by the required two witnesses--Laird and Lady Cowan--held hands across the anvil that, since 1754, had seen many such marriages. Dressed in sober black with a colorful Gracie plaid, the blacksmith pronounced them man and wife in the Church of Scotland, after declaring, "I'll jine ye twa as one, in the heat of the moment," which made Ivy blush and squeeze Jake's hand tighter.

After they kissed as man and wife, the blacksmith brought his hammer down and made the anvil ring, to the delight of the Cowans and the Frosts. After payment of the ritual guinea, Laird Cowan furnished the also-required "wee dram." (Jake Frost could only stare in wonder at Laird Cowan's enthusiasm for wee drams and know he would be a terrible patient for the treatment of gout. At least Cowan was no hypochondriac.)

Then it was back to Lockerbie and a roomful of Jardines, Dicksons, Cowans, and Lauries to dance and drink and then walk the streets with other carolers. Hands still held fast, the Frosts walked with them until they fell back and ducked into a quiet inn. Jake had made his plans earlier on a walk. The smiling landlord found them a third-floor room away from noise.

They did their own celebrating. In the morning, Jake spent luxurious minutes admiring his beautiful wife as she slept. When she woke and stretched, he kissed her heartily and they celebrated some more.

By mid-morning, they were roused by every church bell in Lockerbie, ushering in the birth of the Christ Child. Jake was content to hold his wife, admire the freckles on her bare shoulders, and think about the future. Maybe it was time for a pronouncement. He was a new husband. Did they make pronouncements?

"Ivy, my lovely and bounteous wife-- she giggled at that-- "what now?"

She thought a moment. "I am hungry. Perhaps some food?"

"Yes, indeed. I was thinking a little farther afield, you know, now that I am a husband and a responsible, reliable sort."

"I love you in spite of that," she teased, which meant hair-ruffling, a smooch, and other details.

"As I was saying," he continued an hour later. "I am obviously putty in your hands, so you choose our next move. Where should I set up a practice?"

He thought for a moment that he had made a terrible misstep. Her face grew solemn, maybe even sad.

"But, my love, that's a decision," she pointed out. "I don't know how to choose anything because I never had a choice. Do women make decisions?"

"You could have chosen not to marry me," he pointed out. "I suspect the Cowans would have found you respectable work here in Lockerbie. Really. Choose. I also suspect that my plans to set up a practice in Yorkshire would be, er, scotched by the Baldwins and Pritchards, should I be so audacious. The word is probably already spreading far and wide that I am a bounder."

She consider the matter, burrowing closer. "I can decide where we live?"

"Why not? I know you're bright. You married me, didn't you?" The Frosts both chuckled over that. Ivy said nothing for a while, but he was already coming to understand her silence. Other than running away, he doubted she had done a foolish, impulsive thing in her life.

"Baltimore," she said finally. "I get chilblains ever winter and I am tired of that. My cousin will give us advice, once we're there." She rose up on one elbow and looked at him closely. "Is such a move too expensive?"

It was a consideration. As he frowned over the matter, that peculiar essence that seemed to be governing everything this Christmas, when a Babe was born who would help the blind to see, the lame to walk, and idiots to succeed, continued to nudge him along. War had rendered him blind to goodness. While he would never tolerate the Captain Baldwins of the world, he was beginning to understand goodness. Maybe the Lord did work in mysterious ways.

"Bear with me a moment," he told Ivy.

Jake Frost—a changing man if not an entirely changed one—got up and padded across the room in all his bare splendor to open his trunk. He took out the brown-wrapped package and handed it to her. He tugged a blanket around his shoulders because the room was cold. Surely Baltimore *would* be warmer.

She took out the Gutenberg Bible and gasped. "Where... where...how..."

"A spoil of war from Spain. I can sell it in London for a substantial sum, I believe," he told her. "Enough to get us established in the place of *your* choosing. Merry Christmas. Baltimore, it is. Hopefully the locals will have forgotten that not too many years ago, the British army burned their capitol."

She clutched the Bible to bare breasts. "Are we certifiably crazy?"

"No. We're in love." He set aside the book he had saved from other looters in Badajoz and gathered her close, marveling at unexpected goodness.

Heavenly peace, indeed.

Epilog

O n their way to London and the great auction houses, Ivy tried Jake a bit when she insisted they stop in Brierton so she could make amends with her parents, and hopefully retrieve more of her wardrobe, since their destination was Baltimore. He would happily have avoided meeting what he knew would be irate people, certain he had ruined Ivy's relationship with her parents. At least hanging, drawing and quartering had mostly been abolished in England.

Arriving at Brierton in mid-afternoon, they stowed their luggage with the obliging innkeeper, who grinned when Ivy showed him her wedding ring, newly purchased in Carlisle. Before they started a slow walk to the Pritchard estate, the innkeep gestured them close and spoke in whispers, after looking around.

"There's been a real to-do at the Baldwins, and at your home, Miss, er, Mrs. Frost," he warned. "That's all I know, but I hear it ain't pretty. Have a care, you two."

Jake held Ivy's hand as they walked the two miles. His arm went around her as the Pritchard manor came into view. She had grown quiet and turned away out of habit, something he never wanted to see again. Ah, well. Better face the music.

She hung back when he boldly banged the door knocker. To his relief, Larch opened the door. He gasped and yanked Jake inside, then coaxed Ivy after him.

"I'm glad you're here," Larch said, after making sure they were alone.

"How bad is it?" Ivy asked.

Larch grinned. "Follow me!"

The Frosts exchanged glances and joined hands again. Larch opened the sitting room door and announced, "The Frosts, sir and madam."

Jake's dread vanished when Mrs. Pritchard, dignified woman, shrieked, cast aside her needlework, and leaped up from the comfortable sofa that had lured him into deep sleep only weeks ago. She ran to Ivy and hugged her, laughing and crying. Jake began to relax.

Mr. Pritchard moved more slowly, but in a moment he was pumping Jake's hand, "Thank God!" he exclaimed. "By eloping, you saved my daughter from worse condemnation!"

Jake and Ivy stared at each other. Slowly, then with remarkable velocity, it dawned on Jake Frost that Dame Fortune had smiled again. Or perhaps St. Nicholas had a wicked sense of humor. How was a simple surgeon to know?

Mrs. Pritchard gestured to the sofa and they sat. Ivy looked at Jake, since he was the husband and designated brave man. He cleared his throat. Might as well brazen it through, in case he was wrong. "Mr. and Mrs. Pritchard, I owe you an enormous apol...."

Mr. Pritchard raised his hand to silence Jake. "We owe *you* such a debt, sir," he said. "Not three days after Ivy bolted from the premises, who should arrive at the Baldwins' house than... than...I can't describe her."

Mrs. Pritchard took up the narrative with some glee. "She even called herself Elsie Baldwin!"

Ivy Frost gasped. Ah, the testing point. Was he, Jacob Frost, man enough to admit that he had sent a message and money to Elsie? In that moment, Jake decided, no, he wasn't. Some confessions were better left alone since the whole matter had been a last-ditch effort.

"She called herself Elsie Baldwin?" he asked, feigning innocence. He somehow managed to stop from bursting into hysterical laughter.

"Such a blowsy frump, from what we heard," Mr. Pritchard said. "All bad grammar and making demands. What could George Baldwin have been *thinking*?"

Mrs. Pritchard fanned herself with her embroidery hoop. "And to think our Ivy would have been married to a …a…bigamist! We can't thank you enough, Mr. Frost."

"What happened next?" Ivy asked.

"Daughter, there was such a scene at the Baldwins," Mrs. Pritchard said. "We heard it all from the Baldwins' butler, who told it to Larch."

Jake smiled inside to see his mother-in-law enjoying the whole thing. Perhaps life had been too boring for her lately. "We hear that General Baldwin paid her a huge sum of money to vanish." Mrs. Pritchard giggled. "Apparently she stole Grace Baldwin's Apostle spoons, too."

"And Captain Baldwin?" Jack asked. "The invalid?" (He couldn't resist.)

Mrs. Pritchard leaned close to him like a conspirator. "Apparently he showed a clean pair of heels and dashed away in a different direction. Rumor has it he is sailing to America. I suppose he wasn't as ill as he seemed. You must be an excellent surgeon, Mr. Frost. You cured a scoundrel! We're so delighted with how things turned out."

Poor America. Hopefully, George Baldwin would never appear in Baltimore. There was so much Jake Frost could have said. Instead, he looked at his wife, so pretty and kind, then his in-laws, eager to admire him now. He wondered at his remarkable good fortune and knew his war was over. Christmas was going to be the holiday remembered, loved and cherished.

"Happy Christmas, Ivy," he whispered to his lady, who looked him full in the face, then thrilled his heart by winking her sleepy eye.

"Happy Christmas, Jake," she replied.

YOURS SINCERELY

Chapter One

I need a new dress for Christmas. Come to the manor at your earliest convenience. AC.

That was it, delivered to the Ashfield Circulating Library by a servant from Tifton Manor.

Rose Cuthbert, library proprietor, took her handy broom and tapped twice on the ceiling. The taps landed in the approximate location of the kitchen floor overhead.

Upstairs, Madeline Tifton smiled at her mother over the rim of her teacup. "Two taps means a message. What would you wager that Cousin Amelia Tifton has issued her usual demand and wants her dress right *now*? I've been waiting for such a message."

"She's right on time, which means late as usual, and determined to inconvenience you," Mama said.

Madeline debated between leaving on her slippers, which she typically wore to muzzle upstairs noise, or putting on actual shoes. She decided slippers would do, since it was too early for the circulating library to open its doors.

She was right. Miss Cuthbert handed her the expected note. "A Christmas dress," Maddie told Miss Cuthbert. "She will likely pay me five shillings for hours of work, and dare me to ask for more."

Miss Cuthbert wagged a finger at Maddie. "And she will again get a bargain. You are too timid, my dear."

Maddie shrugged. "It's Christmas and she *is* a relative, no matter how odious."

She didn't mention that at age twenty-six and by now decidedly on the shelf, Amelia Tifton, who never missed a dramatic moment at anyone else's expense, was flat chested and somehow looked sallow in whatever color fabric she insisted upon, in the hopes it might turn her into a raving beauty. She would likely sniff at the exquisite dress, have the footman hand Maddie the five shillings, and blame Maddie when nothing of romantic importance happened this Christmas, one of many so noted.

"You could tell Miss Law-de-dah you're too busy this year," Miss Cuthbert suggested. "Are you?"

"You know I plan my dressmaking better than that," Maddie reminded her. "I'll humor Miss Tifton again because she is a relative, and because I should be charitable at this time of year." She kissed Miss Cuthbert's cheek. "'Do unto others,'" she quoted.

"But no one at Tifton Manor ever does kindly unto you!" the librarian protested.

All I know are ungrateful relatives, Maddie thought. Out of habit, she stopped at the New Volumes bookshelf in the circulating library, not that anything would have changed in the few hours since she had said goodnight and traipsed upstairs.

Miss Cuthbert laughed. "Nothing new overnight," she said. "Imagine a world where that were possible! Go on now!"

It was all in good-natured fun. No matter how many years she and Mama lived upstairs, she knew every day was brighter because of Miss Cuthbert. Grumpy and managing she might seem to the world of Ashfield, Miss Cuthbert was one of Maddie's valued anchors.

Besides, no matter how many furbelows and fancies cousin Amelia wanted on her Christmas dress, she would still be flat-chested and gawky. Not even the prettiest dress in Hampshire could change that. Amelia might blame her, but Maddie knew it wasn't *her* fault that no suitors chased after Amelia, even if she did come from the moneyed side of the Tiftons.

That thought made Maddie shake her head. *I am not homely but have no money at all. I wonder which of us will eventually marry? It won't be I.* She couldn't help a little laugh. *Although I would never settle for an old man with bad breath. Alas, Amelia may have to do just that.*

She showed the note to her mother who tatted by the window now, where the light was best. Mama had her own projects. Between the two of them, they rubbed along quite well in rented rooms and no visible means of support beyond sewing, and twenty-five pounds a year, even if they were poor relations of Peter and Loisa Tifton of Tifton Manor, Hampshire.

Maddie had figured years ago that relatives could be the curse of the earth, or people to be tolerated; she chose the latter. At the ripe old age of twenty-six, her own days of wishful thinking were long over.

She was also not one to put off too many uncomfortable situations, especially since this was business, even if the Tiftons still seemed to think that since she was a Tifton, albeit the only child of the family's black sheep, she somehow owed them. She didn't.

On went her cloak, a sturdy affair she had sewn from a woolen blanket. "It weighs as much as you do," Mama had commented, which wasn't precisely true. Maddie knew it would last a lifetime, and she valued permanence, considering how little of it she felt in her own life.

The bonnet was a new one, a makeover from a lady she sewed for. More than one of her steady clients had remarked how good she was at repurposing items that others never thought twice about discarding. Maybe it was a little wicked of her: Maddie knew her stylish bonnet would rouse envy in her cousin's scrawny bosom. Too bad.

She stood a moment on the front step of the library, enjoying the benefit of new fallen snow, which managed to turn the view of High Street into something befitting--if not the view from Scheherazade's palace--at least a street in *Emma*, Jane Austen's latest novel. The circulating library only had one copy of *Emma*, and it was always lent somewhere. Maddie had at least managed a glimpse inside the cover before Miss Cuthbert handed it to the next paying patron.

"It's so popular, Maddie," Miss Cuthbert apologized, after the patron pounced on the book, clutched it to her bosom, and hurried from the library. "I wish my library budget could have afforded more. I predict *Emma* will be available to you in perhaps 1840."

"Twenty-four *years*?" she gasped. (It was their little joke.)

Maddie had developed patience. When they moved into rented rooms over the library years ago, Mama had worked out a suitable arrangement: Madeline, then six and already a confirmed bibliophile, would sweep, dust and empty the ash cans daily, in exchange for a day or two with the book of her choosing for Mama to read to her. As she turned into the same skilled needlewoman as her mother, Maddie included a new dress a year to Miss Cuthbert's wardrobe. This was paid for in kind, with an actual yearly subscription to the library, except, of course, for brand new volumes. Those still belonged to Ashfield's paying patrons, of whom there were a fair number.

Before Maddie left for Tifton Manor, she swept the walkway in front of the library, another of her duties. There was only a skiff of snow, so she swept a little more, taking care of the walk in front of Mrs. Halton's Pins and Needles, and then further down, a sweet shop.

Number Fourteen came next, a narrow house with one story above the main floor. That was it, a house in a row of stores. For years, Walter Ince had called it home.

At first, no one knew where he came from, but he appeared one day and moved in, an older gentleman who kept to himself, but wore clothes of good quality, according to Mama, who sewed on a few buttons when asked, and turned a collar or two.

There were few secrets in Ashfield. Word got out finally that he was the father of Loisa Tifton, of Tifton Manor. A former Wiltshire landowner of the gentry class, he had soiled his hands with trade, convincing both Peter and Loisa Tifton he was no longer fit company. Maddie thought Mr. Ince looked fine enough, always well-dressed, always with a ready smile, which made him highly unlikely to be related to the Tiftons. As with most gossip, if it wasn't indulged or amplified, it died out, at least to a degree. No one could deny, however, that Loisa Ince Tifton never set foot inside Number Fourteen.

Maddie swept the snow from Mr. Ince's little walk, remembering his kindness. He died three years ago as quietly as he had lived in Ashfield. He had been her special circulating library friend—he loved the *London Times*—and kindly let her read Miss Austen's *Sense and Sensibility* after he read it but before he returned it.

She stood another moment in front of Number Fourteen, thinking of the time she and Mama became his friends after he tripped on a step and broke his ankle, him, with no one to provide home care. It became an easy matter to share their dinners and light suppers: just a knock on his door, a bob and a curtsy, and the handing over of a hot dish wrapped in cloth.

Gone three years and I still miss you, she thought, remembering the letters he had dictated to her, when his handwriting became too shaky. He tried to pay her for this service, but she refused. "Mr. Ince, I like doing this," she stated firmly enough for him to believe her.

She did. Even now, somewhere inside Number Fourteen, there was a pasteboard box with correspondence to an American grandson of his, a seafarer. "Mr. Ince, my world is small," had been her clinching argument to receiving no pay for this. "I enjoy learning about a wider world through these letters."

So there, sir, she thought even now, missing the man and the letters. Hopefully the seafaring American hadn't suffered too badly during those recent years of war between the two countries, when no letters got through. She reminded herself to always sweep in front of Number Fourteen. Call it her gift to someone gone and missed, at least by her, if not his own daughter, now a proud Tifton.

Speaking of which—tape measure in her pocket, along with paper and pencil, Maddie continued down the street. Her annual duty to Amelia Tifton wasn't going to go away, and Maddie seldom avoided even unpleasant tasks too long.

Still, she gave a backward glance at Number Fourteen, then stopped another moment to look up to the window where Mr. Ince used to sit. She looked around. No one was in sight. She blew a kiss to Number Fourteen.

Maddie continued until the High Street turned into the outskirts of Ashfield. Before she wanted it to happen, Tifton Manor came into view. No one was around, so she said what she always did, but under her breath:

"Would a little kindness have been so hard to manage, you Tiftons?"

Chapter Two

Maybe it was her lucky day. Maddie knocked at the servants' entrance and Livingston the butler opened the door. This was always better than either the footman or housekeeper, who both seemed to have been nourished in the belief that if their employers didn't like someone, than they shouldn't either.

"Miss Tifton, what a pleasure," Livingston said, opening the door wide, instead of the usual bare minimum. "How do you do?"

"I do fine," which made them both smile. It was something she had said since she was small and couldn't reach the knocker yet.

He indicated that she enter, and took her cloak and bonnet. Maddie couldn't help but notice all the silver cutlery, knives lined up like a rank of soldiers at attention across the table in the servants' hall, a sure sign of parties and dinners to celebrate the season. She imagined there would be holly and ivy upstairs. She had already noticed the huge wreath on the front door. Who could miss it? Christmas was underway, and it was a ponderous undertaking at Tifton Manor.

Funny notion about that wreath: The first time Maddie remembered seeing one here was in her sixth year, when she and Mama came to the front door. Eyes wide, mouth open, she had gaped at the size of the wreath, which was what Mrs. Tifton never forgot. ("Mouth agape like a half-wit," had been her comment, as relayed to Mama by a servant who liked to embarrass them. Which servant? They were all the same.)

Maddie still didn't want to think about their reception on that doorstep years ago. It lasted less than ten minutes, as long as it took Mrs. Tifton to come downstairs in all her glory and listen to Mama explain that her husband, the wicked brother of Peter Tifton, had died of drink and left them penniless in a Norfolk rooming house.

Mama didn't ask for help beyond what she thought was due to her, and it was probably obvious to anyone with eyes that they needed it. Maybe Mama's Norfolk accent was too strong. Maddie doubted Mama was impolite, because Mama never was. Mrs. Tifton didn't want to hear another word.

"Good riddance to my worthless brother-in-law," had been Mrs. Tifton's comment. "And good riddance to you." The door with the huge wreath had slammed shut on them.

Time might never erase the shock and sadness of their dismissal. The wreath loomed as large today as it did when Maddie was six, so she was happy to take the servants' entrance instead, as she always did.

Today, Livingston offered her tea and cake. "Do you need any help with all this silver?" she asked.

"Oh, no, child. I'll ferret out a lazy servant from somewhere in this vast pile," he said, his eyes merry. "It's a skill we butlers possess. You've been summoned to measure the scrawny Miss Tifton for her usual Christmas frock?"

"Aye, *soh*," she said. It was fun now and then to put on that broad Norfolk accent, which, apparently, was good enough for the late and much-admired Admiral Lord Nelson. "*Prups thee'll announze meh?*"

"*Prups*, miss," he replied with a smile. "I'll escort you up the backstairs."

Up the backstairs, she didn't risk encountering her Aunt Loisa Tifton, as nasty a woman as one could wish to not know. It was enough to catch a whiff of fir and balsam from grand rooms below and know that soon the halls at Tifton Manor would be decked, now that Advent was well under way and Christmas approaching.

Their first Christmas in Ashfield had been dismal, spent in a tiny room over the public house. They only stayed there because they could not afford to go anywhere else. Maddie vaguely remembered a solicitor or two, Mama's tears, and then the scratch of pen on paper. Mama had been forced by want to accept a yearly pittance of twenty-five pounds, instead of the two hundred pounds from her late husband's portion as a Tifton. Mama soon learned of three rooms over the circulating library, at a price she could afford. Eventually, they both had a bed each, and table and chairs.

That was then, she reminded herself as she walked beside Livingston. Through the years, and several redecorations of Tifton Manor, he had quietly sent hand-me-down furniture their way. Luckily, the Egyptian decorating frenzy after Nelson's victory at the Nile was mercifully short.

Livingston took her up the first floor to the catch-all room, where she perched on a second or third-best chair. Tape measure in hand, she waited for her cousin.

She waited more, but not as long as usual. Once Amelia kept Maddie twiddling her thumbs for upwards of an hour, simply because she could, a chip off her mother's block. "As soon's I saw you coming around to the back, I sent Miss Amelia word that you had arrived," Livingston whispered on the stairs. "She probably thinks you've been up here all this time, waiting for her, when you and I were really having tea belowstairs, and a chat. None the wiser, eh?"

"I trust I haven't kept you waiting," Amelia said from the open doorway ten minutes later.

Something happened to Madeline Tifton then. After years of slights and rudeness, she decided not to duck her head meekly and say, "Oh, no, not long at all." Maybe the credit went to thinking of kind Mr. Ince and sweeping snow in front of his empty house. Maybe she finally decided that worrying about what Amelia Tifton said or thought didn't matter. Maybe she was tired of the whole charade. Whatever it was, her response came easily.

"It was no problem at all," she replied. "I had tea with Livingston belowstairs. He is so thoughtful. The usual for you this Christmas? Stand over there where the light is best."

What could Amelia Tifton do but comply? Humming to herself, Madeline measured her cousin. *Scrawny as ever,* she thought, and decided that her own pleasing roundness gave *her* frocks something to drape on without clinging in terror.

"The fashion this year is another inch up from the floor," Maddie said. "What would you like?"

"I prefer the usual," Amelia replied, squashing any change.

Maddie owned to a wicked delight. Usually *she* was the silent one, quiet and head down, a servant and not a cousin. "Are you certain?" she persisted, then lied because she felt suddenly generous. "You *do* have nice ankles, Cousin Amelia."

No, I have never called you Cousin Amelia until this moment, Maddie thought gleefully. *It didn't hurt a bit and it's true.*

"Very well then, another inch up," came the faint reply, followed by an unheard of, "Thank you."

"What color would you like this year?"

"Yellow, of course. What were you thinking?" Ah, the disdain was back. *Quick recovery cousin,* Maddie thought, impressed.

But there it came again, the desire to shake things up a little, and suggest a wiser choice. "What about deep blue this year?" Maddie asked. "It will compliment your complexion." *Anything but yellow,* she thought. *All that does is make you look like a corpse three days dead.*

"I prefer yellow," was the reply, minus the disdain. Was that... could it be...uncertainty?

"Very well. Let me know if you change your mind. I have a lovely blue linen that would bring out the color of your eyes."

That, then, was that. Maddie pocketed her pad and pencil stub. "I'll come by with your dress in a week for a fitting, and you'll receive it a day later. Will that be enough time for you this year?"

"Yes. We have nothing special planned this Christmas."

Maddie heard something wistful in her voice, as if Amelia already knew she faced a future of nothing special. *We are more kin than you realize, cousin,* she thought. *I have nothing special planned, either.* "Very well, then. I will see you in a week. Good day."

That was painless. She went belowstairs, where two maids were sullenly polishing silver now. This was *not* a happy household.

Livingston gave her the high sign and she met him by the door. He had a small wreath in his hand.

"This is for my favorite Tiftons," he said. The wreath was his annual present.

So pleased, Maddie wanted to tell him that the only reason she still trooped here to sew a Christmas dress for Amelia was for his wreaths and other small kindnesses through the year.

He walked her outside and shut the door behind them, in case the maids wanted to eavesdrop, which they often did. "There is an interesting rumor floating about. It involves Mr. Ince." He lowered his voice. "Surely you have heard the rumors that Mr. Ince was Mrs. Tifton's father."

"I've heard something about selling off his ancestral acres in Wiltshire to speculate in some business scheme. He was a lovely man and I miss him," Maddie said with what she hoped sounded like finality, not wanting more rumor about someone she liked so well.

Livingston glanced around as if he expected a Tifton to pop out from behind a bush. "It might involve an American."

This was something. She remembered quite well Mr. Ince's letters that went to an American in Connecticut and occasionally in Boston.

The butler lowered his voice even farther. "The footman overheard comments in the public house from Mr. Clare, the solicitor."

"To what effect?" There. She wouldn't ask anything more, because she remembered kind letters to and from America.

"The story circulating around the manor––mind you, it's rumor and I wouldn't put much credence in anything the footman says––is that Mr. Ince left some money, and it might involve this American."

"Just rumors, sir," Maddie said. *His name is Amos Foster and somehow Mr. Ince is his grandfather*, she could have added, but knew better.

"I suspect as much," Livingston replied. The butler managed a well-mannered chuckle. "I doubt there is anything to it."

As Maddie started down the lane, she thought about the letters that Mr. Ince had written to Amos that he never sent, because of war between the United States and England, which precluded all commerce. If that wasn't enough, the animosity of Napoleon meant that ships sailing from America to anywhere else could be seized, too. The newspapers she read in the circulating library called them Orders in Council, and the Berlin and Milan Decrees. To Maddie it was just one more aggravation of war.

"I will write anyway and keep my letters in this cardboard sleeve," Mr. Ince had told her. "Perhaps someday I can mail them. A war can't last forever, can it?"

Now at last, the war was over, with the French defeated at Waterloo, opening the seaways in all directions. Maybe Amos and the American were one and the same. If he came to visit the Tiftons, she doubted she would ever see him. No Tifton at the manor would ever call attention to poor relatives living over a library.

Still, it would be good to give those letters to the American possibly coming to visit, if he really existed. It was all speculation.

As she passed Number Fourteen on her way home, Maddie resolved to forget the matter.

Chapter Three

Captain Amos Foster heaved an enormous sigh of relief when the *Betty Bright* signaled and was allowed to proceed toward the newer London Docklands. He reminded himself where the West Indies Dock was located. It was one of the first enclosed wharves built in this still-new century, designed to protect cargo from thievery, which his father called "port piracy."

There it was. Captain Foster eased the *Betty Bright* to a safe anchorage, the merchant vessel's first crossing of the Atlantic in five years, brought about by the ratifying of a treaty signed in Ghent with the British, and then the end of Napoleon's romp through Europe at Waterloo. Peace at last.

Amos looked at his lieutenant, cousin Mark Mason. He was a good luff and a joker who rolled his eyes when they anchored. He collapsed into a fake faint on the deck and lay there laughing. "By God, we did it, Captain!" Mark declared finally, then stood up and brushed himself off.

What a relief, indeed. Papa was gone now, but Amos hoped, in some maritime/mercantile theology, that Daniel Foster knew they still had one ship left out of the four in their little fleet. The first sank in a hurricane in the West Indies. The other two were sold for scrap because war had wounded American shipping to the death…. almost. *Betty* alone remained, and she had made an excellent crossing with a hold full of New World cargo that he knew England wanted, and soon: beaver pelts a-plenty, lumber from his country's inexhaustible forests, naval stores of tar and resins, and kegs and kegs of rum, which hopefully hadn't been tapped too often by the crew on the voyage. A little he always overlooked, but not a lot, and the men who sailed with him knew it. He also knew they were as grateful as he was to be in business again.

The next matter of business was as important as this entry into the enclosed dock that had welcome Foster vessels before war ended commerce. Was Pa's London agent willing to be his, as well? Adam scanned the row of houses of business lining the wharf. There it was: Godbe and Sons, Maritime Procurers.

"Tie her up and lower the plank, Mark," he told his cousin. "Let's see if we still have friends willing to trade."

Mark Mason bellowed out orders and the men sprang to their duties. Amos wished he could practice walking up and down the non-moving deck to remind his sea legs to retire now. He remembered the awkward sight of whalers in New Bedford after a three years' voyage, with their curious rolling gait on land. True, this voyage had taken only six weeks, with fair winds.

As it was, he took his papers from his cabin and descended the plank. He took a few cautious steps. It wasn't so far to the door, but his sea legs still moved in that seamen's swagger when he knocked out of politeness, because the sign read, "Do come in."

He did come in, recognizing Gilbert Godbe at his untidy desk – how did the man keep everything in order? – and felt a pang when Mr. Godbe looked over his shoulder, as if waiting for Daniel Foster to appear.

"Mr. Godbe, I wish he were here, too," he said simply.

He recalled Mr. Godbe's inclination toward philosophy, so the maritime procurer's comment comforted him. "Time and tide," was his equally simple comment. A New England minister might have said something about "Ashes to ashes, dust to dust," but this wasn't New England and Godbe was no Puritan.

"Aye, sir. The *Betty Bright* is mine now," Amos said. "Pa taught me everything he knew, howsomever."

"So he did. You are here as proof, eh?"

"Aye again, and ready to bargain, if you and I are no longer enemies."

"We never were, lad," Mr. Godbe said with that familiar twinkle in his eyes. "We'll leave that nonsense to governments. Would you like some tea and biscuits that haven't been in a keg for a month or two?"

"Or two years and then some," Amos said, and felt a weight leave his shoulders. He preferred coffee but this was England, after all. "We just sealed the kegs and hoped for the best!"

The business went quickly. Adam gave the manifest to Mr. Godbe, who read, and nodded, and wasted not a moment in stating his price. The haggling that followed seemed more of a tradition, because the prices offered were evidence that England still needed upstart, raw America and her goods. Done and done.

Now came the next important part, the one that might include a future. To Amos's continued relief, Mr. Godbe wasted not a moment. "Give me ten days and I know I can fill your hold with goods bound at last for America. Are you interested?"

Oh, why hem and haw and hunt around for better bargains, as Pa liked to do? "Aye, sir. Let's fill that hold for a return voyage."

They finished bare minutes later. Godbe wasted not a moment in another signature from Amos, then added his own, as bona fide agent.

"Beyond filling your hold, are you staying long?" Mr. Godbe asked, after handshakes and signing.

He never liked to talk about it, but Adam told his Docklands agent the fate of the other three Foster ships. "War took its toll and I need to keep moving," he said. "I've told the crew we could hope for a week or two here."

"You know where I would house them," his agent said. "What say you?"

"Aye, again."

Mr. Godbe walked him to the door, congenial to the end. No wonder Pa would work with no other. Amos had his own question. "Sir, how are those sons of yours? I want Godbe and Sons to be around forever."

Mr. Godbe's expression changed and Amos wished he had no spoken so jovially. "I mean..."

Godbe's hand on his arm told Amos the measure of his courtesy and perhaps his need to lean for a moment. "War took its toll, as you said. My namesake gone in a battle with France, but his brother still lives. He's lighter a leg from another battle, but game to sit behind this deck someday."

"I'm sorry," Amos said. Time and tides.

Mr. Godbe opened the door, then closed it. He snapped his fingers. "A moment, Amos. I have a letter specifically for you. It's three years old but…wait here."

The agent rummaged, returned, and held out the letter, pointing to the return address. "I always tremble a bit when I see something from a solicitor, but maybe your heart is purer than mine!"

Adam laughed and opened the letter, which bore a Hampshire address. Ashfield. "If you don't mind, sir, let me read this in your presence. I might not know the ins and outs of…we mainly just call them attorneys."

Amos read it twice, then handed it to Mr. Godbe, who did the same. He handed it back. "Lad, it appears that you have some property in Ashfield and a deceased grandfather with you in mind when he made a will. You corresponded with him?"

"I did, at my father's insistence," Amos said. "Walter Ince was my stepmother's father."

"Wasn't there also a Foster Fleet ship named *Cathy Foster*?" Godbe asked. "Just curious."

"Aye, sir. Pa was married first to Betty Mason, my mother. She died too young and he married Catherine Ince. She's your *Cathy Foster*."

"Then the *Betty Bright* is named after your birth mother?"

"Aye. That was Pa's pet name for her. She was a bonny lady, from all reports. I was too young to remember her, more's the pity."

"I recall Cathy Foster. She sailed with your father now and then didn't she?"

"Briefly, and so did I, before my stepbrother and sister came along. Mama – I've always called her that – is still alive and lives in Connecticut. A great and jolly soul."

"I had a stepmother." Godbe shuddered elaborately. "Oof! You were lucky."

"I know. She treats me like her own. Regarding my stepmother, it seems there was a falling out with her sister, who married into a proper family and didn't approve of American seamen. The sister married Peter Tifton, a man as snobby as she is, apparently."

"When did you begin your correspondence with your grandfather?" Mr. Godbe asked.

"I was eleven, I think, and curious to know about my stepmother's family."

"Be careful what you wish for," Mr. Godbe joked.

Amos tapped the solicitor's letter. "I never met my Grandpa Ince. I know we weren't actually related, but he liked my letters and insisted I call him Grandpa. Letters stopped with the war, of course, and I had wondered if he still lived." He looked at the man whom he knew was already adept at guiding him through English maritime business. "What would you do, if you were I?"

"Go to Ashfield and surprise a solicitor," Mr. Godbe said immediately. He glanced at the letter. "I've heard that Tifton name. Heard some rumors. They're rich, but… Maybe you'd best avoid them!"

"I wish I could." Amos smiled. "I intend to be an impeccable ambassador for my upstart country! See you in two weeks, sir, and ready to sail home."

"It'll be Christmas."

"I'll keep my eyes open for the Wise Men, now that shipping lines are open."

"That's a tad flippant, Captain, if I may say so."

"Sir, I have one ship remaining of a four-fleet enterprise," Amos replied, stating his case as firmly as he could without seeming rude. He wanted to add that he didn't have time this Christmas to admire holly and berries, drink wassail and sing carols. He just wanted to get home with a cargo.

Oh, Lord, he said precisely that. Mr. Godbe listened, shook his head, then waggled his finger. "Could be the Almighty will give you something to think about besides commerce."

"Maybe next Christmas, sir," he said. "Aye, next Christmas."

Mr. Godbe shrugged. His eyes were kind, though. "We'll see what the season has in store for you."

Chapter Four

Amos housed his crew where Mr. Godbe recommended, then paid and warned them with serious admonition not to embarrass the United States of America. The innkeep where his crew stayed was good enough to direct him to the nearest mail coach depot. The keep had his own brand of British humor, which involved poking fun at Amos's Yankee accent.

"Yeesh, sor, we turn ye Yanks loose in a strange new world last century ago or so, and whattaya do but start talking funny like," the man said.

You sound a bit strange, too, was what Amos wanted to retort, but Mama raised him better than that. "We're still learning English," was his reply, said with a smile, which seemed to satisfy the man.

Amos did raise his eyebrows when a would-be wit in the pub where the riders waited grabbed a hank of his own hair, took a knife and pretended to scalp himself, all the while dancing in a circle. Small minds. Amos knew the man would turn into a mushy, puking wreck if he actually saw a scalping victim.

He chose to tell himself it was all good-natured ribbing, and not war hatred. After all, the British had burned the capitol in District of Columbia, so who should act out a grievance? Not Captain Amos Foster. Besides, there were more of them than him.

After a longish wait in Aldershot, where another wit wondered what a Yankee could possibly want in Ashfield, the local bone-cracker pulled into said village too late to seek out a solicitor who wasn't already in nightclothes. The public house was quiet enough, suggesting that Ashfield was a sober place and not prone to good cheer much after eight and a half. A quaff in the pub reminded him how good English ale was, plus it furnished him with the direction of the solicitor. It also gave him more insight--wanted or not--into his Tifton relatives.

"'Tween you and me, them Tiftons is the sort what'd step over a pound to pick up a farthing." The keep burped. "And sure as the world, they'd circle 'round to pick up that pound and swat anyone in their way." He leaned across the bar. "'Course I never said this."

"I wasn't listening," Amos teased back, all the while thinking, *No wonder these blokes lost the first revolution. They don't play cards close to the chest.* "I don't think I am involved with the Tiftons in any way, however," he added. "This concerns my Grandfather Ince."

"...whose daughter is a Tifton," the keep informed him. "P'raps you knew that."

"I did. I can keep my distance."

"But will they keep theirs, once they know you're in Ashfield?" Maybe it was time for another confidence. The innkeeper leaned farther across the bar. "I'm too hard on the Tiftons, I s'pose. You can meet nicer Tiftons on the High Street not far from your grandpapa's little house."

"I'm relieved," Amos said, tired and wanting that bed upstairs. "Pull the other leg."

"No, really," the keep insisted. "Maude and her daughter Madeline Tifton live over the circulating library, because that's all they can afford. Apparently Maude married a Tifton rascal who came to a sad but predictable end." He shook his head.

"No fears," Amos said. "I'd better go upstairs now and..."

"Aye, Captain," the innkeep agreed. "But that little Maddie – she still sweeps in front of your grandpa's house when it snows. Word is that they shared their meals with him, when those at Tifton Manor ignored him."

Amos carried that thought upstairs and into bed. He lay in bed a long while, letting the day of travel wash away and wondering about the kindness of a widow and her daughter. He chuckled over the impeccable Tiftons with a rascal in the hedge. Amazing what a person could learn, simply by taking a long pull on ale.

He woke hours later to a light tapping on the door. He had only a slight headache from the night before, but the keep's little maid curtseyed and handed over a small glass of something black and vile.

"It's good for what ails ye," she said, keeping her voice low and confidential. "Master says."

As a matter of fact, it was. He had drunk worse old water at the end of long voyages, so the potion went down easily. He tackled bacon and eggs downstairs with no hesitation, even though the innkeep looked a little groggy.

"Across the street and down a few doors and you'll find our solicitor, you will," Amos was informed.

Snow had fallen, blanketing the street just enough to take away the rough edges of any village a few months into winter. He took a deep breath, always a pleasure after a sea voyage of any length, when the bilge in the hold started to stink.

Papers in hand--something testifying that he was who he said, and not a lunatic--he started for the solicitor's office until his attention was caught by a little miss sweeping in front of what might be his grandfather's house. He smiled to see her, remembering an expression he heard on a coastal voyage to Charleston, South Carolina, during drastic times when there was no shipping to Europe because of war, and he scrambled to find work, any work.

In Charleston, he came across a man watching a boy stacking newly cut wood. "Look'ee there. He goes at that like he's killin' snakes," the man said with admiration.

So was... Maude? Madeline? She didn't waste a movement, but worked with a singleness of purpose like someone, well, killin' snakes. But goodness gracious, she was a pretty thing.

Amos did what any man would do: He admired her. Maude or Madeline was not tall, but she was energetic. Her curly dark hair was tied back simply, curls bobbing as she put her energy into sweeping away a middling amount of snow not sufficient for a shovel. She wore a cloak, a heavy one, which meant he could arrive at no opinion about her figure.

It was enough to see her. She waved to passersby who obviously knew her. Some stopped to chat, even though she continued her task. She paused briefly for a youngish man, good looking and handsome, who stopped and raised his hat to her. Amos felt an irrational jealousy at the man's attention, then reminded himself that he was being an idiot. Maude or Madeline could like whomever she chose.

How did news travel so fast in Ashfield? When he raised his hand to knock on the solicitor's door, it opened. Amos wondered if somehow between dusk and dawn, the innkeeper had spread the word of someone new in the village, bound for the solicitor's.

"Come in, come in, lad," Mr. Clare said. "Seat yourself."

Amos did as he directed. "I am…"

"I already know. Our innkeep loves a good story, and he knew I wanted a chin wag with you." The solicitor scratched his head. "Come to think of it, that conversation may have come up earlier."

"Somehow a brief mention traveled all the way back to Mr. Godbe at the West Indies Dock in London," Amos said, amused. "Rumors travel fast, eh?"

"Lord bless me, that was it," the solicitor said, with no embarrassment.

"He's right, sir. I found your three-year-old letter waiting for me at the dock and here I am. Pleased to meet you, sir." Amos laughed. "Thank you for your patience."

"I'm a patient man, sir. I have a son at sea. I know better than to expect timely communication. And then there was this little war.…What do you think historians in the future will call it?"

"I doubt it will be anything too creative, considering all that Europe has been through, thanks to Napoleon," Amos replied, enjoying this man. "I'd like to call it Here Endeth the Lesson. We two nations, old and new, will hopefully discover we have more in common than otherwise."

"We will." Mr. Clare ran a finger around his spotless neckcloth.

Amos felt only a little shabby in his well-worn navy blues. He crossed his legs, pleased that at least he had set his shoes out into the hallway last night and they were well-polished. Now to begin?

"Here I am, sir," Amon said again. "I have promise of a full cargo, and will stand out to sea in hopefully two weeks. Let me first state that I only really knew my step-grandfather through a lengthy correspondence that began when I was a lad. My father encouraged me to correspond, because he said it was gentlemanly and I might learn something."

"Did you?" Mr. Clare asked with a big smile.

That surprised Amos. He hadn't expected such a question from someone he didn't know, who had business to discuss. He thought about it. "I learned to write a letter, and wish I could have known Grandfather Ince. All I had were letters."

"He was a quiet man who kept to himself." Mr. Clare tapped the sole letter on his desk. "Your grandfather brought this to my office about a week before he died, three years ago." He turned it over and held it up so Amos could read, *This is to be opened when Captain Foster is finally allowed into this country.* "He was quite adamant that it was for you."

"Can't imagine why, really," Amos said. "I doubt he was prosperous. Maybe he has a book for me. He knew I liked to read."

"Captain, he also gave me a letter with the direction of your shipping agent at the West Indies Dock, which, obviously, was finally delivered to you a few days ago."

"Indeed it was."

"Well, sir, open the envelope. I own to some curiosity."

Mr. Clare handed Amos a letter opener. He slit the top and pulled out another envelope with more writing on it. Amos angled it on the solicitor's desk so they could both read it. *This is my last will and testament. I would like my daughter and her family present, as well as her husband's Tifton relatives, at its reading.*

Mr. Clare leaned back in his chair, "This is singular, indeed. Captain, gossip and speculation make their rounds in small towns. Word has it that the Tiftons of Tifton Manor made a point years ago not to have anything to do with Mr. Peter Tifton's brother, who was a rascal. His widow and Madeline live here."

Hah, so Madeline is the pretty daughter, not Maude, Amos thought. Not that it mattered. He meant it when he said two weeks was all the time he could spare for England. Perhaps he could at least meet Madeline. "So the keep informed me. Over the library, he said."

"The very place." The solicitor allowed himself a smile. "Ashfield is full of, um, information."

"What's the proper thing to do here, sir?" Amos asked. "I don't know any of these people. Could you…would you send a note to …to Tifton Manor, is it? You know, explain the situation?"

"Such a missive will be in their hands by luncheon," Mr. Clare said. "I can do the same thing for Maude Tifton, although I know she and Maddie are afraid of the other Tiftons. They might choose to have nothing to do with this." He grew conspiratorial then, much like the innkeep across the High Street. "Word has it that after her spendthrift rascal of a husband died of the drink, Mrs. Maude Tifton came her with her little daughter, asking for help, and was turned away."

How cruel, Amos thought. He tried to imagine his own mother or stepmother doing such a thing, and couldn't. "No wonder they might be reluctant to participate in whatever this is," he said, and tapped the will, securely bound with a cord.

"This will give Ashfield something to gossip about for a while," Mr. Clare said. "So will you." He opened his desk drawer and took out a key with a note attached. "Here is the last part of this intriguing task of mine. Go on, take it. The notes says this key opens that little house at Number Fourteen. It's yours for the moment. Move in, lad, even if it's only for a couple of weeks."

Chapter Five

The solicitor was right. Duffel in hand, his account closed at the inn, Amos had barely let himself into Number Fourteen when someone knocked. He smiled to see an out of breath domestic in some sort of livery holding out a letter.

Amos invited him in, apologizing for the house closed up for three years. He took the letter, noting the expensive envelope and Tifton Manor in imposing letters in the left-hand corner.

"Do at least sit down," Amos said. He removed holland covers from furniture in the sitting room, and both of them coughed.

"Thank you, sir," the servant said when he could speak. "If you please, Mrs. Tifton said I was not to leave until you read her invitation and wrote an answer."

"Very well." Amos read the letter, which began, *Our very dear Captain Foster,* making him wonder at so flowery an address from someone who had never clapped eyes on him before. The note was short but included an invitation to dinner at the manor, and then their total honor and delight if he would stay with them until the matter of "my dear father's will was read."

Hmm. Hadn't the solicitor just told him that the Tiftons of the manor had chosen not to deal with Grandpa Ince? And hadn't the innkeeper warned him about them, too? Best get this business done soon and return to London.

"Very well," he said to the servant, who had recovered from what must have been a dead run from the manor--wherever that was--to Ashfield. "Please tell your master and mistress that I will be delighted to dine with them tonight at...." He looked at the note. "...six of the clock. As for staying with them, I prefer to remain here."

The servant's eyes widened in disbelief. "Not...not...stay there? You are *refusing* Mrs. Tifton?"

"Yes. I am here at Number Fourteen and that will do." Why was the man so suddenly terrified? "They certainly don't need to go to any bother over what is probably a trifling matter."

"I daren't tell her that!"

This was strange. "I am afraid you must," Amos said with some sympathy, but also the firmness that came from conning ships and knowing his own mind. "Dinner, yes. Lodging, no. Good day."

Amos stayed at the door as the servant left, head down, visibly distressed. Amos decided that Mrs. Tifton obviously never entertained the notion of someone refusing her.

Puzzled over the matter, he opened curtains in the sitting room, coughing down the dust, and opened windows to remove the musty odor. Luckily, the day was sunny and the walls painted in light colors, so he could see the place.

He went from room to room, admiring a little dining nook and an adjacent kitchen. There was a small room down the corridor which appeared to be an office. The desk was clear of clutter, causing him to reflect on the occasional simplicity of death, when a man had time to get affairs in order. Life at sea had acquainted him with the opposite--pirates in the Indies, smugglers in the Caribbean, war and its adjacent terrors. "Grandfather, I suspect you were orderly in life," he announced, then felt silly, until a warm, odd comfort settled on him, as if Grandpa Ince was approving and agreeing. Rational man, Amos knew that was impossible.

There were two bedchambers upstairs, both well-organized. He realized that he was looking at good furniture and handsome curtains throughout Number Fourteen. The thought beguiled him that this was not the abode of a poor man, and yet, hadn't the innkeep said last night that his own daughter disdained him, and Maude and Madeline brought him food?

What to do? He knew he needed a temporary maid to clean and dust. Perhaps the innkeeper could loan him a servant. He let himself out and locked the door, also realizing that he needed directions to Tifton Manor. He knew the innkeep would be his man of information.

He quickly found himself in front of Ashfield Circulating Library a few doors down. A wave of shyness washed over Amos which made him argue with himself a moment, until he reminded himself that he was an adult man looking for cleaners to tidy up Number Fourteen. Maybe the Tiftons who lived upstairs? Everyone said they had to pinch pennies.

An older woman looked up as he entered, and closed the book she was reading. She rose and said in a forthright manner, "I am Miss Cuthbert, proprietor. You must be new in town, sir."

"New and temporary, ma'am," he replied. He briefly considered the way news seemed to fly about and decided to add to her knowledge. "I am Captain Amos Foster, from America. Walter Ince was my step-grandfather and he lived at Number Fourteen. I received word in the London docks that Grandfather's solicitor has been attempting to reach me for three years."

"Yes, yes, that pesky war," Miss Cuthbert said. "Mr. Ince was a lovely man and a subscriber to my library." She put her hand to her face to hide a smile. "Mainly he liked that wonderfully comfortable armchair by the window where he would sit and snooze. Between you and me, sir, I think the book in his lap was merely a ruse."

Amos laughed at that, charmed at this homely vignette about someone he wished he could have known in person. "I've done the same thing, even aboard a ship tossing about in the Atlantic. Needs must, you will agree."

"I will, indeed. How may I help you, sir? 'Temporary' suggests you are not moving to Ashfield."

"Alas, no. Apparently Grandfather left some sort of will, and I am here for its reading. That is all. I'll be sailing back to Boston in two or three weeks with a cargo of goods from *your* shores."

"Captain, you are welcome to visit the library on a temporary basis. Free of charge. Our newspapers are current." Her glance at the tidy pile told him she read papers, too, not a lady's occupation. "I mean, it is the least we can do, since British soldiers burned your capitol in 1812, I believe."

"A patriotic gesture on your part, madam," he replied, amused. "There is one thing more, a small matter."

"We specialize in small matters in Ashfield. Say on, sir."

"Um, my other relatives in town want me to stay with them at their manor, and I'd rather not. I am looking for a dependable woman to clean and dust Number Fourteen so I can be comfortable enough there. I can probably take my meals at the inn, so that isn't a concern. Do you think—I hope I am not misreading any of this—that the Tiftons upstairs might help me?"

"Mrs. Tifton at the manor was an Ince, wasn't she?" Miss Cuthbert commented, her face sober now.

"He was her father." He could see this wasn't a subject Miss Cuthbert relished. Time's a-wasting. "About the Tiftons here? All the house needs is a lick and a promise."

Miss Cuthbert looked at the ceiling. "I think they can accommodate you, provided they're not too busy sewing for Christmas parties."

"Ma'am?"

"They're both seamstresses, Maude and Madeline. That's how they earn a living." Her smile disappeared. "Years and years ago, Mrs. Tifton upstairs and her small daughter came to Ashfield in hopes of help. Mr. Peter Tifton's rascally brother had married Maude, then abandoned her and their child and died of the drink."

Nope, no secrets in Ashfield. This was the same tale, slightly altered, he had heard from the keep *and* the solicitor. He shook his head in sympathy, growing more intrigued by the minute.

"They eke out a decent living with sewing and whatnot."

"Cleaning my grandfather's house might fall under whatnot," Amos said. "I will pay them, certainly."

He could see Miss Cuthbert was wondering if she was doing the right thing. Long years at sea in the business of trade with sometimes unscrupulous merchants had taught him to study faces. *Let her think*, he told himself, then realized he didn't have much time for Ashfield. There were moments when something stronger than a hint was in order. "I'm only here for a few days, and I need help."

"Very well, sir. I'll go upstairs and ask." She pointed to that armchair by the window. "Have a seat but stay awake!"

He smiled that she could still manage a joke. She left the shop and he heard her on the stairs, then a door opening and voices. He sat down and applauded Grandpa Ince's taste in comfortable chairs. It would be hard not to sleep in this one. He leaned back, settled in, and wondered how much Miss Cuthbert might charge him for this chair. It would be a tight fit, but he could wrestle it into his cabin aboard the *Betty Bright*, which was, he knew, a total fiction.

He heard more than one person coming down the stairs, so he stood up and tugged on his uniform, which was nothing fancier than navy blue trousers and coat, much worn. He had left his white shirts at a laundry at the docks, and this blue and white checked shirt didn't precisely shout out *Here comes the captain*. Needs must, he reminded himself as the door opened on the prettiest female he had ever spotted since only earlier than morning, when she was sweeping in front of Grandpa's house.

As he stared in utter admiration, she came forward. "I'm Madeline Tifton, and I can clean your house, sir. Shall I begin now?"

Chapter Six

Madeline didn't know what to expect when she came downstairs behind Miss Cuthbert, but she was pretty sure it wasn't Captain Foster. Maybe she had thought he would look like Mr. Ince, since he was that good man's grandson, but Amos Foster was of middling height and lean, with an intensity in his dark eyes made more pronounced by the wind scours around them. She knew this was a man used to being outdoors in all weather. Mama always said that Mr. Ince looked like he was built for comfort, but that wasn't Captain Foster. He looked like a man accustomed to enduring.

Before she turned away because of an engrained unwillingness to be scrutinized, she noticed something more than mere scrutiny: he appeared interested in her. Why, she couldn't imagine, except that the notion was flattering. He needed a haircut, and somehow, that simple detail, quickly noted, touched her heart. It made her wonder if he ever had time to think of himself. It also made him human.

Should she curtsy? Should she extend her hand? What did ladies do in America? *You're being silly*, she told herself. What should she even say? Miss Cuthbert said he was interested in someone to give Mr. Ince's house a quick clean. "He called it a lick and a promise," Miss Cuthbert had said upstairs, and they giggled together. Perhaps it was an American term.

"I already know you," she said impulsively, then put her hand to her mouth. 'Well, I do, sir. I wrote some of the later correspondence to you from Mr. Ince. I don't precisely know you..." Why was she getting so flustered? There was something about this American she liked on sight. Heavens knows what, but she was turning into an idiot. She gave up and held out her hand to him.

He shook her hand. "I regret I never met him."

That, then, was that. "You would have liked him," Maddie said. "I know I did."

Miss Cuthbert had gone ahead into the library. "Tea and biscuits," she announced. "You have time for that, Captain Foster."

"I think I won't argue with her," he said, when he nodded and the librarian returned to her kitchen.

"Wise of you, sir," Madeline Tifton replied. She went to the window and sat on a stool beside the comfortable armchair.

"This is the better seat," he told her. "You should sit here."

"Captain Foster, I have tried that armchair. Once I am in it, I sink in and need assistance getting out of it."

He leaned toward her and tried to sound conspiratorial. "I'm trying to think of a way to whisk it from the library, stick it on the mail coach without anyone's notice, and get it back to my ship and into my miniscule cabin. If you think of a distracting diversion, do share it with me."

"I will point out to the street, and scream that the horses are loose from the posting house," she said promptly, her eyes lively. "It will be a brief diversion, and you will be on your own!"

It was a silly conversation, but the captain didn't seem to mind. When tea arrived, he took a sip, and became all business. "Apparently, I am here because the solicitor has been keeping my step-grandfather's will, which must mean I am in it; heaven knows why. I don't suppose he reckoned on war, so some considerable time has passed. Mr. Clare gave me the keys to Grandfather's little house, where I want to stay. It's only a matter of a few days, but I'm already sneezing from all the dust."

"We will both be happy to redd up the place for you," Maddie said. "Mama is sewing a row of tatting to the annual Christmas dress I make for Miss Amelia Tifton of Tifton Manor. When she finishes, she can help me at your Number Fourteen."

"I will pay you four pounds for your efforts, Miss Tifton."

Goodness. You Americans are perhaps easy to cheat in the market, Maddie thought, astounded at such a sum. "Captain, you would be grossly overpaying us," she said. "Five shillings will suffice and we'll be glad of it."

"But *I* wouldn't be glad of it," he countered. "Don't argue, Miss Tifton. I will pay four pounds."

It wasn't said with any meanness, or really, any emotion at all. Maddie decided that sea captains must have a certain command that was hard to dispute. "Very well, sir," she replied, "as long as we do not put you in the poor house."

"You will not." He took another biscuit. "When can I expect you next door?"

"Now," Maddie said, still stunned by the idea of that much money for doing so little. "I'll wrap a scarf around my hair and get some cleaning supplies." She couldn't help herself then. "Is there a password after I knock that allows me entrance?"

He thought a moment. "Swordfish," he said, which struck her as hilarious.

"Oh, you have a better one?" he teased back.

"Thimble."

"Thimble it is."

Maddie knew Mr. Ince's house well. Perhaps she should tell Captain Foster that she and Mama had cleaned it many times when the old man started to fade. She put on her oldest dress, knocked on his door and said "Thimble," when he opened it and laughed, which gave her the giggles.

But there was work to do. She went right to the closet off the kitchen, with its mop and bucket, and something evil-smelling that cleaned floors and walls.

"I can help."

She handed the captain a broom and dustpan, and he went to work alongside her until the kitchen was in order. The sitting room was a larger dust repository, which meant the captain was soon sneezing and helpless.

Poor man, Maddie thought. *This will never do*. She had a task for him upstairs. "I can finish this," she said. "Captain, please go upstairs and take the sheets from the beds."

"I already looked. No need. They've been covered by bedspreads."

"…Which are full of dust. It's been three years."

When he appeared inclined to argue, she took a page from his own book. "You told me not to argue about wages," she reminded him. "Don't argue about housework, Captain. I probably know it better than you do."

"Yes, ma'am," he said meekly enough. He whistled his way upstairs, which suggested she had not wounded his pride overmuch. Poor fellow. She heard him sneezing almost immediately.

The sitting room was also a nightmare of dust, even for Madeline. She took a large handkerchief from her pocket and tied it over her nose and mouth, which helped. She dragged the area rug outside. She swept, then began to mop, when the captain came downstairs with a load of bed coverings. When he looked in on her in the sitting room, he dropped his bundle and raised his hands. "Is it my money or my life? Both?" he asked.

She had never enjoyed cleaning out a dusty house so much in her entire life, and all because Captain Foster was hilarious. When his hands were still raised, she threatened him with the wooden end of the mop. "Neither of those, sir," she said, then felt supremely shy, because she wanted to tell him that his good humor was buoying her up as nothing had in her years of poverty and humiliation at the hands of relatives. It wasn't something she could tell anyone, much less a man she barely knew.

But I do know you, she considered later as she tackled the book room. On her direction, Captain Foster had taken that area rug to the backyard clothesline and was tormenting it with the rug beater. *I know you from the letters than Mr. Ince dictated to me, then stowed in that pasteboard box because he could not mail them.*

The box. Where did he put that pasteboard box? She would have looked, but a knock on the door meant Mama's arrival. Like her daughter had done, Mama walked through the main floor, remembering its former owner, dabbing at her eyes.

By the time Mama's inspection ended, Captain Foster was in the pantry, emptying out old flour and nameless food that had seen better days. "I'm not in my element here," he admitted to Maddie.

There was no real need for an introduction. "You must be Mrs. Tifton," he said to Mama. "Is Hampshire famous for its handsome ladies?'"

Those wrinkles around his eyes deepened, and Maddie revised her opinion of them, and him. Maybe they were smile lines. "Three or four days should finish my involvement in Ashfield, or as long as it takes for Mr. Clare to read the contents of Grandpa's will and testament. Can't imagine why he needs me for that, but here I am."

Thinking of the will seemed to remind him of the time. He pulled out his pocket watch and frowned. "Time and tides wait for no man. I am to have dinner at Tifton Manor in one half hour," he told them. "I wish I had a better shirt than a flannel one and this sorry specimen rejoicing in blue and white checks."

"I can find one of your grandpapa's shirts," Mama said. "The other Mrs. Tifton is a stickler for proper social spheres and good manners."

"I doubt she will be impressed with my social sphere," the captain said cheerfully, leading Maddie to suspect he didn't give much thought to rank and style, if any. "A shirt here?"

"We used to wash and iron your grandpapa's linens," Maddie said, feeling her face turn rosy because the subject seemed intimate. A glance at the captain only showed her an interested face.

"We still have a shirt or two at our place," Mama said. "I never had the heart to return them, once he was gone. There is this, too." She reached in her pocket. "Here's the key he left us. We didn't know who to give it to. But then, you must already have one."

"Aye. The solicitor told me that about a week before he passed away, Grandpa took a will to him, plus a key. You hang onto yours, Mrs. Tifton," he told her. "I don't know what is to happen to this place." He looked around. "It's a nice house."

Mama left to get the shirt. Captain Foster watched her go. "What happened to you and your mother?" he asked quietly.

He sat down at the dining room table, and she felt obliged to sit, as well. "Mama met Mr. Peter Tifton's younger brother in London at the home of mutual friends. Apparently he was a charming person, and Mama quite a beauty."

"She still is," he interrupted, then startled her by looking at her with that same scrutiny that had surprised her earlier. "And you resemble her. Ah yes, go on. I interrupted you."

"They married, and it was a mistake from the start. He was under the impression she had some wealth--Mama does carry herself well--so imagine his surprise when he learned how little she had."

"Mr. Clare said he drank and gambled and died, leaving you in ruins. Do you remember your father?"

"All I remember is someone who came by now and then, and finally stole Mama's two remaining gold necklaces to pawn." She went to the newly cleaned window, uncomfortable with the subject. "I remember a cold ride on the mail coach, then walking to the manor and a door slamming in our faces. I was six."

What he must think of us, Maddie thought, unwilling to say more. "We manage well enough now," she added quickly. "Please don't feel sorry for us."

"I won't," he said. "Now I must dine with people who already don't impress me too much. So Mr. Peter Tifton is lord of this manor, and his brother was the rascal?"

"Aye, sir," She took a liberty and leaned closer. "Between you and me and probably everyone in Ashfield, Peter Tifton has been cowed by your step-aunt for years. I doubt you'll miss Ashfield when you leave."

He started to reply, but Mama came into the room. She handed him a neatly folded shirt, kept in their lodging over the library, and not dusty. "It might be a little large."

"But there are no blue and white checks," the captain said. "Wish me luck, ladies!"

They did, and left after Mama gave him directions to the manor, just a mile further west. "Stay on this street and you'll get there," she said as he walked them to the door. "After you leave, Maddie and I will return and finish tidying up this place."

"I'll find that pasteboard box with the rest of your grandpapa's letters," Maddie said.

"What? What?" he teased. "Neither of you are willing to stay here to make sure my neckcloth is straight, there is no tooth powder on my nose, and my jacket well-brushed? How can I possibly impress those other Tiftons?"

"I could have told him that no one can impress those Tiftons," Mama said as they strolled home three buildings away, where Miss Cuthbert was turning the sign from Open to Closed, Come Again. "Maddie?"

"Oh. Yes. No one," she said, surprised to find her mind busy with the enjoyable fiction of making certain Captain Foster's neck cloth was squared away and his suit jacket tidy. She had long since given up the notion that she might ever do that for a man someday. She thought she had resigned herself, but apparently wishful thinking poked its way out of dusty corners to look around.

He's only here for a few days. Don't be silly.

Chapter Seven

Grandpa's shirt was a little large, but far superior to blue and white checks. The bedchamber had a mirror over the bureau, and he frowned into it as he fidgeted with a neckcloth, wishing someone *could* help him with something so simple. Then he remembered numerous fraught moments at sea. Surely he could manage a yard or so of stupid cloth.

The bed sheets and coverlet had been whisked away, making Amos regret that his almost next-door neighbors were obliged to keep cleaning while he had dinner elsewhere. Then again, in the stillness of his grandfather's house, he had a moment to think.

He remembered a conversation years ago when his father captained the *Betty Bright*, and they were lolling along in the dog latitude where not a single puff of wind came their way. "Pa, if you could be anywhere but here, what would you be doing?" had been his boyish question.

Pa's answer was prompt. "Probably sitting in the kitchen at home, watching your stepmother get dinner on the table. Or maybe sitting with her of an evening. She'd be knitting and I would be reading."

At the time, there off the humid coast of Brazil, Amos had thought that answer perfectly stupid. He was too polite to say that, because he loved his father. Standing in front of the mirror now, he recalled what he did say. "Pa, I thought you'd rather be bartering with traders in the East Indies. I know you like a good barter."

"I like your stepmother much more," Pa had replied, amused. "A quiet dinner with her means the world to me."

After all these years, Amos understood. Too bad those damnable times and tides meant his father lived at sea and died there, too, killed by a fever off Barbados four years ago, when their shipping business was starting to wither and die. Now the seas were Amos's again, and he wanted to forget it all and sit down to dinner with Madeline Tifton.

"Pa, you were right, in this and in so many other ways," he told the mirror.

He considered the matter as he walked the mile to Tifton Manor, enjoying the bliss of walking and walking without confining himself to 25 feet in one direction on his quarterdeck, and 25 in another. This was bliss, or would have been, if he could have avoided a dinner which he was already wary of.

There it was, Tifton Manor, an imposing three-story property on a small rise, with a pretty row of trees leading to it. Come spring and the return of leaves and nesting birds, it would be beautiful. A curved driveway graced the front, and there were candles in each of the ground floor windows. The effect was charming and Amos's natural inclination to optimism rose. Maybe this evening would be one to remember, after all.

He could scarcely have been more right and wrong at the same time.

The butler who opened the front door looked pleasant enough. He handed Amos's well-worn cloak and lid to another liveried man who must be a footman. "This way, sir," the butler said and proceeded at a measured pace.

Perhaps the butler moved too fast. When he knocked lightly, then open the door, four sour faces stared back at Amos, which made him want to run back to Ashfield and catch the nearest conveyance to London. *You're braver than that*, he told himself, and smiled at all the Gorgons.

"Captain Amos Foster," the butler announced.

To Amos's continuing surprise, the expressions changed to something almost human. The young lady and her obvious, if overweight, brother, smiled outright. The other two, likely the parents, smiled as if practicing this display of goodwill.

The butler gestured. "Captain, Mr. and Mrs. Tifton, and Amelia and Cosmo Tifton."

When Amos still hesitated in the doorway, the butler gave him a push into the room, not a push anyone watching would have noticed, directed as it was to the small of Amos's back. It got him into the room. The door closed quietly behind him, so he could not leave.

He bowed, which always felt artificial. "I'm delighted to meet you all."

"Yes, well," the lady of the house said, which sounded hardly reassuring. "Do be seated, Captain Foster."

What now? Amos asked himself. Everything he knew about these people had come from the innkeeper, Maude and Madeline Tifton, and the solicitor. He was no fool. Since the Tiftons seemed to be looking at him to discourse eloquently, or twirl plates, or dance a jig, perhaps he should attempt an explanation. He cleared his throat and began, certain this could not be as bad as anything he had every faced before, up to and including cannibals in the South Pacific.

"I gather Mr. Clare has informed you of my arrival in Ashfield, in answer to a letter I received in the London Docks." He would have said more, but some part of his comment had turned them sour again.

If Amos could do anything, he was able to read a room. *Let's see: stickler, snobs. What else?* he thought. Ah, the London Docks. Perhaps never before had anyone heard those words in this manor. All he could do was forge ahead.

"Apparently, Walter Ince, in actual fact my step-grandfather, is your father, Mrs. Tifton," he said. "At least that is what Mr. Clare told me."

"Yes."

He needed more than one syllable. Maybe it was time to use that firm jawed, raised eyebrow "captain" look that commanded attention from many a crew of his. "Then, madam, please tell me why I am here. I have no family ties beyond the affection he always showed me."

He said it nicely, but he knew how to get people's attention. Mrs. Tifton stirred in her chair, her expression hardened, and then changed to…something. "You are correct. Mr. Ince was my father."

And? And? He wanted to say. *Is Hampshire rationing words?* "Catherine is your sister then? She married my father, David Foster. You are my Aunt Loisa."

Ooh. He felt the back of his neck curdling. "I am Mrs. Tifton to you," she replied. He heard the icicles hanging off the sentence. "My mother always regretted sending Catherine to stay with friends in London, who had ties with America we were unaware of." He could tell she had the obvious question. "We knew my sister had several children, but she never mentioned one named Amos."

Ah, that was it. "I am not related to an Ince or a Tifton. Betty Mason, my father's first wife and my mother, died shortly after I was born. He met your sister Catherine in London, as you have said. Let me add that she is still alive, living in Groton, Connecticut, and a wonderful stepmother. She has always let me call her Mama."

"Then you and I are not related," Mrs. Tifton replied. He heard distinct relief in her voice.

"No, we are not," he said, and felt distinct gratitude.

She wasn't done. "Does my sister ever speak of me?"

Amos decided he wasn't done, either. "Mrs. Tifton, in all my life, I do not believe she ever received a letter from *you*, her older sister, although I know she sent a few. She's a kind, forgiving lady and I owe her a great deal." Could Mrs. Tifton stand *this*? "She loves me as one of her own."

"But you are not."

Ouch. "My late father took good care of your sister," he said cheerfully, which earned him a stare that could have cut through iron. "If I could apologize for the recent war, I would. This matter of a will should take no time at all and I will be on my way."

Mr. and Mrs. Tifton exchanges glances. "You have no plans to, er, contest anything that should be contained in it?" Mrs. Tifton asked.

REGENCY GLADTIDINGS • 99

So that was it. Amos gave a mental sight of relief and relaxed.

So that was it. Amos gave a mental sight of relief and relaxed. "Heavens, no! When I arrived at London Docks"--Ha, he admitted saying that again just to watch ol' Loisa cringe – "I had no idea there would be a letter for me from Grandpa Ince. It must be a small matter. Perhaps it's ownership of the house on the High Street." He couldn't resist then. "I doubt he had many possessions. It's a small house."

What happened next made him open his eyes wide and wonder if he could edge toward the door. Mrs. Tifton turned to her husband, who appeared to have perfected a semi-cringe when she looked at him. "There! I told you, Peter! This is what happens when an otherwise sensible man like my father dirties his hands with common trade!"

"Yes, Loisa," came Mr. Tifton's quiet reply. "Certainly you were right, Loisa."

"Someone had to hold the line," she said in triumph. "To make matters worse, husband, your own brother ruined himself with drink and tried to foist his widow and daughter on us, but I held the line there, too!"

"Yes, my dear."

This next barb came low, but he knew he was supposed to hear it. "And now we have to deal with an, an *American*! I am not even related to him!"

Amos stared in amazement as Mr. and Tifton engaged in a venomous, low-voiced conversation, and their children looked stony-eyed at each other, as if this was a too-common event. *What a miserable bunch*, Amos thought. *This matter of an estate can't be settled too soon.*

He debated between staying and finding a way closer to the door. The son--Cosmo?--gave him a desperate look as if he wanted to escape, too. It was hard to tell about the scrawny daughter.

Amos decided to chance it, and why not? He had stood up to the French in Polynesia, and some Chinese merchants ready to steal his cargo in Indonesia. This squabble embarrassed him, and made him sad at the same time. Life had taught him when to abandon ship. He stood up slowly and edged toward the door, the combatants seemingly unaware of his escape. The closer he came, the wider the door opened.

Two more steps and he was safe in the corridor. The butler closed the door on the sitting room and ushered him quickly toward the entrance.

"It seemed a little loud. I was about to announce dinner, but thought you might prefer a rescue," the butler said, handing him his cloak and hat.

"What sort of place is this?" Amos whispered. "And what is your name? I like to know who my rescuers are."

"Livingston. It's an unhappy place, sir."

"I don't doubt it, Mr. Livingston."

"Livingston," the butler said. "Just Livingston."

"No, *Mr.* Livingston," Amos said firmly. "Pardon me, but you look of an age to perhaps know my stepmother, Catherine Ince Foster."

Livingston opened the door and ushered Amos out, closing the door on the two of them. "Your mother was a sweet lady, and so jolly. We as live belowstairs were happy for her when she eloped with your father to Gretna Green and followed him to America. Mrs. Tifton never spoke of her."

"Eloped, did they?" Amos asked, diverted by this notion. "She never would talk about it! I'll have to tease her when I see her in a few months."

"She still lives?"

"Yes, although my father is gone now. She is in Connecticut."

"Do tell her hello from those of us belowstairs."

"I will." He started down the front steps. "Now I am running away like a coward. This matter with the solicitor had better be a paltry one quickly over and done." He laughed. "It's a good thing the crew of the *Betty Bright* can't see me."

"Wise of you to flee," Livingston said. "Goodnight."

Chapter Eight

Amos realized how sad it was to walk into an empty house. When in port and he had some time, he lived with his stepmother in Groton, Connecticut. She always had a cheery word, whether he was back from a six months voyage or a trip to the pub. He was never alone aboard the *Betty Bright*, either, because of close quarters and the nature of his work.

This was different. He was in a strange country, a strange village, and had suffered through a strange dinner than never happened, because the people inside Tifton Manor were vipers. He wanted--needed--someone to talk to, at the very least. At the very most, he needed someone to soothe his heart. There. He admitted it to himself.

Either Madeline or her mother had left a lamp burning in the kitchen, so he didn't feel entirely cast away...and look, under a cloth was a loaf of bread and jar of jam. He set aside the cloth, saw the note, and pounced on that. He was more starved for companionship right now than any food he had missed.

As kind as her mother is, please let it be from Madeline, he thought. He looked to the signature first and sighed with relief. He sat down, propped his feet on an opposite chair, and read her note. It was prosaic beyond belief, except there was a small matter that flew into his heart and lodged there.

Dear Captain, he read, *We hope all went well tonight. Mama has a little more Christmas sewing, but I will be by in the morning to finish tidying. I found your grandfather's pasteboard box where he stored the letters he couldn't send because of the war, and those few he dictated to me when he could no longer write with a steady hand. You'll see the box upstairs. I miss him. Yours sincerely, Madeline.*

After such an uncomfortable evening, Amos was inclined to grasp at straws, so grasp he did, noting that she signed only her first name. He followed an arrow, turned over the note, and his heart settled itself in his chest again, because, well, because.

He smiled and re-read her postscript, running his finger lightly over the writing. *We didn't have time to wash the bedding, so what you have is some of ours. Call me silly, but I tried out both beds and decided on the one you might like. That's the bed I made up. MT*

As he thought, he made himself a jam sandwich. There was a pitcher of water and a glass by the dry sink, so he drank deep. His neckcloth came off, to be left on the rail at the bottom of the stairs.

The pasteboard box on the dresser practically called his name, but he sat on the bed first. He glanced at the pillow. His heart and soul were touched by what he saw: an indentation of someone's head, as if Madeline had made the bed, then wanted to make sure again that it was the right one. He settled himself into her little well of pillow comfort.

He closed his eyes and slept. The letters would wait. He wanted, needed, to treasure this moment of kindliness after a terrible evening.

He woke up to a soft morning, as sun streamed in the window. With hands behind his head, Amos took a mental inventory as he thought through favorite such mornings in more exotic places than Ashfield, Hampshire. Usually he began with Tahiti, then moved to forested realms and mountains reaching down to the sea in America's Pacific Northwest where a mighty river named Columbia flowed into the ocean. Mornings on the Spanish Main were noisy with birds calling to each other, and monkeys offering rebuttals.

He went farther this time and imagined a morning in his own bedchamber in Groton, Connecticut, where the family lived when Papa married his second wife, Catherine Ince. Family lore testified that Papa carried her across the threshold, then left her weeping there three days later for a voyage to take rum to Bristol. Stepmama still lived in Groton, even though more of their business was transacted in Boston, Massachusetts, these days. She laughed now about those early tears, but before Amos left on this voyage to England, she told him, "Hurry back. I don't like an empty house."

Grandpa's house was empty, and Amos knew what she was really saying: Empty can mean lonely. He heard a clock ticking somewhere. He shook off that lonely feeling by imagining himself carrying Madeline upstairs to *this* bedchamber. The mere thought of it got him downstairs to cold water in the bathing room off the kitchen. To his relief, the sudden chill dragged his mind back to the business of the sea, and his own mandate to spend no more than two or three more days here. He simply couldn't stay longer, when he had a fleet to resurrect.

He wasn't so certain he liked the notion. Not at all.

Mama seemed to be spending more time than usual finishing up that last Christmas dress. "You'll have to get that bedding back to Number Fourteen on your own," she said serenely. Amazing how Mama could speak so distinctly, with two or three pins in her mouth.

It was no chore, really. The sheets and pillowslips folded down to neat little packages, and the blankets were manageable. Still, it was a chore to go up the three steps to the front door, and Madeline couldn't get the key from her apron pocket.

Since she doubted Amos Foster was a morning layabout, Madeline knocked. The captain opened the door, smiled at her predicament, smiled wider when she said "Thimble," and relieved her of the blankets. Without a word, he took them upstairs. She thought to follow with the sheets, but shyness intervened. It was different in the house when they were cleaning it. Now someone lived here, a single man. She left the sheets at the bottom of the stairs and knew she had no business lingering.

He came downstairs soon enough. "Good morning, Miss Tifton," he teased. "How do you do? Lovely weather we're having."

What he said struck Madeline as hilariously formal, and she laughed and curtseyed. In turn, he bowed, and any shyness left her. "You found the letters?"

He gestured to the sitting room. "I am enjoying them, and also my early poor attempts at correspondence. He was kind to save them. Stay a minute."

She needed no more invitation than that, and followed him into the sitting room. He had made himself at home in his grandfather's armchair, and the paper clutter around the chair took her back to those days when Walter Ince ruled his little domain sitting there. The thought made her dab at her eyes with her apron, which caught his attention.

"You have good memories here," he said, and it was no question.

"The best ones. Mama and I loved to bring over meals and sit and listen to his stories about people he knew. Mostly he talked about the eccentrics here in Ashfield. He would clear his throat most dramatically, then raise his hands as if outlining his words: 'Ashfield, the village where your business is everyone's business.'"

He indicated the footstool close to the chair, which made her dab her eyes again. "What's the matter, Madeline?" he asked, then seemed to know. "Did you usually sit there?"

She nodded and wiped her eyes. She gestured around him. "This stool, the paper clutter that drove Mama to distraction. Captain Foster, I miss him."

"Please call me Amos," he said. "People call me Captain Foster because they must. I like to hear my name."

"Everyone calls me Maddie. I...I think I prefer Madeline, because I am no child," she said, knowing that something between them was changing. She liked it, even though it frightened her a little, because she wasn't used to change in the unvarying chores and challenges of her life. He didn't need to know that. Better change something else: the subject. "Wh... what have you read here?"

"I glanced at my poor and naïve letters, but I have been reading the ones he never mailed, when I was a lot older." He grinned at her, which made her smile back. Some grins were infectious, apparently. "Between you and me, I think I know more about the goings on of Ashfield than people who live here."

"He was a keen observer," she noted, happy to be on more solid ground again. "Remember, your business is my business."

"I wish I knew more about him. Speaking of business, did he ever tell you what business he was involved in, if any of that is true and not just an Ashfield rumor? Whatever it was, set him crosswise with his own family, I gather." He indicated the clutter. "In all this, he speaks so movingly of the land."

"He may have mentioned it to others, but little came to our ears here," she said, then brightened, as a similarity struck her. "Actually, it was water, same as you, except much, much narrower. Something to do with a system of canals throughout England. He mentioned that a few times."

"I imagine people have lost fortunes over such schemes. Or made fortunes."

"You know more than I do. I imagine you got quite an earful last night at Tifton Manor."

She meant it in jest as idle conversation, but his face darkened. He looked at her, as if measuring how much he wanted to say to someone also related, and with the same last name.

"I shouldn't have asked. It is none of my business," she said quickly, wanting that stricken look on his face to go away, and knew she had caused it. "I should go..."

"No, most emphatically no," he said. He held up his hands and dropped them in his lap, as though there weren't sufficient words to convey anything. "I should be ashamed to admit this, but I am baffled. My crew would never believe that. They think I know everything." He shook his head. "I don't."

Madeline knew better than to say anything. Beyond sewing lovely frocks for women of Ashfield, she and Mama did not mingle in society. No door ever opened to them, and they had not the means to move away. Still, this kind man--what told her he was kind escaped her, except that she knew he was--deserved her attention. On impulse, she reached over and touched his arm, just a small touch. She knew that wasn't good manners, but he need a human connection.

It was enough. "Madeline, I ran away before dinner even started. Yep, sidled out of the room and darted away."

She gasped. He rolled his eyes. "I would never tell this to anyone else."

"Then why me?"

She hadn't meant to be so personal, but seriously, why her?

He touched her hand briefly, almost as briefly as she had touched his arm. "I feel comfortable with you," he said softly. He managed a slow wink, which made her rosy up. "And you will never, ever breathe a word of this to my crew, who think I am a fearless leader."

"Cross my heart," she vowed. "I already know the Tiftons are mean and small."

Simply put, she gave him permission to crawl out from under this boulder of shame. "They...they were going at each other, hammer and tongs, over the fact that Mr. Tifton--Peter--had a drunkard brother and how...how your mother tried to foist herself on them. And then that...that vile woman turned on *me*, because I had the nerve to be an American!"

"My mother did not foist herself on anyone," Madeline said in a soft voice. "She came here asking for very little. She had in her possession a letter from...from my father, something about an inheritance coming to him from another relative. It wasn't much beyond two hundred pounds annually, but it was owed to Mama, since she was his widow."

"I'll wager your mother never saw a penny of it," he managed to say.

"We have no proof of that letter. Right there on the doorstep-- we never even crossed the threshold--Mrs. Tifton snatched that letter and ripped it to pieces." Madeline put her apron to her eyes again. "God help us, but every year Mama has to go to Mr. Tifton and grovel for twenty-five pounds a year. She wouldn't do that if she didn't have to. And there is Mrs. Tifton, gloating about the matter as Mama grovels. Twenty-five pounds!"

"These are terrible people," Amos said, after a long silence that made her wonder how many curses and swear words he had to wade through to reach something so innocuous as a merely *terrible people*. "My aunt--ah, but I am to call her Mrs. Tifton--also wanted to know what my share would be from any inheritance. I assured her we weren't related, but maybe I would get this house. What else did he have?"

"He used to be landed gentry in Wiltshire," Madeline said, "the same as Peter Tifton is here in Hampshire. A gentleman who didn't have to work. I assume he sold all that land and sank the proceeds into canals that were never built."

"And she never forgave her father."

"Never," Madeline said. "I am certain she never set foot here. Her own father!"

She looked down. Captain Foster held her hand so gently. For the first time in her life, she knew she wasn't alone. "Thank you," she whispered. "I'll be praying for you when you have to face the Tiftons in his office and listen to a will."

The knowledge she wasn't alone came with another benefit, one that grew slowly until it filled her. "The strange part is that I think I feel sorry for her."

"You're a better person than I am," he admitted.

"No, I'm not," she assured him. "I've been around her longer, is all."

He untangled his fingers from hers, which came as more of disappointment than relief. *Don't ever let me go*, she wanted to tell him, but he obviously knew better.

That was it. He looked at her as perhaps an old brother might look, who wanted to tease her. "Let's do this: Since I am certain there will never be a huge amount of money from whatever is in that good man's will, we can joke about it. Ahem, pay attention. Once I am the proud heir to a king's ransom, what gift would you like from me at Christmas? Make it something grandiose, Madeline. I am certain I will soon be rolling in pounds sterling."

She laughed along with him. "A palatial estate on riverfront property."

"Done! Riverfront property for you! And what will you give me?"

"I'll think of something equally grand, sir, but you must wait." She glanced at the clock. "It is time for me to screw up my courage and take Amelia's Christmas dress to her. Good day."

He gave her a friendly salute as she left, and returned to the letters before she was out of the room.

Mama had ironed and boxed the dress. Madeline sat with it a moment in the circulating library as Miss Cuthbert dusted. She knew Amos had agreed to her imaginary riverfront property, and she should reply in humorous fashion, but she couldn't, not then. Once he left on the mail coach, she would never see him again. If she decided, for one time in her life, to express herself with honesty and not fear that what she "gave" him would be too much or too little, what did it matter?

"Miss Cuthbert, do you have pen and paper? I need to write a note to Captain Foster. It's all a tease."

The librarian handed her both, and directed her to the table and chair where paying customers sat. Madeline looked around, not wanting to usurp anyone. The room was empty, except for the two of them.

"Very well, then," she said, thought a moment, and wrote: *Captain Foster, my gift to you is the sure knowledge that wherever the sea takes you, there is someone of no importance or acclaim in Ashfield who is always going to wish you well.*

It needed no signature, so she wrote, *Yours Sincerely, Happy Christmas.* She blew on the note, folded it, addressed it and didn't know what to do next. She scanned the row of books until she found one that she knew no one ever checked out, *Fox's Book of Martyrs.* To be certain, she looked at the pasted page opposite the frontispiece that listed all checkouts and returns. Perfect. This book hadn't been checked out since 1798.

She tucked the note inside, ready to retrieve it later and keep it. She could put it in a wooden box of hers and treasure forever the thought that a man had once held her hand, and maybe even almost looked like he wanted to kiss her.

Chapter Nine

But there was a dress to be delivered. Madeline enjoyed the walk to Tifton Manor even less than usual. She knocked on the servants' entrance, hoping to see Livingston. To her disappointment, the housekeeper opened the door, and not the butler.

"What do you want?" the woman growled. Madeline could have sworn she smelled brandy on her breath.

"Ju...just to deliver Amel...Miss T...T...Tifton's Christmas dress to her," she stammered. "I...I know she wants me to make certain it needs no alterations."

"Follow me. Be quick about it."

They went up the back stairs of the grand house, the housekeeper silent. Madeline's left shoe needed a new heel so it gave off a merry "click tap, click tap" down the corridor. *Don't say anything, Mrs. Bower*, she thought.

No such luck. "Get your shoes mended," the woman hissed at her, then knocked on Amelia's door. There was a faint "Come in," which made Madeline wonder if her cousin was as terrified of the housekeeper as she was.

"Do your business and don't dawdle or you won't be paid," Mrs. Bower snapped and pushed her none too gently into the room.

"We'd better hurry," Madeline told her cousin.

The dress slipped on easily and fit precisely as Madeline knew it would. The Tiftons hosted the shire's best families for a holiday dinner and she knew there would be no prettier frock on any lady's back than one of hers or her mother's. She gave herself a mental shake, wondering why Amelia insisted on yellow, instead of the more flattering blue that Madeline suggested. The curtains in the Tifton formal dining room were a similar pale shade. Amelia would simply disappear. Perhaps that was the point. Maybe Mrs. Tifton was just mean enough not to want any competition, even from her own child.

"What do you think, Miss Tifton?" Madeline asked, wondering if this pale spinster about her own age had an opinion of her own.

"It's well enough, I suppose," Amelia said, sounding almost as listless as she appeared.

"I could add a blue sash that would really set it off," Madeline suggested.

"Yes, that might...." Amelia brightened momentarily, looking almost animated, then reconsidered, probably out of fear for her mother's opinion. "No. This will do."

"Very well," she said quietly. "I will leave the receipt with you."

"You're to leave it with the housekeeper."

Madeline's sighed inwardly. Something told her that Mrs. Bower would ignore it. She had done that several years ago. Usually the payments came after several attempts, and even then, it was never the full five shillings, never mind that a similar dress in London, or even Portsmouth would earn her twice that amount.

"I will leave it with you," Madeline repeated firmly, even as her heart sank lower.

She let herself out of Amelia's room and started for the back stairs.

"Stop!"

Startled, Madeline turned to see Mrs. Tifton bearing down on her. She felt her hands turn into fists. *Does she think I'm stealing spoons?* she asked herself.

She did something then that went against all her own recent personal admonitions to abandon daydreaming and wishful thinking. Just this once, she decided to pretend that she was married to a kind and capable man who would protect her from all the ills of society and the position in life where she found herself, through no fault of her own. She drew herself up, pretending that if she took a step back, Amos Foster's comforting arms would be around her. Maybe just this once, she could fool herself into thinking she had someone on her side, besides her equally powerless mother.

"Yes, Mrs. Tifton?" she asked, keeping her voice steady. This was no time to stammer and look afraid. "Your daughter has approved of the Christmas dress. I left my bill with her. How may I help you?"

Her serenity must have thrown Mrs. Tifton off her usual vitriol. She stared and then her eyes narrowed. If Madeline could have dug her feet into the carpet to remain immovable, she would have. As it was, she clasped her hands together, not daring to look down to see how white her knuckles were. She decided not to give Mrs. Tifton that triumph.

Her aunt came closer and closer, but Madeline refused to back up. When they were nearly none to nose, it was Aunt Loisa who stepped back. Her words came out low and menacing.

"I demand to know what that uncouth sea captain is doing in my father's house," she said.

Oh, that house you never visited, even though Mr. Ince was your father? Madeline wanted to say. She refrained, only because she knew that the invisible Amos Foster protecting her would have roared out a protest in his best command-in-a-gale voice. No. Wait. Something – a Christmas blessing? A gift better than waterfront property? This was telling her that she refrained because she knew she could manage this on her own.

"He is merely staying there, with permission from Mr. Clare, the solicitor," she replied calmly. She felt Amos's imaginary strength turning into her own, and it felt real.

"He's not looking for money stashed here and there?" Mrs. Tifton asked. Her expression turned conniving. "Or did you and your foolish mother already steal that?"

You are a dreadful excuse for a human, Madeline thought. *Isn't she, Amos?* "We would never do such a thing. If you'll excuse me, I have work to do elsewhere."

"Someday you will go too far!" On any other day, that would have struck terror into Madeline's heart. Now it sounded like the bleating of a desperate woman. Perhaps someday she might feel pity for her aunt, but this was not the day.

Without another word, she turned on her heel and forced herself to walk to the backstairs, and not run down in a desperate attempt to get away from the evil in what could have been a lovely home.

She walked back to Ashfield, never once turning to look behind her. By the time she arrived in the High Street, she resolved to never again go to Tifton Manor to make a Christmas dress for Amelia. There would be some way to make up for the lost shillings. She would not be that desperate again, no matter what happened between now and next Christmas.

To her infinite relief, Amos Foster stood in the doorway of his grandfather's house. Without caring if anyone saw her, she went directly up the steps and into his open arms, which was a good thing, because her legs suddenly failed her. She started to sag.

Without a word, he scooped her up and carried her inside, setting her on the sofa.

He sat beside her on the floor. "I asked your mother where you had gone," he said. "When she told me, my blood started to run in chunks."

As calmly as she could, Madeline told him what her aunt had asked. "She seems to think her father has squirreled away wealth here, and that either Mama and I through the years, or you now, have been using it for our own purposes. She is a pathetic woman."

"You're too kind," he said drily. He stood up and held out his hand. "Let me walk you home."

He helped her up, and there was no mistaking his concern. "I don't know if you need a hug, but I do."

It started out as a simple hug, but the idea of letting go of the man whose invisible presence she had called on during her encounter with Mrs. Tifton seemed silly. She clung to him, and with a sigh and the simple utterance, "Madeline," he clung to her.

When she started to shake in the aftermath of her ordeal or maybe a lifetime of ordeals, he put his hand to the side of her face and pressed her even closer to his chest, shutting out the fear that threatened to overwhelm her. In another moment, she was calm. She stepped back, not because he was too close--she loved every moment of that--but because she knew that when he left, she would be on her own again. She gently shooed away wishful thinking, and sent it back to whatever corner of her mind it usually temporarily inhabited. In that moment, she grew up.

"I needed that," she said softly. "Thank you, Amos. I think I will be all right now."

Just like that, she was gone, staggering a little, but quick to take possession of that steely will he recognized in other ship captains, soldiers he had met during the war, his own father, even. *Am I as strong as you, dear lady?* he asked himself, knowing that when this bit of nonsense involving his grandfather's will was read and certified, he had to return to London and the business of cargos and trade. A few good years might mean he could add onto his fleet of one. He saw nothing but a lifetime of hard work ahead; he had no choice. He toyed with the idea of asking Madeline if he could write to her, as he had written to his grandfather, but no. He knew what he was like when he was busy. There wouldn't be time for letters. Again, no choice. He had to leave, and that was that.

Amos took himself to the inn for supper, needing to be with a noisy bunch. He could drink some ale, and maybe watch other men and their wives banter about and flirt with each other...and envy them. There. He had thought it.

He was halfway through a mound of shepherd's pie when the solicitor approached. "Captain Foster, Mrs. Tifton said I might find you here."

Amos flinched. Mr. Clare noticed and reassured him. "No, no, not that harpy on the hill. Mrs. Maude Tifton."

"In that case, join me," Amos said. "I can't begin to eat all this. Lizzie? How about another plate."

Lizzie brought a plate and Mr. Clare joined him in finishing the shepherd's pie. The solicitor gave a sigh of contentment. "My cook at home isn't nearly this good."

He seemed to recall why he was here and not at home eating poor victuals, but Mr. Clare still didn't speak. Amos took matters into his own hands, as he would aboard the *Betty Bright*. "Mr. Clare, do you have news for me? I hope it is that you've peeked at the will and I have nothing to do with the contents therein. I need to return to London."

"That's the funny thing, Captain," the solicitor said. He burped politely--"Excuse that"-- then leaned forward. "I opened that second envelope to prepare myself, and there was this note. Took me a moment to decipher it. Poor old fellow's handwriting was quite gone."

"That's why he had Mad...Miss Tifton write for him," Amos said.

Mr. Clare pushed the scrap of paper across the table. From reading a few of his grandfather's letters this afternoon, he was already familiar with the spider-like scrawl. He read it, then read it again. "My grandfather wants Mrs. Maude Tifton and her daughter to attend the reading, as well?"

"So it would seem. The reading is tomorrow in my office. Will you somehow convince those two ladies to attend the reading with you? I know they are terrified of the nasty Tiftons. The reading will begin at nine of the clock. I doubt it will take long."

Amos leaned back in his chair as another thought about his uncle's will took hold. "Could it possibly be..."

"It seems unlikely," Mr. Clare said hastily, as if wanting to discard the notion. "He might have promised Maude and Madeline the house at Number Fourteen. Partly I am here to cushion *you* against such a personal disappointment. You've told me about your own shipping woes. Selling that house might have brought you a little relief in a nest egg toward future shipbuilding."

"There are worse things," Amos said. "Actually, I rather like the idea of two kind ladies getting a roomier place to live."

"I like it, too. I wanted to warn you against getting any hopes up." He held out his hand. "Whatever happens tomorrow should end your need to remain here. You'll be able to go on about your business. I do wish you well in future enterprises."

They shook hands. "I know they'll be reluctant, but I will have both Tifton ladies in attendance tomorrow."

The solicitor left. *And how, Genius, do you plan to convince Maude and Madeline to join you tomorrow?* Amos asked himself sourly. He did what all men do in a crisis. He held up his empty tankard. "A little more if you please, Lizzie."

Chapter Ten

It took all his paltry powers of persuasion that evening to convince Maude and Madeline Tifton to let him escort them to a meeting they dreaded to attend.

The circulating library was long closed, but he returned there and banged on the door until Miss Cuthbert, wearing a sour expression, opened the door. When she saw who it was, her irritation changed to worry.

Amos apologized and explained. She hurried upstairs. In a few minutes, Madeline came down, her hair around her shoulders, her robe carefully cinched. He knew he was unlikely to ever see a more lovely woman, even if his searches for cargo took him around the world.

He saw the worry in her eyes, but he saw something else, a certain strength he had not noticed earlier that day, as if she had made a personal decision that included no one but herself. Odd, that, because even as he felt some relief, he also felt his heart sink.

There was no point in mincing words, not that he was ever good at it. "Mr. Clare told me at the inn that you and your mother are also requested to be in attendance at tomorrow's reading of my grandfather's will."

Madeline took a deep breath. "We will be there, but why?"

"There is no guarantee what Loisa Tifton will do," he cautioned.

"There never has been," Madeline replied. Her agitation showed when she twisted the long hair by her ear into a curlicue, but her hand did not shake. "Every year when Mama must abase herself for 25 pounds, I am certain it will be the last time. I suppose we'll find out after Christmas."

Should he? Why not? "Mr. Clare wanted to cushion me against the idea that the house might be going to you and your mother, and not to me. I assured him that was a wonderful idea."

"That is so kind of you, but with 25 pounds a year, if we're still fortunate, we cannot maintain it."

How could her eyes look so kind, when everything pointed to ruin? *The lessons I could learn from you, dear woman*, he thought.

There wasn't any more reason for him to stay. "Let us walk over together tomorrow."

"Let's. Goodnight, Captain Foster."

He watched the gentle sway of her hips as she walked upstairs, sad beyond belief because she called him Captain Foster, and not Amos. She was already steeling herself for his inevitable departure. Hadn't he said over and over how eager he was the return to London, his ship, and his life? Gad, what an idiot he was.

After thanking Miss Cuthbert for her forbearance, he let himself out. He knew sleep was impossible. He reached for Grandpa Ince's box of letters, finally nodding off in the chair after the clock chimed four. In consequence, his backed ached when he woke up.

He rubbed his eyes and put the letters back in the box. All that remained was a final letter to read. Madeline had numbered them meticulously, perhaps mindful that someday the mysterious "Dear Amos" might appear. He had, and done little good for her. He toyed again with the idea of asking if she would be amenable to correspondence. If Grandpa did will him the house, he would sell it and give Madeline the profit.

"That's the best you can do?" he asked the supremely unhappy face in the mirror. "I'm surprised you can hire a crew to walk across the street with you, much less sail an ocean."

Smile and put on a happy face, he ordered himself as he opened the door to the circulating library and two worried faces looked back at him: Maude Tifton and Miss Cuthbert.

Amos Foster knew right then that if he lived to be an old, dribbling, doddering antique, Madeline's serenity would be something he wanted to carve as figurehead on every ship he built and sailed. *How do you do it*? he asked himself. She was the only calm presence in the room.

Leaving for the solicitor's was a trial. Maude burst into tears, which meant her daughter spent a moment with her arms tight around her. He heard, "Mama, we always have a home here. There isn't anything your sister-in-law can do to us."

"Then why this summons, daughter?"

"Maybe she wants to gloat about her good fortune, should Mr. Ince's house come her way. Be brave."

"How do you do it?" he asked simply.

"Amos Foster, how on earth did *you* survive a ship sunk in a hurricane, two other ships rendered unseaworthy, and a war?"

It was easy enough to tell the truth. "Simple, dear heart," he began. (He couldn't help a little unholy glee when she rosied up at that.) "I drank too much rum, gnawed my fingernails off, suffered through spells of diarrhea, and those were the pleasant things."

He hoped she would laugh, and she did, a laugh that he wanted to hear again and again until he died. Yes, he would ask if he could write to her. But she hadn't answered his question. "I've bared all my indignities, Miss Tifton, and it was ugly, you will agree. Confess to me how *you* stay so calm."

She must have given the matter some recent thought. As pretty as she looked, he could tell her eyes were tired, too. Maybe *she* had stayed up all night. "I decided yesterday that no matter what happens, every day has twenty-four hours and there is always another sunrise to try again."

"Touché, Miss Tifton," he said, humbled as never before. *I used to feel that way*, he thought. *When did I change? Can I get that back?*

He crooked out his arms. "Ladies, let's go. This can't take long."

A pretty lady on either side of him, Amos admired the Christmas wreaths on many doors. "Do you have any amazing Yuletide traditions that we uncouth Americans haven't reckoned on?" he asked, hoping to put Mrs. Tifton at ease. He could feel her trembling.

"I suppose not," Madeline replied. "Our door-to-door Christmas carolers probably sound no better or worse than yours across the Atlantic. Many people steam a Christmas pudding here, and I suppose you do, too."

He nodded. "Mama wouldn't miss it. Is yours ready?"

"Sort of," she said, her eyes merry. "Since there are only two of us and we're not noted gluttons, we save money by drawing a picture of a Christmas pudding."

Lovely, kind, gallant. He leaned closer and whispered in her ear. "Madeline, would you think me uncouth and rude if I asked to correspond with you? Think of the practice you have had with my grandpa."

She whispered back. "I will enjoy that."

Up ahead, the Tifton coach was pulling up to Mr. Clare's modest office. They waited until Mr. and Mrs. Tifton were ushered inside by the solicitor.

They went in next, Maude hanging back until she took several deep breaths at her daughter's suggestion. Mother and daughter's heads were close together, but Amos heard their exchange. "I usually only see her when I go to the manor for my twenty-five pounds," Maude whispered. "This will make twice this year."

"I can go in your place, Mama," Madeline said. "I should have offered to do that before. In fact, consider it done."

In silence, they removed their cloaks. He saw them as they were, two little people who had been dealt a wicked hand years ago, but who did not break under it, reminding Amos all over again that his trials were no better or worse than anyone else's. He had known ship captains who had lost less than Foster Shipping, but who had turned into broken hulks. He had seen other men receive mercy somehow, who then turned on those lower down the ladder of life and extracted their pound of quivering flesh.

He vowed to read his Bible more often, mainly because he was forgetting the lessons found there. And here it was, nearly a Christmas he had forgotten. The unjust practices foisted on powerless women were of great concern to Him whose birth the world was poised to celebrate. There would always be a reckoning, whether in this life or the next. Madeline's greatest gift to Amos Foster was her example of courage in the face of adversity. He would never forget her.

Mr. Clare cleared his throat to get their attention. He looked around at the small gathering. "I will dispense with preliminaries," he said. "You know me. I know you. This letter and accompanying will is dated June 26, 1812, a week after the war between our countries began."

Using a wicked-looking letter opener, the solicitor sliced the packet in front of him. He slit through twine, and broke open Grandpa Ince's seal that Amos was already familiar with, having opened many of those himself in that period before all mail stopped and war began. In silence, Mr. Clare spread out the document and began to read to himself. His eyes widened and he sucked in his breath, which made Loisa Tifton lean forward, triumph all over her face. "See there, Peter, you worried for nothing," she said softly.

Mr. Clare gave her a sharp look, until he started to smile. He shook his head and finished reading the closely written page. His smile grew wider.

Amos twined his fingers through Madeline's. He squeezed and she squeezed back. "Better breathe, Amos," she whispered. "You're turning red."

He took a breath. "Yes, ma'am, thank you, ma'am," he teased.

"Read it, man," Peter Tifton demanded.

"With pleasure," the solicitor said firmly. "I hope all of you are ready for this."

"Certainly," Loisa Tifton said sweetly, but with an edge of malice. "I know my dearest father would not torment us as you are doing."

Dearest father, my ass, Amos thought. *You never once set foot in the house that is probably yours now.*

Or was it? Mr. Clare puffed his cheeks and blew out a column of air, as he seemed to calm his own nerves. "Mr. Ince was a bit of an eccentric," he began. "I know there were many of the landed gentry in our shire, and his own, who washed their hands of him when he sold his land and invested in canal stock. Yes, that was it." He glanced at the Tiftons, husband and wife. "I always had the feeling he was hounded from the district by censure from people who felt he brought shame to their social sphere."

"Papa did make it difficult for us," Loisa Tifton said. She dabbed at dry eyes.

"Be that as it may. Your father moved north to a small house in Yorkshire near Leeds. Bless my soul if he didn't do a little digging, himself. He was a man of great enthusiasm."

"Canals! We have enough of those already!" Mrs. Tifton declared. "I told you he was a fool, Peter. When I think of the land he sold and the money he lost, I am appalled."

Mr. Clare held up his hand in a placating gesture. "Now, now." He looked her in the eye, quelling her commentary. "*Au contraire*, madam. According to this will, Walter Ince made a fortune by investing in *more* canals well-suited for commerce."

Amos had to admit that Mrs. Tifton recovered in spectacular fashion. "Dear, dear, father," she cooed, even as her face turned an alarming red. She dabbed at her eyes again, but with more energy. "I didn't want him to soil his hands with trade, and embarrass himself. I was thinking of him. How much….what did…"

"This is where it gets interesting." Mr. Clare looked at Amos. "Here is what he wrote, ""In appreciation for years of charming letters beginning as an eleven-year-old boy and then a growing lad turned to the commerce of the sea, and then a master and captain in his own right, my step-grandson Amos Foster did me a signal honor with his letters. I wanted to do something fitting for a man who probably will have his own trials in coming years, if this war is a long as the revolutionary one. I do not have a crystal ball. I have no idea when this war, now begun, will end. When it does, Amos Carter will find the sum of …"

Mr. Clare paused dramatically. Amos wondered how it was that the solicitor avoided a life on the wicked stage. ""…of twenty thousand pounds sterling.""

Amos had no plans to faint, but he did see little sparkles of light jostling each other across his vision, then skipping around.

Madeline took his arm. "Breathe, Amos," she said, but not in a whisper this time. "In and out, in and out."

"This is impossible. He is not even his grandson," Mrs. Tifton said. "My dear, dear sister Catherine had the raising of him!" She tried to snatch the papers on Mr. Clare's desk, which he now held close to his chest.

"Be seated, madam," he said. "I will continue with this sentence. Let me see… 'twenty thousand pounds sterling currently residing in the Bank of England. It is to be used at least partially to increase and maintain his fleet, no matter how or when this war ends. I trust him with his decisions.'" The solicitor's eyes softened. "'This is in grateful thanks for hours of wonderful letters from a grandson who let me know I had not been forgotten by my family.'"

"What a kind man," Madeline said. "Amos, you'll have all the ships you want."

Amos doubted he could even speak, but he managed. "I wish I could have met him." Tears gathered in his eyes. Madeline pressed her handkerchief into his palm.

"This cannot be!" Mrs. Tifton shouted again. "It cannot be legal."

"It is legal," Mr. Clare said. "Mr. Ince was entitled to leave his fortune wherever he wanted." He read ahead. "There is more to come." He looked at Madeline this time, the very act of which made Mrs. Tifton set up a howl. She stamped her feet like a child, and glared at Madeline, who leaned away from the woman. Amos put his arm around her protectively.

"'Maddie, dear Madeline,'" Mr. Clare began. He pointed to the document. "That's how he addresses you." He looked at Maude Tifton, his expression equally kind. "'Madam, this is to both of you, but he specifies Madeline.'"

"He should," Mrs. Maude said. "She took him meals and read to him, and still sweeps the snow from before his house. She wrote his last few letters as he dictated them to her, when his handwriting failed."

"You raised an excellent child, madam, and you did it with no help or resources from anyone." Mr. Clare said. He accompanied this with a measured glance at Loisa Tifton. "Deep breath now:

'To Madeline Tifton and her mother Maude, I bequeath the sum of 5,000 pounds. Used judiciously, this should provide a tidy sum to live on.'" He read on and chuckled. "Wouldn't you know it? He added, 'Maddie, beware of fortune hunters, won't you?' And this: 'You may also have deed to my house at Number Fourteen High Street.'"

Madeline put her hand to her heart, then turned her lovely eyes on Amos. "Mr. Ince was so easy to care about. I, too, wish you could have met him."

"I learned a lot reading his letters last night," he said, knowing this wasn't the place or the time, but not sure when or if that would ever come. "He mentioned you many times. Hey now, don't you cry."

"I'm not crying," she said. He returned her handkerchief, which she accepted gratefully, adding her tears to his, which did something to his heart. Gad, but he was a soft touch.

"That is it," Mr. Clare said. "He is allocating me the sum of two hundred pounds per annum to continue overseeing this will and testament, which I am legally qualified to do." He slid a pasteboard business card toward Amos. "When you go to London in a few days, you are to visit this man. He will guide you through the process of acquiring your legacy. Maddie, I can manage yours here, if you so choose."

"I do," she said softly. "I have a request right now. From my share, could I give the sum of 500 pounds to Miss Cuthbert? She has charged us so little through the years, and I want to share some of this." She laughed. "Knowing her, she will probably use some of it on more copies of Jane Austen."

"It can and will be done." He pointed to the document again. "There is still the sum of 10,000 pounds set aside for future investments, and they will be handled by that same man you will see in London, Captain Foster. It's early days, and who knows if *this* modern scheme will someday overtake canals in popularity: Mr. Ince wanted to invest in railroads. He states that if anything should come of that--and who knows?--the sum will be divided between you and Madeline and Maude."

"Fair to me," Amos said. "And you, ladies?"

The ladies nodded. Loisa Tifton set up another howl and stamping of her feet, while her husband looked on in alarm, and then casually moved his chair farther away from hers. "But I am his loving daughter!"

In what galaxy would that ever be true? Amos thought.

Mr. Clare looked down at the page again. "He did write something to you, Mrs. Tifton. I will not read it beyond saying that he quotes Shakespeare's tragedy, *King Lear*." He looked her in the eye. "Something about a thankless child and a serpent's tooth. The Bard did have a way with a phrase. Good day to you all."

Chapter Eleven

Amos's good fortune sank in after he escorted two excited ladies back to the circulating library and Miss Cuthbert, who went into raptures over the news. She burst into tears and protested when Madeline, also in tears, told her that 500 pounds was coming her way soon for her unparalleled kindness through the years.

"But for you, we would have been on the street or in the poorhouse years ago," Madeline reminded her, which meant more tears. Her simple comment made Amos's blood run in chunks, because he knew she was right.

"I'll be back later today," he promised, and hightailed it to Number Fourteen, where he could close the door and weep. The awful burden of watching Foster Shipping sink closer and closer to ruin had been a bitter pill. His father died in his arms, but with trust in his eyes, as if his son could somehow stop the turmoil of war and make things right with his ships and crews. He felt himself relax, really relax, for the first time since war was declared, because that burden heavy as an anvil was lifted.

Amos could by no stretch of his imagination call himself a righteous man--no one swore better than a sailor, unless it was a dairyman. His was an admittedly odd kind of faith that seemed to lead back to one thing he had never found in reading the Bible. Nowhere did it say, "Things most generally turn out all right."

As he sat in Grandpa Ince's comfortable chair it occurred to him in a blinding flash that maybe that was the whole point; things most generally did turn out all right. He already knew that the

Lord loved effort. That tenet had come with his birth, and earlier lifetimes of his Puritan and Separatists ancestors, who expended massive amounts of effort in all they did, for the glory of God.

He now had money to rebuild his father's fleet, and then some. It was the "then some" that told him he could leave a little more with Mr. Clare for Maude and Madeline Tifton. Life could go on pretty well for them and he would not have to worry about people he had come to admire.

"Gadfreys you dope, admit it," he said out loud. "You're in love with Madeline Tifton."

He was. The idea of leaving––he was free to go––smacked him where it hurt. The rational side of his brain told him this was not the time to court and marry, considering that she lived in England, and he in New England and involved soon in rebuilding a fleet, a years-long effort. When he wasn't sailing, he had to supervise at the dry dock. Heavens, he could build his own drydocks with this largess, which would amount to more work. And yet…

The idea of life without seeing Madeline every day was a poor life, indeed. She was first of all lovely to look at––naturally that had caught his eye because he was a man. Then he saw her kindness, followed by courage and gallantry and every single quality he yearned for in someone he knew he must trust completely, because his work might take him away from home for months at a time.

He leaned back in Grandpa's chair and closed his eyes. He had seen something in her face yesterday, before today's reading of the will, that infinitely smoothed her path. He saw that she did not need him. He saw that no matter the challenges, things would most generally work out for her, too, and she understood it now. How, he didn't know, but she did understand.

"That is the supreme irony," he announced. "A seafaring man needs a wife who can stand on her own. She can't be the clinging type. She doesn't need me. I need *her*."

He would definitely write to her. That would be a start.

He finished the packing he had started earlier. The beauty of a duffel bag meant he could cram things inside and there was always room. He looked long and hard at the box of letters and set it aside, because it belonged here in Number Fourteen. He wrote a note on the box. "Please take good care of these, as you took good care of my grandfather. Sincerely, Amos Foster."

He returned the box to the sitting room and recalled one remaining letter, the only sealed one. He chuckled. Maybe it was something manly that his Grandpa didn't want a tender woman to read. It went into his duffel. He shouldered it, looked around one last time, and locked the door behind him.

He dreaded stopping at the circulating library, but they needed to know he was leaving. When he opened the door, Miss Cuthbert looked up from the row of books she was perpetually dusting. "I'll use my broom," she said, her expression a study in sadness.

Three taps on the ceiling. Madeline came down first, followed by her mother. Her face fell when she saw his duffel. "I thought you would stay at least through Christmas," she told him. "Christmas is tomorrow, after all."

"I have much to do," he said, and hated his cowardice.

Bless her heart. She let him get away with that, offering her hand and a bright smile. "I owe you more than I can say," she told him. "What's that expression? Fair winds and something else."

"Following seas." He gave her hand a good shake and writhed inside. "I promise to write to you."

"I hope you have time." She kissed his cheek. "Do look out for the French on your shipping line. They signed no treaty."

"Napoleon is done. Your navy has'm," he said, keeping it light, because she did.

"I believe he is headed farther away than Elba this time," Madeline said, then blushed. "Miss Cuthbert insists that I read the newspapers."

He could linger and make it worse, or leave. "I will be in touch. Good day and God bless you."

Madeline opened her mouth to say something, and couldn't. She fled up the stairs, her mother following more slowly.

Miss Cuthbert remained, glaring at him as if he didn't measure up, which he didn't.

"I don't know what to do," he said. It sounded so lame.

"Yes, you do," she replied. Ouch. He headed for the door before she threw him out.

"Just a moment. Take this."

She held out a folded note. "Maddie wrote this. You and she were teasing about what to get each other for Christmas."

"I remember."

"Thank goodness you remember something! She wrote this to you and stuck it in a book no one checks out. I am certain she meant to retrieve it, but forgot, in all this excitement."

He put the note in his pocket by the sealed letter, and couldn't leave the library fast enough. A quick walk took him to Mr. Clare's office, where he picked up a packet of intimidating documents, specific directions, and an address. "Make this barrister your London agent, and you'll sail through any release of funds," Mr. Clare promised.

"And you'll remain my agent here," Amos said. They shook hands.

The mail coach was on time, so he only had a brief word with the innkeeper, who took considerable delight in telling him that his daughter Susan, who worked at Tifton Manor, had a story about vases thrown, and Mr. Tifton making a quick retreat by post chaise to Brighton for a repairing lease.

"Dunno if he'll return," the keep said. "I wouldn't! Susan said Mrs. Tifton looked angry enough to chew on the carpet. G'day now, Captain. Come and see us again."

To his infinite relief, the mail coach was not crowded. He shared it with an old couple who woke up, looked around and returned to sleep.

Amos debated a stupid amount of time whether to read the folded note that Miss Cuthbert had thrust at him. *Are you a man or a mouse*, he thought. A mouse was the answer, but he took out the note finally.

What beautiful handwriting. He had commented on it to her when he started reading the letters Grandpa Ince had dictated to her. Madeline's note made him stare out the window for a long, long time: *Captain Foster, my gift to you is the sure knowledge that wherever the sea takes you, there is someone of no importance who is always going to wish you well. Sincerely yours, Happy Christmas.*

"I'm doing the right thing," he muttered under his breath, which made the old man wake up, looked around, fix him with an owlish glare, and return to sleep.

Amos didn't even debate on whether or not to read the last of Grandpa's letters. He needed a soothing letter from a man he wished he had met, had things been different. He opened the letter, mindful that it was the only one of the box that had been sealed. He chuckled to himself. *Keeping secrets from your pretty scribe?*

He was. As he expected, the letter was in Madeline's writing, but he read Grandpa's longing in it for more life, even as his aches and pains increased. Amos sighed to read, *I wish I could have met you, lad,* and then, *With love, Grandfather.*

All of that was in Madeline's now-familiar handwriting. What Grandpa must have added after she left for the day was not. A scrap of paper remained to be read.

I suppose he knew it was his last letter, Amos thought. He had only a little challenge deciphering Grandpa Ince's scrawl. The letter was simple and to the point, with no chance to misinterpret or cavil about. He understood why Grandpa had sealed it, which must have been his own wishful thinking. How would he know if his correspondent ever received it? *When peace comes, get your sorry carcass here, you American, and marry my Madeline. She'll make a better man out of you than you probably deserve. WI*

Grandpa was right. Peace had come. He was here. Life would be busy. Madeline would make all of the work worth it and all of the long-overdue joy not only possible, but certain. No one but a fool would think otherwise.

He left the mail coach at Hemphill and promptly paid for a ticket back to Ashfield. "Didn't ye just come from there, laddie?" the agent asked. "Forget something?"

"Aye, sir, I did."

Back in Ashfield, Amos left his duffel at the inn, surprised that the innkeeper made no comment about his unexpected return other than, "I thought you forgot something. Happy Christmas." And this hint: "Pretty much everyone is at church except us sinners."

He sat in the back of the Anglican church, only a little appalled at the incense and other evidences of high church so foreign to his upbringing. He wondered what Madeline would make of the New England economy of words and simple music of his Congregational Church in Groton, when he was in port for a more lengthy time. Madeline might like Groton better than Boston. He knew he did, but she could decide for them both.

Sitting at the back, he was the first one out the door when the service ended and the night air filled with bells pealing to signal Christmas Day. He had seen the love of his life sitting closer to the front with Maude, because he knew Maude was hard of hearing. He still didn't know what he was going to say to his future wife, if she was of the same mind as he.

There she was, her eyes wide and mouth open at the sight of him, standing there hat in hand like a penitent. He said nothing, but held out Grandpa Ince's last letter, with its immortal postscript.

"I understand why he sealed it," she said, after she read it. She laughed softly. "'Sorry carcass.' He had a way with words."

His heart lifted when she put her hand on his chest, the gesture intimate. "He seemed to know you better than you knew yourself, Amos Foster. Welcome back."

He didn't care who watched, even if it was most of nosy, gossiping Ashfield. He gave her a scorching kiss right there in the church yard. She returned it with similar vigor, and they stared at each other as if wondering, *What in the world was that?*

He didn't let go of Madeline, but he held her off. "You don't need me. Be honest now."

He saw momentary confusion on her face, and then she understood. "No, I don't *need* you. I would have managed, no matter what happened."

Better and better. "You realize that makes you the ideal wife for a seafaring man," he said, as his confidence grew. "And by the way, I do have riverfront property in Groton, Connecticut. Good Lord, it's even called the Thames River. But you don't *need* me."

She put her face close to his until he grew almost cross-eyed looking at her. "Captain Foster, there are needs and there are wants, and they are not the same thing. If you don't propose to me right now, I will."

There was snow on the walkway, much like the snow she had swept so meticulously through the years at Number Fourteen. He knew he was going to soak his trouser leg, but he went down on one knee. To his amusement and undying affection, Madeline Tifton promptly sat on his knee. The parishioners still leaving the church laughed and he proposed.

She nodded. "Well done, Captain," she whispered in his ear. "The answer is aye."

He kissed her again, to general applause this time and whispered back, "Yours sincerely, Happy Christmas."

Epilog

Groton, Connecticut
February 1817

Dear Mama,

The first new ship of the Foster Fleet went down the ways in Groton before the turn of the year. The rigging was set with great efficiency and she is a thing of beauty. Amos is conning the shakedown cruise, which will eventually take him to Ashfield and the circulating library, once he makes the London Docks. (I sent this letter a month before he is due to sail. You should be getting this letter a little before he reaches England.)

I do hope your bags are packed. You promised they would be, in your last letter. No fears, please. You will like our riverfront property on *this* Thames River! You will also like my husband's stepmother. Indeed, I have come to love Catherine Foster. This is a big house and there is room for all of us.

Having said that, Amos had real trouble prying himself away from us. Yes, us. You are now grandmama to a boy. We decided upon David Ince Foster. He is the most handsome little one I ever laid eyes on. I am not even slightly biased, am I?

Oh, and this: My dear husband christened this first ship the *Maddie Mine*. I cried over that, but then, before David was born, I cried at nearly everything. The midwife assured me that's what ladies-in-waiting do. Heavens.

But here we are, and eager to see you soon. America might

seem raw and a bit primitive, but the people are stalwart and kind. You'll feel at home here very soon. I did.

Love,

Madeline Foster (a.k.a. *Maddie Mine*)

P.S. We are both delighted that you have given Number Fourteen to Ruth Cuthbert. She will take good care of it. A suggestion: Do you think Livingston, the butler at Tifton Manor, would like to do some light work for her, in exchange for lodging in our old rooms over the library? I've heard rumors that Mrs. Tifton is ready to turn him off, and you know that will come with no compensation, even after all his years at the manor. (My husband is going to arrange a stipend with Mr. Clare, so Livingston can leave Tifton Manor with dignity.) Just a thought.

M

PICTURE A CHRISTMAS

Prologue

October, 1809, Plymouth

All Luke Wainwright wanted was a quiet evening by the fire. He had the satisfaction of knowing that the banking firm of Biddle and Bancroft was inching closer to funding the remainder of what Magleby & Wainwright Shipbuilders needed to add another drydocks at Devonport's South Yard. It was amazing how Devonport and nearby Plymouth had grown large enough now to compete favorably with the drydocks at Chatham.

Luke had more numbers to add and subtract to complete his father-in-law's upcoming presentation, but it was nearly midnight. As his late wife would say, "Love, this bed is getting cold."

To say that even after six years he still missed Clarissa was no exaggeration. So many were willing to tell him that life goes on. At some level, he knew they were right. He had his doubts, even though he tried not to argue with well-wishers. Luke knew they meant the best.

The house was quiet, his daughter Sally long abed. His small staff of a cook, a maid of all work, and a nanny appeared sufficient unto the task. Luke had to admit one thing: He still didn't think of his house as a home. That would probably come in time, too, and truly, they had been comfortable, living in Devonport with the Maglebys, Clarissa's parents.

He knew his life was too busy, but war with France meant money to a shipbuilder in good odor with the Navy Board and Lords of the Admiralty who paid for the frigates and larger warships that went down the ways, then out to sea and battle. Only now and then did he ask himself, *Luke, my boy, are you busy for busy's sake?*

Maybe solitude and nightfall, with his ears free from hammering, sawing and the constant need to hurry also made him more personally honest. *Why aren't you happy?* he asked himself. *You come from a plain and ordinary family and you are on the way to wealth and success. You have everything to make this a Happy Christmas, indeed. What's the matter with you?*

Chapter One

Mid-September 1809

Papa was a man of his word, if not a particularly successful tenant farmer. "Aye, Squire Banford, I'll have the oats in before the weather changes, just like me father and his father before him."

He did, enlisting Mary Cooper, his daughter, plus other field hands to scythe and winnow. When all was done to his satisfaction, tenant farmer Cooper on the Banford estate lay down and died.

Mary never knew what caused his death, beyond a stomach complaint. There was no money for a doctor. Like many of his social sphere--non-existent--Frederick Cooper was not a man to rail against fate; he didn't put up a struggle. Besides that, Mary knew how much he missed Mama.

She sat beside her father's bed a long while, aware that her days were numbered in the crofter's cottage where she was born. She was also aware that she would soon have no home, no prospects, nothing. Because of this, she continued her vigil until morning, then gave herself a shake. Perhaps it was a reminder that she was alive, and full of fortitude, even if no one knew it except her.

She straightened Papa's nightshirt and brought the blanket up to his neck, because she couldn't bear to cover his face. She sat a moment more, then felt her resolve return. She searched their cottage and found one sheet of paper, torn in half. She smoothed the edges, then found her prized possession, a drawing pencil.

"I won't forget you, Papa," she told him as she sketched his peaceful form, "but I do know that after a few years, the memory dims. I need your image."

She had done all she could for her father. Now it was time to notify Squire Banford, knowing what would happen to her when he knew her father was dead, and had no son to follow in the work of the land. True, she helped around the estate whenever needed, but it wasn't the same as having a son.

Outside, she raised her face to the sun, equally aware that the harvest was over and winter on its way. She felt the smallest edge of the season's change, knowing that next week might bring falling leaves. She had an instinct about trees and small animals, and when it was time to fly away, burrow in, or shed.

It was a short walk to the manor. She was used to walking. *What will I do?* she asked herself. She stared up at the squire's manor and her courage nearly failed her––nearly but didn't, Mary reminded herself as she walked around to the servants' entrance and knocked.

She told her story simply to the housekeeper, who ushered her in, sat her down, and provided tea. She sent word to the squire, then handed Mary a cleaning cloth and pointed to a row of knives. She set to work polishing, noting the housekeeper's nod of approval.

"Do you have any family around here?" the housekeeper asked.

"No, mum," Mary said, and couldn't overlook the worry-frown on the woman's face.

When the knives sparkled and Mary had started on the spoons, the butler signaled for her to follow him upstairs. Her own unease increased when the housekeeper had a whispered word with the butler, who shook his head. Mary heard, "Too many here as it is," and she knew there wasn't a place for her in the squire's household, even though her father had been raised on the estate and Coopers had farmed here for three generations.

She had never been upstairs. She kept her eyes down as she followed the butler through the immaculate corridor and into the squire's bookroom. Before the butler left, Squire Banford told him to get some men to help at the cottage. With a sinking feeling, she knew when she returned home, Papa would be gone.

The squire didn't say anything for a few minutes. He finished some work on his desk, then looked up. "Mary, I am sorry for your loss," he said. "Fred Cooper was a good and loyal worker." He didn't smile, but his eyes were sympathetic, to her relief, which gave her the smallest, tiniest hope. "He never said much. Not a waster of words, he."

She nodded. Papa was a man of few words--even fewer after Mama died--who worked with his hands and not his mouth. When he dispensed praise, Mary never forgot it.

His expression changed and she braced herself for the worst. "Mary, there is no place for you on my estate now," he said. "What with the war on, times are tough all around."

Not in your house, she thought, but not with any rancor. She knew her place well enough. She said nothing, and made herself look him in the face. *I won't beg, but please, Squire, please.*

She knew her greatest fear was unvoiced, but the squire seemed to hear it anyway. "Mary, I...I hope I can find a better place for you. No guarantees."

At least he didn't say the word poorhouse. "I hope you can, too, Squire Banford."

"I'll think on it," he said, then made a slight shooing motion. "All the same, better pack whatever you wish to take with you. We'll bury your father tomorrow morning after breakfast. Good day."

He left unsaid where she would go. Mary gave him a grand curtsey, but the squire had already returned to perusing his ledger and didn't see it. Other crofters were removing Frederick Cooper when she came home.

When you have nothing except another dress, apron, chemise and your mother's brush, packing takes no time, particularly if there is nothing to put it in. Mary remembered Papa's canvas seed bag that he carried over his shoulder during sowing time. Perhaps it belonged to the estate; she decided she didn't care. Papa's only possession of any value were his boots, but she had no use for them, and left them beside the now-empty bed. Her clothing went into the seed bag, followed by Mama's Book of Common Prayer, where she stashed the two small sketches of her parents.

She debated whether to add Shakespeare's sonnets. Years ago, in a deed uncharacteristic of her, Mama had stolen it from the squire's library, where she had been sent to dust. It was the book she used to teach Mary to read. No one ever claimed it, but Mary squashed it deep into the seed bag, where it couldn't possibly be seen. She couldn't leave it behind.

That was that. She would pack Mama's teacup tomorrow after her breakfast of toast and water and go...somewhere.

She didn't expect any of her neighbors to offer her supper and none did. She knew they preferred to ward off death by keeping its closest relatives away, too. She read a page in her sonnets. The sun set and she was in darkness. She cried for Papa one last time, or maybe she cried for herself, since there had been no word from anyone about work.

Papa was buried in the morning at the back of the squire's large plot. There was space beside Mama, so in he went, wrapped in a winding cloth, fair game soon for worms, which were more ambitious than ashes or dust. The pastor rattled off something about ashes to ashes, and man born of woman. In minutes, she was the only one standing in the plot behind the church.

Where to go? Mary had seldom been off the estate, but she knew the village of Liddiard could be reached by walking east. For years, she had seen people going that way, and now it was her turn.

She slowed down as she passed the squire's manor, hoping he might send a servant out to invite her in, because they had found a place for her, but no, that was wishful thinking.

Still, the day was warm and the sun shone down on her, which she considered nature's kindness. The last thing she wanted today was rain.

After a half-hour's walking, she came to Liddiard—houses closer together, and then a few shops on a single street. There was an inn or public house, a church, a tearoom, and four other businesses. She looked in each window for a placard advertising for workers; no again.

It was then that panic set in. She swallowed and swallowed, uncertain what to do. She had no money. Papa had certainly earned something from his last harvest of oats, but the squire had said nothing about payment. She looked up at the modest spire of St. Andrews--Liddiard was modest in every way--and knew it was time to throw herself on the mercy of the church. She never attended much. She remembered the frowns of other parishioners who assumed they were better--at least better dressed--than her or Mama. Without question, she knew the vicar would send her to the poorhouse.

"No, please, God," she whispered. "I need something else." She stopped. It seemed like a wicked thing to ask for. She never asked for anything, because there never was anything. This day, in the deepest part of her heart, she knew there had to be something else.

Mary looked across the street at another store. She looked closer. A simple sign overhead announced, Notions. *I've had plenty of notions*, she thought, wringing wry humor out of a terrible day. *None of my notions have got me anywhere.*

Was that a placard in the corner of the display window? She crossed the street for a better look. "*Help wanted, but you'd better be useful*," she read. She couldn't help a slight smile. "I am useful," she declared out loud, after looking around to make sure there was no one else in sight. "I never met a more useful human than me."

She tried the doorknob. Locked. If the sun wasn't fading from sight, and she wasn't desperate, she never would have knocked. Nothing. She knocked louder.

Mary cocked her head, listening, and heard a firm tread. "Please, God," she whispered.

The door opened on an old lady even smaller than she was. "Well? Well?" the woman asked, and none too kindly. "Mostly your sort just knocks, throws dirt clods, and runs away."

"I would never do that," Mary said, more forcefully than she should have. "I saw your placard and I…I think I am the help you want."

The woman looked where Mary pointed. "I should have taken that down years ago. I thought I had. Hmmm. That's a bit of a mystery." She glared at Mary as if it were her fault that the sign was there. "I don't need help."

"The sign says you do," Mary persisted. "Whatever it is you need, I can do it."

"No one visits my store. All I get are arguments and contention when they do."

What did she have to lose? Mary looked into the store. "I would start by dusting and tidying a bit. Perhaps a better arrangement in the window display." She turned her attention to the woman herself, whose lace cap was skewed at a strange angle. "You could use some tidying, yourself."

Before the woman could object, Mary straightened her lace cap. "There now. That's better. I'd call it a world of difference."

Obviously no one had spoken to the woman like this before. Mary persisted. "I think you need me."

"I need someone who can make things beautiful again so people come to my store," the woman insisted. "I don't think that's you. You're shabby and belong in a poorhouse. Go away."

Please, God, Mary thought again, in utter desperation. *Please*.

"Take this sign with you!" the old woman demanded. She yanked it from the window. "There is nothing beautiful in Liddiard."

She thrust the sign at Mary Cooper, who had suffered all the indignity she ever wanted. All she had was another dress even more shabby than the one she wore, and a drawing pencil. She took the placard and turned to leave.

As she turned, she noticed the sunset, reminding her all over again how lovely Devonshire could be, when it wasn't treating her cruelly. She took the pencil from her seed bag, wishing for crayons to do it justice, but possessing none. She turned over the placard and drew the gentle slope of the terrain, and the sun setting behind the church. She smiled to see the River Plym in the distance, a ribbon of water sparkling as the sun reflected and made it dance.

It was only a rough sketch, but her heart started to beat again after the sorrow at Mama's death and now Papa's, and the scarcity of everything except worry and want. There now. She had done all she could. She would leave this rough-drawn landscape with the old lady, and keep walking.

"Here you are," she said, handing it over. "Something to remind you that Liddiard is beautiful. Good day."

Was there another village farther on? Mary had run out of village here, but she was a good walker. The idea of the poorhouse was as repulsive as ever. She was hungry, but not so hungry that she couldn't keep walking.

"Wait there, you."

Her mind already on what lay ahead, Mary stopped in surprise. "Me?"

She stood her ground when the old lady came closer and closer. Her heart softened when she realized that the woman's eyesight was rudimentary at best. "Yes, ma'am?" she asked, in a kindlier tone, because one old woman was no one to fear.

"Don't just stand there. Come inside."

"Why?" Mary asked. "You said you didn't need any help."

"Possibly, I was wrong," the old woman said. "I am Miss Wainwright."

"I am Mary Cooper."

"Well, get inside, Mary Cooper!"

Chapter Two

To call Luella Wainwright a taskmaster would be gilding a vaseful of lilies. After two days of skinny meals and little sleep after Papa's death, Mary was certain of one thing: there might be food. Beyond that, she didn't care.

She saw actual drawing paper in the shop, which contained random bits of nearly everything of modest price. It was as if a cosmic hand had scooped up a wad of this and that, jiggled it a bit, then tossed it on the shop like dice on a green felt cloth.

But first things first. "Can you cook?" Miss Wainwright asked.

"Aye," Mary said. "If there is food."

"Follow me."

The kitchen was spartan, at best, but there were pots and pans, which suggested food. "I'll fix you a nice porridge," Mary said, seeing oats in a glass jar. "Is there milk?"

"A farmer delivers it twice a week, plus eggs," Miss Wainwright said. "Check the pantry. See what you can do. I'll be in the dining room."

Mary couldn't help herself. One egg went down raw, apparently liked her famished stomach, and stayed there. Soon there was porridge and two boiled eggs to take into the dining room, a grandiose name for a little alcove off the kitchen. The tea was a nameless brand, but it was tea.

Miss Wainwright surveyed her efforts. "Two eggs is too much for me," was her only comment.

"One is for me," Mary said firmly, "and half the porridge."

Miss Wainwright ate in silence, yawned, and took herself

to bed somewhere in the back of the shop. Mary let out a sigh she had been keeping inside her for a week at least. She took up the lamp from the kitchen and returned to the shop itself. She surveyed the dusty shelves with sewing notions, skeins of yarn and knitting needles, stationery, and other bits and pieces of what ladies probably shopped for.

"Underneath this dust is a genteel business, Miss Wainwright," she said, looking back to the rooms beyond the kitchen where the old lady had disappeared. "Now, I wonder..."

She traveled the narrow corridor, please to see a little sitting room. She sat on the sofa and decided it would do for the night. She knew better than to plan much beyond a night's sleep, but at least she wasn't out of doors, hungry, and wondering what wild beast—man or animal—might grab her in the darkness.

She began work in earnest in the morning after breakfast, which was more porridge and eggs. Mary had no idea what Miss Wainwright thought, but she launched her campaign. "I can tidy your store and get it ready for customers," she said.

"No one ever came," was the grim reply from Miss Wainwright. "Or will."

"I can change that." How, she had some ideas. As uncomfortable as the sofa was, Mary knew it was better than anything in the poorhouse, a place she devoutly wished to avoid. "Let me tidy up the shop and see what happens. In the meantime, I will cook for you and run any errands you like."

"How do I know you won't cheat me?"

She already knew that Miss Wainwright liked her conversation straight up, with no bark on it. "You don't," she said quietly. "I can tell you that I am desperate for a place to sleep. I don't eat much, and I expect little."

She noticed a softening of Miss Wainwright's expression. It was brief, but she noticed it. She knew better than to rush into plans she hadn't even hatched yet. "You tell me what you like to eat, and provide me the money to buy it, and you will never be disappointed in me."

"You seem sure of yourself."

"I'm not," Mary replied, "but I plan to stay alive."

Tying up her hair in a length of cloth and finding an all-encompassing apron, Mary tackled the shop after Miss Wainwright retired to the sitting room, a book in hand. A mop and a broom plus something that smelled like cleaning powder stood at attention by the back door. She carefully dusted all items that looked like merchandise and set them in two pasteboard boxes. They went into the hall, as she swept, mopped, sneezed, and rubbed dust from her eyes all morning.

By noon, the results were gratifying and so Miss Wainwright told her when she looked into the shop. "I have some wood oil for the counters," the old lady said, "and ammonia for the display glass and window." Mary listened, and there it was: a thawing of Miss Wainwright's unhappiness, slight but there.

After a sparse lunch of buttered bread, cheese and tea, Miss Wainwright opened a door off the kitchen. "I keep more merchandise in here. I have a lot of yarn and knitting needles."

In addition to yarn, the storeroom yielded buttons, thread, pins and needles, yards of ribbon, and lace to sew onto hems and camisoles. It was all of good quality, but simple. Liddiard was not London, after all.

Miss Wainwright chose not to return to the sitting room, which both surprised and pleased Mary. She seemed to enjoy finding forgotten treasures in the storeroom. She exclaimed over the pin cushions, which she must have forgotten. "They are silk and they came from China," she said, taking them from a box and setting them on the counter.

"My, that was a long voyage," Mary said, as she finished mopping her way out of the dusted shop.

"My nephew in Plymouth sailed aboard a merchant vessel then," Miss Wainwright said. "It was before the French stopped maritime commerce and Napoleon made everyone dance to his tune."

"I imagine your nephew has changed professions now," Mary said, happy to pause for a moment in conversation, happy that Miss Wainwright wasn't looking at her with suspicion. Why the change? She was too shy to ask.

"Now he builds warships in Devonport," the lady said. She sighed. "What has the world come to?"

It was a good question. Mary thought about it as she put the final touches on the shop, finishing with ammonia and water on the window and buffing it with old towels until she was satisfied. She considered how little she knew about world events, and realized her major concern had been another meal, and not the dealings of tyrants and kings that she could do nothing about.

She sniffed the air, remembering that the proprietress of the tearoom brought over soup and bread for supper. They ate in silence, Mary not exclaiming over the wonderful soup, even though she wanted to. Pieces of meat floated in the broth. After Miss Wainwright yawned and retired to her room, Mary knew she could wrap up in her cloak again and sleep on the sofa in the sitting room.

Before sleep, Mary restocked the glass cabinet and wooden shelves along the wall. Miss Wainwright had already grouped the sewing supplies in the glass cabinet, with the Chinese pin cushions in a prominent spot. Mary brought out the yarn, which went on the shelves at the wall. She arranged it by colors, and stuck knitting needles here and there, liking the effect. She added a wooden bowl full of yarn to the window display.

To her surprise and delight, the next morning Miss Wainwright found a little display easel for her small sunset sketch, drawn in desperation. She set it in a prominent spot on the counter, then looked at Mary, her eyes lively. "I am having fun."

"I am, too," Mary said.

The lady stood a moment longer in contemplation of the sketch. She held up one finger and hurried into the storeroom, returning with what looked like a pencil box. She held it out. "For you. Open it."

Mary did, and gasped. "Miss Wainwright! The colors!"

"Crayons. I believe they came from France, that poxy country," the lady said. "Or perhaps Germany." She said in a gruff voice, "Don't be a watering pot over crayons."

"No one has even given me anything in my entire life," Mary said, when she could speak.

It was Miss Wainwright's turn to struggle. "I...I think you should take that thicker paper over there--if it doesn't look too old--and draw some more small scenes. We can display them in the window. It'll be an artful touch." She touched the crayons, too, and her gaze turned wistful. "I was going to give these to my nephew's daughter, but...but...they haven't come around lately."

"I imagine he is busy building ships," Mary said gently, wondering at the change in this frowning, grouchy soul who had come so close to forcing her from the store.

"It's more than that," Miss Wainwright said in a soft voice. "I gave up after my sister died--my nephew's mother, and then my brother. My nephew and his little one are all the family I have remaining, and I pushed them away. I wonder why I did that."

"Grief is a strange companion," Mary said after long thoughts of her own in the quiet shop. "My father is gone, and I had nowhere to go." She smiled at the sunset sketch. "I'm not a pushy person, but I so want to stay here. Did I *make* you employ me?"

"I believe you did," Miss Wainwright agreed. Mary heard no rancor now. She couldn't help smiling.

"We'll have to make this little shop a success, then. Let's eat."

Miss Wainwright had an arrangement with the woman who ran the tearoom to provide food on most days. Chicken and wild rice soup with crusty bread chunks to dip in it came with its own drama. Mary ate slowly, but couldn't help glancing at the pot on the hob. She knew there was more, but she wanted to get up to check, anyway.

She wasn't aware that Miss Wainwright was watching her until her employer brought the pot to the table and ladled more of the soup into Mary's bowl.

To Mary's horror, she burst into tears, crying, "But there won't be enough for tomorrow! We'll go hungry!"

Miss Wainwright shook her head. "I'll send you to the tearoom tomorrow and you can buy more soup. No one goes hungry here," she said, giving Mary a little shake that was more of a caress. "Dry

REGENCY GLADTIDINGS • 151

your eyes and finish it. When you're done, there is another matter that I should have addressed sooner."

Mary did as she was asked, trying to control her fear about the "other matter." Maybe now that the notions shop was put to rights again, there was no need of her presence. She dipped the bread, chewed and swallowed, trying to appear calm, even as she dreaded what worse thing would come her way, now that she was warm and well fed.

Finally Miss Wainwright pushed away from the table. "Come along," she said.

Mary closed her eyes against the next terror--eviction. Maybe she should have worked more slowly with her tidying, drawing out that time until the shop was in good order again. She headed toward the front door.

"Mary Cooper, turn around!" She did, her eyes downcast, unable to meet Miss Wainwright's gaze. The woman was entitled to whatever she did.

"This way." Miss Wainwright gestured toward the back of the shop. "I could kick myself for making you sleep heaven knows where the last night two nights," she was saying. "I didn't even furnish you with a coverlet. Here."

She opened the door on the bed chamber next to hers. Mary peeked inside to see a small but serviceable room. True, there was hardly space to turn around, but she saw a narrow bed, a dresser to hold extra air because she had no possessions, and a rag rug.

"You're small. You'll fit," Miss Wainwright said in that gruff voice Mary was coming to recognize as the prickly woman's way of deflecting gratitude.

"I will," she said simply. "I will."

She couldn't sleep that night. She sat in bed, the lamp hanging overhead, and drew a series of scenic views of their valley around Liddiard, the only place she knew. Outlining with her pencil first, she colored with the magic crayons, giving to her by a woman Mary had forced, in her desperation, to employ her.

By morning, she had six country vignettes four inches by four inches, because she had to conserve the paper. Quietly, she tiptoed

down the hall and into the shop, where she propped them against
carefully arranged mounds of embroidery thread. She went back
to bed and slept two hours, exhausted, but with a smile on her
face, her heart in tune with whatever lay ahead.

What lay ahead exceeded her modest hopes. The women of
Liddiard came shopping.

Chapter Three

Devonport – Late October

Blast and damn, but Luke Wainwright did not have time for an old maid aunt. Her letter came to the drydock with the usual mail, which was much more important to him. It was simple to slip her letter to the bottom of the pile, knowing it could keep until he went home.

Home, hardly. It was just a house where he lived with his daughter Sally. Home meant a wife who in some mysterious way made everything better, simply by her presence. Clarissa had been dead six years, almost since Sally's birth. Her father, a ship builder, had taught him everything he knew, except how to manage without a wife.

From his blueprint-filled office at Magleby & Wainwright Drydocks, he looked out across that stretch of the bay from South Yard, pleased to see work underway. It would have embarrassed him to admit that war paid so well, except he knew that the frigates that came down the ways from M&W Drydocks were things of beauty and menace, ready to strike the French fleets wherever they sailed.

Mr. Magleby's drydocks had begun life as most of Devonport's drydocks: a place to repair ships, both Royal Navy and merchant vessels. War changed everything as the need increased for quicker repairs, and then new ships to fight the French. M&W was modest enough; not for them the two and three-decker builds. All the same, no one could lay a keel and send a smaller frigate down the ways faster and better than M&W, and in the doing, they prospered.

A merchant mariner, Luke had met Clarissa Magleby at an *al fresco* luncheon, when he was a guest and she sat on the ground next to an ant bed. They laughed about that for a long time. He got to know the family, and found a shipbuilder with ambition in Clarissa's father. One thing led to another, and now the firm was Magleby & Wainwright. (By age and ability, Mr. Magleby ruled the roost.)

No doubt Luke Wainwright had married well, and even better, he loved his wife. If only Clarissa had lived longer. If only if only. In this generation of war, he didn't have time for if only. No one did.

Now here was this letter from Aunt Luella, his late father's sister and his only living relative. He felt a guilty pang as he opened it. Liddiard wasn't that far from Plymouth, but he hadn't seen the old rip in three years. Partly, he hadn't wanted to. During his last visit at the death of his uncle, Aunt Luella's brother, it was obvious she had let herself go to an alarming degree, the shop in shambles. Always a prickly woman, she was even more so, to the extent that the few mourners sidestepped around her, he among them.

Three years ago, he had done what duty required for her after the funeral, which involved a visit to Mallard's counting house where she had funds. All appeared in order, especially since her late brother had willed her what remained of his own funds. She was well set up, to Luke's relief. A few words to the proprietor, and he need not give her much thought. Mr. Mallard would take care of her.

Relieved to be kept from squandering his increasingly scarce time, that changed with the receipt of this letter, the first in three years. She started by scolding him for neglecting her, which didn't surprise him – yes, she was prickly, and yes, he *had* neglected her. The rest of her letter put him on alert and ready to pack a bag.

Luke, my way was smoothed a month ago by a young person who literally forced me to hire her, he read, to his alarm. *She set my shop to rights and works in it with no complaint. She bullies me to eat and rest, and I can even put my feet up and read, now that Mary is in charge. Yes, in charge. I tease her about robbing from the till, and she merely smiles and waggles her finger at me.*

"Oh, Aunt Luella," he said aloud, which made his daughter Sally look up from her book as she sat tucked close beside him. "What have you done?"

"Papa, it's only a letter," she reminded him.

"It's from my Aunt Luella, and she appears to have been taken in by a shady character."

He took a short moment to explain shady character to his daughter, which he didn't mind. At least she was speaking. Of late, she had become quiet around him, even as she wanted to cling. He was as patient as he could be. Truth to tell, he enjoyed how she burrowed close to him on the evenings he was home, and not puzzling over specifications for the next build. If only he understood why her eyes welled with tears when he left each morning. If only. There it was again.

"What will you do, Papa?"

It was on the tip if his tongue to say that Aunt Luella could extricate herself from her own problems because there was a war on. He changed his mind; guilt drove him to it as did a reminder of his inadequacy only last night.

He had been walking past St. Michaels, his head full of a million details concerning the latest frigate. His mistake was ducking inside to sit a moment in solitude with no one asking him stupid questions, or demanding his time for a trivial argument.

It must have been choir practice. They were attempting to sing "God Rest Ye Merry Gentlemen, Let Nothing You Dismay." All that ran through his overworked brain was how on earth anyone could be merry in this year of 1809? Colonel John Moore was dead at Corunna and full-blown war had come to Spain, as Napoleon sent in his generals. Luke sat there in silence, ashamed of himself and sad. By the time the carolers did their best and finished, he wondered if he was turning into a sour man, old before his time.

"Papa?"

He looked down at his pretty child – thank God Sally looked like Clarissa – and asked himself if a few days in Liddiard would cause the ship underway, demanding his attention, to come crashing down from its stays. The idea was ludicrous. His second in command was steady and knew how to keep the men sawing and hammering. Liddiard was less than half a day away. He could take a post chaise, look over his aunt's situation, and dismiss the encroacher – what was her name? Mary – close up the shop if things were out of control, and take Aunt Luella back to Plymouth.

"I'm going to Liddiard to rescue my spinster aunt," he told his daughter, surprising himself. "You'll be fine here for a few days."

She gave him a bleak stare, and then her lip started to tremble. "It's only a few days," he pleaded, wanting solitude. When she sobbed into his sleeve, he altered his sudden plans. "Oh, dash it. You can come, too."

He saw relief in her eyes that gave him something else to worry about. He wasn't an attentive parent and Sally needed him. God Almighty, everyone needed him. He sighed and resolved to do better.

"Certainly you can come along. You've never met my Aunt Luella."

"Is she good to little girls?" Sally asked, which gave him more cause to worry. He dismissed it, reminding himself that his daughter lacked for nothing. She had food, clothing, and people to look after her.

"Good? We shall see," was the best he could do. It sounded lame to his ears.

"Papa, you say that when you mean no," Sally murmured, already turning away.

What a craven lump he was, what a poor excuse for a father. God certainly needed to rest *this* merry gentleman, who was letting everything dismay him.

"We're both going," he said firmly.

He decided it would be a surprise visit, the better to see just what sort of trouble this Mary Whoever was causing. His father-in-law's only comment was, "Lad, you should've done this sooner. I can manage. What's a toothache, after all?"

"Are you sure, Father Magleby?" Luke asked. Poor man. His father-in-law must have the worst teeth in Devonport.

His father-in-law laughed. "Believe it or not, I knew how to run this drydocks before you came along! Go save your aunty."

In midafternoon, a mere three days after he received his aunt's disturbing letter, the post chaise dropped him and Sally off in front of the little shop with its cryptic sign, "Notions." Aunt Luella never was one to use two words when one would do. And look, the sign appeared to have been touched up and painted a bright blue. All Luke could hope for was that the painter hadn't cheated her, too.

He peered in the display window, which, to his surprise, was sparkling clean to a fare-thee-well, and not dingy with road dust and rain spots. Hmm. He saw inside the shop, where a woman in a preposterous bonnet was pointing to something inside the glass case next to the counter. Someone behind the counter was reaching inside.

"Papa! A cat!"

Sally pointed this time. Sure enough, an orangeish feline of no small proportions slept in the center of a wooden bowl of yarn. He stared, remembering how much Aunt Luella hated cats, and so she had told him on one of his obligatory visits, when his uncle still lived and Mama insisted he take an interest in old relatives that interested him not at all.

"Please may we go inside?" Sally asked. He nodded, and she darted ahead, which set the doorbell tinkling.

He followed more slowly, then stopped. He took a closer look at the skeins of embroidery thread and packets of pins in the window display. Interspersed with a dainty cup on its side with thimbles pouring out, and tiny scissors used in some sort of needlework that was a mystery to the manly mind, were miniature landscapes. Ordinary, prosaic crayons looked like the medium. *How could someone do such detail and remain sane?* he asked himself. He stared, and felt himself beguiled by the order around him. The window display was perfection.

The bell tinkled again when he entered the shop. Sally had already planted herself in front of the sleeping cat, which opened its eyes and stretched. He heard the clink of coins as they passed from one hand into the hand of the shop clerk who had straightened up and slid the glass cabinet shut. Was this Mary Cooper?

She was a pretty thing, but too slim, a contrast with the customer, who was overstuffed and overdressed. Her dark hair was braided, with the braids done up smoothly and held in place somehow. Luke was no arbiter of fashion and its trends, but he knew this style was an old one. She wore a dark blue dress and white apron with a pinafore top. He had to admit that the overall effect, from head to heels, was charming. She was neat as a pin.

"May I help you, sir?" she asked. "Something for your wife?"

He heard the West Country burr he was familiar with from all of his drydock workers. She was plain and simple Devon. Generally an honest man, he had to admit he saw only kindness in her eyes.

"No," he said. "I'm Miss Wainwright's nephew from Plymouth," he heard himself saying. "She wrote about a tyrant bullying her in her shop and I wanted to see such a spectacle with my own eyes." Good Lord, couldn't he stop? Apparently not. "I'm her only living relative, and I don't want her cheated."

The light went out of her eyes and he hated himself.

Chapter Four

"It's not as bad as all that," Mary said, suddenly unsure of herself. "She had a placard in the window, advertising employment. I answered the ad."

The man took out his aunt's letter and handed it to her. "This is what she wrote to me. Read it. If you can read, that is."

That stung. Mary read the letter. She looked up at the man, noting the hardness in his eyes. In his own way, he looked as resentful as his aunt, when she first approached the woman and begged for work. Maybe suspicion was a family trait.

She saw something else that touched her more than she wanted it to, considering what a menace he was to her remaining employed. She saw the exhaustion of someone who had no idea what a day off, spent in leisure, might look like. What approach should she use?

She tried humor. "I do bully Miss Wainwright to eat and rest. And for stealing from her, I would never do that."

"Why not? She is likely an easy mark."

Even mild humor was making no impression. It embarrassed her, but total honesty might be best. "I was hungry," she told him simply. "I had nowhere to sleep. I thought I could put this little shop to rights, and that is what I have done. Excuse me, sir. I'll go find your aunt."

She wanted to slap him silly, but she knew better. She turned toward the back of the store, but stopped instead to watch the child, who seemed to know just where a cat luxuriating in a pile of yard wanted to be scratched.

"Handsome, isn't he?" she asked. "Do you like cats?"

The little girl nodded. "I wish I had one," she confided.

"He's a stray like me," Mary said, on more sure footing now, for no discernible reason, except that she liked children. "He wandered in a few weeks ago, caught a mouse and ate it on the spot, then curled up in the yarn. He needs a name. Miss Wainwright hired him, too."

She thought she heard a chuckle behind her, but it must have been her imagination.

"I am Sally," the child said.

"I am Mary. Now I must find Miss Wainwright."

"I'll find her. I know this place," the man said, brushing past her and into the back of the shop. Mary stared down at her hands, wondering why it was so easy for some to create a problem where there was none. Still, she thought he had laughed.

She soon heard the murmur of voices behind her in the sitting room, just a murmur, no shouting. When the front doorbell tinkled again, she pasted a smile on her face, even though she wanted to find a dark corner and mourn the probable loss of her job. "Good afternoon. How may I assist you?" she asked the prospective customer, who, to her surprise, turned out to be Squire Banford's wife.

"I know you," Mrs. Banford said.

"My father Frederick Cooper was one of the Squire's tenants," Mary said. "He died and I work here now."

"My husband could have found something for you to do on the estate," Mrs. Banford replied, as if it was Mary's fault.

"She's working for my aunt here in this shop, madam," Mary heard behind her.

"I was only saying…" Mrs. Banford appeared surprised to be addressed by a stranger. "Never mind, sir. I have a matter to discuss with Mary Cooper."

"Discuss away," Mr. Wainwright said agreeably.

He didn't back off, or leave the room. Mary felt herself relaxing. She wondered if this was what it felt like to have someone on her side. But that was silly. He was only trying to hurry things along so Mrs. Banford would leave, and he could fire her.

"Very well, sir, although I do not care for your impertinence. We have not been introduced," was Mrs. Banford's last shot across the bow. She returned her attention to Mary. "May I contract you to draw me ten such landscapes?" she asked, picking up one of the cards. "I will pay you three shillings."

"I accept, Mrs. Banford," Mary replied, stunned. "Wh…when would you like them?"

"The end of this week? I will pay you when I pick them up." Mrs. Banford glared over Mary's shoulder, which made her wonder if Mr. Wainwright was making faces. The squire's wife picked up the scene with a house and smoke spiraling from the chimney. "These will make excellent decorations on Christmas packages." She looked closer. "Imagine. Done with crayons?"

"Yes, Mrs. Banford," Mary said shyly. "It's what I have."

"I like them. Good day."

Luke Wainwright stood behind Mary. She addressed him without looking at him. "When she or her servant brings the shillings, they will go into the strong box with everything else." No comment. "And do you know one things else, sir? In two short weeks, I have sold twenty little landscapes. All the money is in that box."

Silence. He picked up that same landscape. She battened down her courage and turned around to see him smiling. He cleared his throat. "Miss Cooper, I owe you an apology," he said. "My aunt tells me your miniatures have created more sales than anything except skeins of yarn, that is, when she can get the fat cat to budge off the merchandise."

Mary laughed, which dissipated the tension in the shop to a noticeable degree. Or it may have been because Mr. Wainwright sounded completely sincere. He looked her right in the eye, and she saw lurking good humor, again something she did not expect. "Aunt Luella assured me that every word she wrote is true. You do bully her to eat and rest – thank you for that, by the way. She also admitted that the only person robbing the till was herself, most recently this morning when she arranged for a beef roast to be cooked at the public house and brought over here tonight."

"A beef roast? From the public house and not the tearoom?"

"Aye, miss. She said the public house does a better job," he told her. "She declared that you are skinny and need feeding up." He looked around a moment, as if embarrassed. "Thank you, Miss Cooper, for coming to her rescue when I did not. What is that expression I see?"

"A woman astounded that a man would ever apologize for anything," she said promptly, which increased the size of his smile.

"Then I am a rare fellow."

And he was, Mary decided, right down to fetching the beef roast himself from down the High Street, if such a street could be so distinguished in tiny Liddiard. He also proved remarkably adept at peeling carrots to simmer in the pot while Mary sliced and fried potatoes until they were brown and crispy.

She counted it surprising enough that a man could ever admit to a wrongdoing without sulking. Here he was, working alongside her in the kitchen while his daughter hovered close by, not wanting anyone to come between her and her father.

Mary remarked on Sally's devotion when Aunt Luella coaxed the child into the shop to help sort a jumble of embroidery threads the postman delivered. "She's your very own shadow," Mary said to Mr. Wainwright.

"Aye, she is, and that worries me a little," he said, wiping his hands on an improvised apron made of a dishcloth. "I recently moved a little farther away to Plymouth. We had been living in my father-in-law's house in Devonport, but I wanted a place..." He moved the carrots slightly off the hob so they would simmer now. "There are many distractions in a household of that importance. I confess to needing some peace and quiet." He chuckled. "Or as Sally says, 'A piece of quiet.'"

"Did you find it?" she asked, intrigued by a man who only an hour ago had been ready to bite her head off for ill treatment of his elderly relative. Then, he seemed to be someone with the weight of the world on his shoulders. Now, not so much. "You know, your piece of quiet."

"Yes and no. I have a good-enough cook, a maid of all work, and a nanny to tend to Sally." He sighed. "Perhaps I should have stayed in the house of my late wife's father. I confess I am not around as much as I should be. Did Sally prefer the…the noise? There is so much for me to do at the drydock." He looked toward the shop. "I am not certain that Sally is happy. And so she clings. As the sole parent of a young one, I am baffled."

"That's honest," Mary said. She fried the last of the potatoes, then transferred them to the oven alongside the roast to stay warm. She turned around and bumped into Mr. Wainwright.

"It's a tight space," he said, cheerful even as his face reddened.

"Aye, sir," she agreed. "I just remembered something I needed to ask your aunt. Excuse me."

She could have argued with herself that it was agreeable to share a tight space with someone she knew well, except that she didn't know Mr. Wainwright at all. Besides that, she needed to know where these additional Wainwrights would sleep that night.

Miss Wainwright was in the shop, where Sally chatted with the cat, a one-sided conversation except that the cat seemed to be listening. Mary came closer. "Miss Wainwright, where will we put them tonight?"

"Oh my, I hadn't thought…. When they visited before, they stayed in the room you now use. I have a folded cot under that bed." She put her hand to her mouth. "What will *you* do?"

"I will do quite well on the sofa in the sitting room again," Mary assured her. "I'll get Sally to help me, while you visit your nephew. Sally, you and I have work to do. Follow me."

"I will help if Gargantua comes, too," Sally said.

"Gargan…" Mary laughed, which surprised her. When had she last laughed? "He *is* getting rather stout on scraps and left over dinner. Where did you ever hear of Gargantua?"

"Papa named him a minute ago," Sally whispered. "He told me it was from a book not intended for little girls."

They laughed together, conspirators. "Never mind. It is the perfect name, and I have been wondering what to name him." She touched Sally's shoulder, only a light touch, which made the child flinch. *What is this?* she thought, then covered up her surprise with a laugh. "Well, it is. Let's get to work."

The three of them went into Mary's room, after she grabbed

some sheets from the storeroom. As she stripped the sheets from her bed, Mary felt her old anxiety return – homeless, no food, no place to sleep. She swallowed it, reasoning with herself that this visit was not a permanent one and there would be a place for her again.

"There's not much room," Sally said. She brightened when Gargantua curled up on the cot. "Perhaps there is enough, if Gargantua can squeeze in."

"Cats do that," Mary said, even as she thought, *And so do people, when they are desperate enough. I squeezed in.*

Dinner was a delight. Mary ate more than she should have. She excused herself by crediting her appetite to the growing fear – she couldn't help herself – that from a bed on the sofa again, the next direction was out the door.

Sally started drooping when Mary removed the plates and brought out the pudding, which perked her up noticeably. Mary noticed nothing like that in Luke Wainwright. He ate with a certain absentminded mien, as if food was needed to stay alive and that was all. He appeared preoccupied and eager to get away, which told her worlds about his responsibilities, left behind in terms of distance, but obviously not in terms of never-ending worry, which she knew was more portable. Who knew that frigates bound for His Majesty's Royal Navy could fit inside a builder's over-active brain?

But this was not Mary's worry. True, he showed all the signs of a man ready to bolt back to his duty, now that the mountain he had imagined in Liddiard was not even a molehill. Or so she hoped. But were there other Wainwrights lurking about, waiting to pounce on a simple position in a quiet town? Her position?

Oh, enough. She could point out the obvious. "Mr. Wainwright, Sally is drooping. I can easily tidy her for bed, if you help your aunt in the kitchen." She bowed to the inevitable. "I suppose you have matters to discuss."

"I do," he said, which confirmed Mary's fears. He leaned across the table and touched his daughter's cheek. "Very well, missy. I will tuck you in after I break a dish or two and Aunt Luella never wants to see me in a kitchen again."

Mary knew all the signs. Mr. Wainwright had come here with questions, and she could tell he had plans, even if his initial worry had proved unfounded. He probably thought Aunt Luella was too old to be on her own, even with help.

"Come along, Sally. Let's see if Gargantua is sleeping on your cot."

The child danced ahead of her, but paused in the doorway for another look at her father. "My da won't go anywhere while I am with you, will he?"

It was an odd question. Mary shook her head. "I don't think your fathers knows anyone in Liddiard. Where's your nightgown? I'll get a little warm water from the kitchen."

When she returned to the kitchen for warm water, a towel draped over her arm, Mary knew she had interrupted conversation more important than idle chatter. She apologized, got the water and hurried out, but she had heard Mr. Wainwright saying, "... room for you in Plymouth."

"I can't reach my back buttons," Sally said as Mary returned, tears in her eyes, and shut the door. "Well, only one or two." She turned around dutifully and Mary unbuttoned the pretty dress.

She sucked in her breath and stared at Sally's back, wondering at a series of bruises, as if someone had pinched her over and over.

"I can do the rest now, Mary," the child said. "I'm no trouble. Really, I am not."

"Oh! Certainly you are no trouble, my dear," Mary said, regaining her composure. "I can help, though. Raise your arms."

Carefully she lifted the dress over Sally's head, noting more such bruises along her upper arms, places where ill-use wouldn't show. Too shocked to say anything, she hummed softly to herself, which, up to now, soothed her. No, not now.

She buttoned Sally into her nightgown, pushing back her sleeves, and noting with sorrow bruises around her wrists, as though she had been grabbed. Gently she touched the bruises, silently observing that like the bruises on her back, they would not be visible under clothing.

Unsure of what to do, Mary did what *she* would have wanted – she took Sally in her arms and hugged her close. She held her off a little, looked deep into old eyes and asked, "What happened to you?"

Sally shook her head. "She told me that I was a wicked child and not to ever say anything to my father," she whispered.

"You're not wicked," Mary said. Gently she pressed her forehead against the child's forehead. "You're good and true and look how much Gargantua loves you." It was completely illogical, but Sally sighed with relief and gathered the meaty cat close to her.

"Is it your nanny?" Mary asked.

Sally nodded, after a look around the room to make sure her nanny hadn't suddenly materialized. "She likes to drink after Papa leaves in the morning, and the maid is busy. The first time she saw me watching her, she pinched my back." She winced. "It doesn't hurt now, but it did." Tears came to the surface. "I shouldn't have said anything to you. She made me swear I wouldn't tell anyone."

Mary kissed her and tucked her in bed. "It's not going to happen anymore."

"Are you sure?"

"I am certain."

Chapter Five

Luke had taken advantage of the time when Sally and Mary Cooper were in the other room. "Aunt Luella, you are welcome to come to my house in Plymouth. Perhaps you shouldn't be alone in Liddiard."

"I'm not alone now. I have Mary."

"Aye, but I mean family. There's room for you in my house. Mary's not family."

If a glare could have cut through lead... "She's not, Aunt Luella," he protested, but it was a weak protest. Truth to tell, he was getting a little tired of himself, too.

And there she was, standing in the doorway. He hoped she had not heard that low-voiced exchange, but...He took a closer look at her, startled to see her set expression, with her eyes so wide and her face drained of color.

"Mary?" he asked tentatively. "You don't look well. Sit, please."

She did as he said, perching on the edge of a chair, almost as though she would take flight if she heard a disparaging word.

"Mary?" Aunt Luella said. Luke heard all her concern for this small woman, this waif.

Mary seemed to gather herself together. She spoke to him, her eyes boring into his. "Is Sally generally in bed and asleep when you get home?"

He didn't expect that, and it set him on the defensive. "I have important word, Miss Cooper," he replied, biting off his words. "It often keeps me from home until late. Sally is in good hands. You shouldn't think that I leave her alone. Don't be impertinent."

She winced at his sharp words, but the stricken look did not leave her eyes. "I care not how you feel about me. Perhaps I *am* an encroacher." She sent a fleeting smiling in Aunt Luella's direction. "It hasn't been long, but I like it here and I have done some good."

She returned her gaze to him. "Sally is probably asleep now. Go to her. Push back the sleeves of her nightdress. If she is turned the right way, see if you can look at her back."

"By God, you *are* impertinent!" he exclaimed, but he felt a great foreboding as he left the room. He stood a moment in the hall, trying to calm his fears. He opened the door to see Sally curled up with Gargantua. Her sleeve was pushed back, revealing exactly what Mary Cooper noticed – a ring of bruises around her wrist, as though someone much stronger had squeezed her tight, no affection involved.

Shaken, he leaned over her and saw a series of bruises on her back. He wept as silently as he could, but only briefly, because he had no time for tears. He dried his face and returned to the sitting room, well aware of his failure as a father.

"I had no idea," was all he could say, before he sat down heavily, as though his legs would no longer hold him. Aunt Luella took the candle from him and hurried from the room. While he waited for her to return, he could barely bring himself to look at Mary Cooper, who sat in silence, contemplating her hands.

"What must you think of me?" he finally managed to say.

Bless her heart. She was too kind. "You are a busy man doing a hard job," she said, as if she wanted to apologize in his place, to spare him any self-recrimination. "I do understand how hard it is to do everything and have no help."

"*Try* to do everything," he corrected. "I can't."

"Who can?" she questioned in turn.

Yes, she *was* kind, but he didn't intend to absolve himself so easily. "I should have known…Sally started clinging to me…I suppose she didn't want to be near Miss Templeton," he said, shuddered, then turned on himself again. "I am a fool and my daughter has suffered because of it."

He hoped she would say something else, some kindness to further excuse him. Drat her, she gave him that level-headed, entirely benign look of someone who…. He paused there, forced to acknowledge the obvious: She didn't know any of them. Even more to the point, she was completely powerless and dependent upon *them*. He continued the thought, a beguiling one: She knew it, and was willing to risk her own security for someone equally powerless. For Sally.

He surprised himself then. In the middle of his self-recrimination and misery, he saw how lovely she was, and how kind. He wished there was a way to know her better, despite the fact that his daughter and his ships remained his major concern, and she was, by anyone's reckoning, a complete nobody. Granted, his own social sphere was hardly exalted. Hers was non-existent.

He couldn't help his smile, rueful as it must have appeared to her. "I have a problem, haven't I?"

"Life's full of those, Mr. Wainwright," she replied, with unmatched serenity. "Sometimes we have to ask for help. I did, and I found it here. Perhaps you can, too."

Ridiculous, he thought, *simply ridiculous.* Help from a shop clerk one step from total ruin, and an old lady? "Perhaps," he replied lamely.

Mary Cooper was kind enough to say nothing.

When his aunt returned to the sitting room, her expression as bleak as his, the three of them sat in silence. Luke waited for Aunt Luella to speak first, and she did not fail him, even though he knew he had also failed her by leaving her alone in Liddiard. Good God, she had to be seventy, if she was a day, and he was her only living relative, poor lady.

"Nephew, this is a wretched turn of events," she said finally, which wasn't precisely what he wanted to hear.

That was it? Luke knew he needed a solution to his problem. Dash it all, his daughter was being abused, but the business of war edged everything else aside. King, country and the Royal Navy demanded his total attention. Didn't they?

He glanced at Mary Cooper and saw something in her eyes

that suggested – oh, it couldn't be – that she was smarter than he was. "What would *you* do, Miss Cooper?" he asked, not disguising his irritation.

"Do you truly want to know, Mr. Wainwright?" she asked in turn, but she was serious, and not sarcastic, as he knew he sounded.

"I believe I do," he said quietly, even humbly. "I know I do."

"Were I you, I would leave Sally here with Miss Wainwright and me, fire that excuse for a nanny, and build your ships," she said.

Drat that woman again, but she must have seen the skepticism in his eyes, even though every word she said was a solution to his immediate problem. "Miss Cooper…" he started.

"Just Mary," she replied. "I harbor no illusions about my place."

By God, she didn't. He strongly suspected that only truth would come out of that mouth. Well, all right then. "Just abandon my only child to an aunt getting on in years – I apologize, Aunt Luella, but you know this is so – and someone I don't even know?"

He winced inside when he saw massive, but momentary, sorrow in her eyes. "It's true," he said.

"Aye, it is, but that is precisely what I recommend you do," she told him, her words firm. "When matters are better in hand, you can find another, more qualified governess, or perhaps even marry a good lady who will smooth your path, because that seems to be what women are allowed to do. You can go merrily on, building frigates."

Did he sense a little sarcasm from her? He did, and he knew it was well deserved, if impertinent. Dash it all, she was absolutely right. "I should take your advice?"

"*I* would," she replied, a smile in her eyes.

"I will," he said. "Done, Mary. I will be in touch."

Luke steeled himself for the ordeal of telling Sally about the practically spontaneous plan for her to remain in Liddiard. He settled down in the bed beside her cot, where she slept with Gargantua, who apparently adopted her with all the ease that Mary Cooper had moved into his aunt's home and shop. Personally, he hated cats.

He slept surprisingly well, all things considered, and woke before Sally did, content to watch her peaceful face, relaxed in slumber. Clarissa had a similarly peaceful approach to mornings, allowing them to arrive gradually, and give her time to stretch and contemplate. He saw the same thing in Sally. He smiled, remembering.

For some reason, Gargantua had changed addresses at some point in the night and lay at his feet. As much as he disliked cats, Luke had to admit that his feet were warm for the first time since Clarissa's death. She had never minded his feet on her legs, another thing to admire about his late wife. Gargantua must have been a living furnace, because he performed his magic on top of the covers.

It pained his heart that the first thing Sally did after opening her eyes was to look around in fear, as if expecting the horrid Miss Templeton to materialize and abuse her for some miniscule infraction.

"No fears, Sal, my dear," he said. "It's just you, me and uh, Gargantua." He held out his arms and she joined him in bed. "Things are going to be different for a few weeks," he began, then told her of his plan to leave her in Liddiard for a short time.

She appeared relieved at first, then the fear returned. "Is Miss Templeton going to come here to teach me?" she asked. Luke heard all the worry.

"No. She will be making other plans," he said. "I will find someone else for you." He thought a minute, wondering how much the maid of all work, and even his cook, knew about what had been going on. How to ask? He settled on a way that even Mary Cooper would approve of, that is, if he was even slightly concerned how Mary would handle this matter. "The maid will stay of course, unless you might like her to find another position. You tell me, please."

"I…I would like it if she leaves along with Miss Templeton," Sally told him, confirming another suspicion.

"Excellent. I'll see that she finds another place to work."

Sally snuggled closer, reminding Luke of earlier, lovelier days when she had stomped her imperious way to their bedchamber and held up her hands to him or her mama. As he hugged her, Luke knew how much was missing from his life, and hers.

His daughter wanted to placate him. Women, even little ones, seemed to have a sense about that. "Mary said she would teach me some Christmas carols." She clutched the front of his nightshirt. "You *do* remember that Christmas is coming?"

God forgive him, but he had forgotten. "A father doesn't forget Christmas," he lied. He thought it best rise and shoo her from the room, before he told too many more lies. "But now I have to hurry back to Plymouth." *And fire two odious woman from my employment and see if I still have a cook*, he didn't add. "There's a ship to build and three frigates to repair. Promise me you will continue being helpful here."

"I promise, Papa," she said and kissed his cheek.

"Write to me," he said, feeling monumentally unsure of himself at this moment, as if he were abandoning his daughter. To his relief, she nodded, after a reminder. "Christmas, Papa."

After she left the room in search of breakfast, Gargantua trailing along behind her, Luke took a hard look at himself in the small hand mirror someone, perhaps Mary Cooper, had hung over the water basin. A worried man looked back at him, staring long enough to find him wanting in every way.

Accompanied by Aunt Luella, he spent the early morning visiting Mr. Mallard in his counting house, where he made arrangement for funds from Carter and Brustein, his Plymouth firm, to send a modest sum to Liddiard. "Just in case you have any extra expenses," he said. "Don't argue."

Other than give him the fishy eye, she didn't argue. When they returned to the shop, Sally, under Mary Cooper's direction – her hands gentle on his daughter's shoulders – was showing a customer the yarn. Gargantua had worked his way into the window display, which made Luke smile, even if he didn't like cats.

"We will manage quite well," his aunt assured him. "Straighten out your own household, and then perhaps we'll return Sally to you."

He thought about that when he leaned back in the post chaise an hour later, bound for Plymouth. *Perhaps, eh?* he thought, not sure if he should be ashamed or amused.

Leaving had been rendered easier by Mary Cooper. When Sally started to cry, he liked the way Mary's arms naturally enveloped his little one. "Go get your father's briefcase, my dear."

Sally nodded and went into the sitting room, giving him a moment to gather himself together. As poor as his management had proved, one thing had never wavered. Perhaps he should mention that to Mary, in case she was inclined to pass judgment.

"I love my daughter," he said simply. "I never realized how hard leave-taking would be."

She did something that he knew had to be spontaneous. Before he had a moment to react, she grasped him above the elbows, her touch firm but brief. "I have no doubt of that, Mr. Wainwright," she said in her quiet voice. "You need a little help right now. That's all. Good journey to you."

She was gone before he could say anything, which was just as well, because he had to swallow a few times and compose himself, all because someone had touched him. No one touched him. He laughed when Sally lugged in his briefcase, and made certain to hold her close for a moment, then kiss her cheek. When the post chaise pulled away from the curb, he looked back to see Mary Cooper standing in the doorway. She raised her hand as if to wave, then seemed to change her mind, as if she didn't want to intrude.

He sat back and closed his eyes, relieved to know that Sally was in a safe place. After a moment, he opened his briefcase, with its ship drawings. There, among the blueprints and his own crude drawings, was a sketch of his daughter done in crayon with a sure hand. Sally smiled at him in her shy way and he smiled back.

Chapter Six

Luke Wainwright had never been inclined to fire workers in anger. After all, people could make mistakes they regretted immediately, and never repeat the offense, if given another chance. When letting go of hired help, he was happy to leave that distasteful task to Mr. Magleby, the controlling half of Magleby & Wainwright.

This matter within his own household was different, more personal. Miss Templeton had harmed his daughter. What about the others? Sally had mentioned the maid, too.

He arrived home when his staff was expecting him, paying off his post chaise driver at the curb with more than the designated fee, because the driver was reliable and treated his horses well.

He looked up at his house, a pleasant, two-storied stone structure on one of Plymouth's quieter streets leading up from the Barbican, the old city center, and less than two miles from the South Yards in Devonport. He couldn't help it. Every return, after even only a few days away, made him pause and remember carrying Clarissa up the steps that first time, because her always taxed heart made her weaker every day. Thank God Sally's heart beat steady and true, like his. Such a memory. He would happily replace it with another.

The house was quiet as usual. He set down his grip and went to the kitchen, with its pleasant odors. Although he was now aware of her cruelty to his daughter, it saddened Luke to see Miss Templeton, hand pressed to her forehead, being force-fed a dark and odorous brew by Cook, as the maid of all work watched in consternation.

Aye, he thought, *t'master will be home in no time.* He stood in the doorway, unnoticed, because all the attention focused on the woman heavily hung over. They all knew. Everyone knew except him, the neglectful father.

"You are all let go, as of this moment," he said quietly from the doorway.

The maid shrieked in surprise, as noisy as a fishwife; the cook tried to babble an explanation; the governess was too far gone to do anything except drop her head lower to the table. They were history inside of an hour, after he retrieved all their keys and paid them off, which was more than most employers would have done.

Face set in firm lines, he walked in the rain to his father-in-law's house and laid the matter before him. He minced no words over his own neglect, and asked him and his mother-in-law who joined them, to locate a housekeeper who would manage the house and him. He ate dinner in the kitchen with the Maglebys, where all of them felt at home, and discussed the business of ships.

Buttered rum in the kitchen was next – Mrs. Magleby was a dab hand at such things – followed by a hearty goodnight. Roger Magleby hung onto his hand a little longer. "What's *your* plan, lad?" he asked.

"After I find my house organized and safe, I might invite my aunt in Liddiard to come with Sally and stay. There's ample room, and she's not getting a minute younger."

"It is a good plan." Magleby gave his shoulder a pat. "But what about you?"

"I'll do well enough," Luke said, offering nothing else.

The rain had stopped. He walked home, at peace with himself. He trusted his mother-in-law. Soon there would be a martinet of a housekeeper to manage his domestic affairs. Sally would be happier under a better regime. He thought of Mary Cooper, then reminded himself that she seemed good at making her own plans.

He thought of Mary Cooper again when the sun came up. It was that luxurious time of day when he woke up early, and had a moment to think whatever he wanted, before the business of the day started doing a little dance off stage. He decided he would like to get to know Mary better. Maybe Aunt Luella would leave her in charge of the shop – it appeared that Mary already ran it – and he could drop in every now and then to visit. He could use the pretext that he wanted to check in to see that all was well with Aunt Luella's funds in Mallard's counting house. He could ask her to dinner. He could possibly court her. There might be time for all of that. Anything was possible, before breakfast and the business of the day. Afterwards, never. What was he thinking, anyway?

At work, he picked up where he left off, spending long hours aboard the current frigate in the dry dock. He noted that the frame was solid and true, while chaos ruled and nothing appeared to be going as planned. This was typical and he knew it. He stepped around piles of rope and wood stacked in locations where it would turn from lumber into a quarterdeck. He sniffed the tar cooking, which meant that the lower decks were on schedule.

A short sail across the bay – the chop was up, signifying the beginning of winter – took him to a battered frigate, snugged tight to a temporary dock and waiting her turn for the W&M brand of surgery. In a sharp encounter with a Spanish ship of similar build and guns, the Spaniards had fought well. Better cannon work from the British gunners eventually sent the Spanish ship aground off the Canaries, but it meant a long limp home for the HMS *Peregrine*.

Luke knew he would find the sailing master and the second luff aboard, men with families, yes, but only a short walk into the Barbican for the lieutenant, and a post chaise in two weeks to Scotland for the sailing master. As he walked the deck with them, he took notes of work done, work to be done, and work to re-do. He ate supper with them ashore at a grogshop rejoicing in the dubious name of Neptune's Nipples, which, amazingly, turned out fine food and occasional back-alley mayhem. But that was Devonport.

He came home to a cold, empty house. He nearly laid a fire so he could at least warm up enough water to fill a bottle and keep his feet toasty. He decided it was too late. He kept his stockings on and found another blanket.

As he lay in bed, staring at the ceiling, he thought about Christmas, mainly because Mrs. Magleby said two nights ago that it might be hard to find a housekeeper at this time of year. "What time?" he had asked innocently.

"Christmas, you heathen," she joked, with her usual good humor. "Seems like the parties start earlier and earlier."

"It's barely November," he reminded her. His mother-in-law shrugged.

At least he was smiling when he finally fell asleep, thinking of Mary again. Why was that?

His fortunes turned in mid-November, when the postman delivered the usual mail to the W&M office, usual in that there were bills to pay, and Royal Navy edicts – so he called them – more-than-suggesting that two more battered frigates were coming his way. He would find room for them somewhere and hire more laborers. God knows they needed that new drydock.

The sweetest moment was a letter from his daughter, or so the left-hand corner of the envelope announced. The first thing to extricate from Sally's envelope – well made, to suggest more skilled hands at work – was a pencil sketch of his Aunt Luella, looking less forbidding than usual, and even of pleasant demeanor, dare he suggest lurking good humor? He could almost see Mary Cooper telling her a funny story and sketching like mad to capture Aunt Luella in a good mood.

Aunt Luella had included a note, complaining about constant headaches and low appetite, but stating in the next paragraph that all was well. She had set Sally to the task of needlework, which was not received with much joy from his daughter. (Luke smiled at that.) Then this: "Sally has challenged Mary to draw a ship for you. When Mary protested and said she needed at least a ship's model to work from, Sally brought out that silly wooden ship you gave me in jest once, announcing that it was for use in a bathing tub only."

What came the next day to his Plymouth house was a combination housekeeper and cook, a woman of fierce expression and determination in her eyes, sent by his mother-in-law.

"Caldwell is my name," she announced to Luke when he came home that night, reeking of fried fish from the pub. She sniffed the air around him with some dissatisfaction. "I'll feed you plain food that won't mess with yer innards as much as fried fish."

"You'll get no argument from me," he said hastily, already half afraid of her.

"I'll have two maids here as soon as possible." She sniffed the air again. "Your house reeks. The maids will change that."

The maids descended upon his house two days later, proving as formidable as the housekeeper, who happened to be their aunt. "They're good girls, they are," Mrs. Caldwell said. "From Norfolk same as me. Nieces."

Order reigned supreme the next day: ne'er-do-well rugs taken outside for a good thrashing, floors cleaned, some curtains washed and others waiting their turn, and walls wiped down. In the entry hall, there was mail on a table that positively luxuriated after the application of furniture wax.

He looked around in appreciation, wondering why in the world he had suffered the indignities of his recently fired domestics. A person, let's say for argument's sake as tidy as, well, Mary Cooper, would see this order and be sufficiently impressed.

Thinking of her returned his attention to the table with mail. He could have let out a most improper yell in this impeccable house to see M. Cooper in the return address, but he refrained himself. He set down his briefcase right there and could have sunk to the floor in delight to see a letter opener right on the table, waiting for him. He resisted the urge to go outside for a good look at the façade of his house. Did he go into the wrong house by mistake? No. Same house, but under new management.

It proved to be a small note – too small, in his opinion, but no one asked – accompanying a wrapped sheet stiffened with pasteboard. *Be careful what you ask for. All is well here. Mary Cooper*. That was it. He opened the pasteboard took one look, and laughed.

My, but you are a clever lass, he thought, as he held up her drawing, larger than some of the others. The little wooden ship he had given Aunt Luella years ago when he was of more jovial mind, was half-sailing, half-sinking in a bathing tub, with someone's bare knees drawn up, the spectator. He peered closer, and smiled to see a very small captain saluting on the deck as the toy ship appeared to sink as a bar of soap floated by.

It was hilarious and spontaneous and exactly the antidote he needed to drive away a headache caused by fourteen hours of hammering, sawing, and nautical swearing. He turned it over, hoping for more somehow, and was rewarded with three inked-in camels and the notation: "An early Christmas present, Mr. Wainwright. We are doing well. MC."

He didn't think the drawn-up knees were Sally's, which led to impish thoughts. He tacked up the droll cartoon next to his shaving mirror and slept peacefully for the first time in many weeks.

Everything changed a week later with another note, this one delivered by express while he ate breakfast. That kind of express always alarmed him. This one did more than that.

He recognized Mary Cooper's distinct handwriting, as unique as she was, but the news, oh, the news. *Terrible tidings, Mr. Wainwright,* he read. *Your aunt has died in her sleep. She had been complaining of headaches, and even the physician was baffled. His only remedy was to bleed her. Oh goodness. Please come to the funeral and take Sally to Plymouth. I have made arrangements here. The funeral is the day after tomorrow. Mary Cooper.*

He sat back, stunned. "I must go to Liddiard now," he said to his housekeeper. He handed her the note.

She read it. He saw the sympathy in her eyes. "Was she ill?"

He gathered together his jumbled thoughts, thinking of Aunt Luella's complaints through the years about her heart, or her liver and lungs, or that pain in her back.

"She complained about everything," he said, and looked at the note again. "And nothing. I suppose I never knew what to believe." He managed a smile. "I know she enjoyed these last few months, what with the rejuvenated shop, and Sally in her care." *And Mary,* he wanted to add, but didn't.

"You'll be leaving tomorrow?"

"Yes, certainly. I have to fetch my daughter, and see what else needs to be done. My aunt had no other relatives."

He decided to walk to Devonport that morning, his eyes down at his shoes mainly, thinking of everything he had to do, wondering what he could postpone at the drydocks for a few days. He looked up now and then to see wreaths on many doors, as Christmas approached. He noted that last night when he returned home, late as usual, the lamplighters even tipped their hats and wished him Happy Christmas. A cynic might think they were extra cheerful because they wanted tips from the patrons on each block. Luke thought otherwise. Who didn't enjoy the respite that was Christmas? He had hoped to celebrate it this year, but now...

He should have hurried, but he slowed down, remembering Aunt Luella's querulous summons that had introduced him to Mary Cooper, then more recently, Sally's happy note about walking outside in Liddiard with Gargantua, "...because he is fat and needs the exercise. Papa, cats don't like to walk outside if it isn't their idea. That's what Mary says. I think she is right."

What would he do now? Sally would return to Plymouth, of course, but what about Mary? He stopped. *What about Mary?* he thought. He stood there in misery, watching a young couple hurry in the rain, his arm around her waist, her head close to his. They were laughing and he envied them, at the same time thinking that in another day he could be seeing Sally, and Mary.

He took the matter of a few days off to his father-in-law, who shook his head. "Lad, don't you recall? Biddle and Bancroft will be here tomorrow for the presentation on building another drydock. Did you forget? We've been preparing those numbers for months. You have to be here." He gave Luke a friendly pat. "You never even mentioned your aunt until a month or so ago. And look at your note. Mary said she would make the arrangements. She can send Sally back to us after the funeral. You've told me several times how dependable Mary is."

"Aye, but..."

"You're needed here more, Luke," Mr. Magleby said, his voice firm, his mind made up. "Everyone will understand." He patted his jaw tenderly. "And suppose my tooth takes a turn for the worst and I have to summon that officious man with a dental key?" He shuddered.

Everyone will understand except me, Luke thought in misery of his own, minus a toothache. *And Sally. And Mary.* "Sir, I am pretty sure Mary and Sally need me. Give me a day or two."

"Look, lad, she said she would make arrangements! There's a war on and we need that third drydock. We need it now! I tell you, everyone will understand."

No one will understand, Luke told himself. He walked home in the dark and cold that night, thinking of all the nights ahead that would be dark and cold. He stopped on the corner, stared at his house, and allowed himself another thought, one that came out of nowhere, unless he had been hiding it from himself. Between war and work, he was tired. Maybe he had given up.

Mary could have made this a home.

Chapter Seven

Sally didn't understand. Neither did Mary. "I know Papa will come," Sally insisted, right up to and including the graveside service two days later for Luella Wainwright. It was attended by none except them and the publican and his wife across the street, because aye, Miss Wainwright was a prickly woman and aye again, no one had come to know her as well as Mary in the last few months. She and Sally both mourned in honesty and solitude.

Mr. Wainwright, you did not come, Mary thought. Thank God there was money in the strong box to purchase a modest coffin, grave clothes, and a spot in Liddiard's cemetery. A tombstone would have to wait. Mary knew Aunt Luella had funds in the counting house, but they were not hers to access.

"It is this way, my dear," she told Sally as they walked home from the cemetery. "I have a few more Christmas landscapes to draw, which I will finish today. I will use that money for the mail coach to get you to Plymouth."

Sally took her hand. "What about you, Mary?"

"I don't know, Sally."

Sally started to cry. "I will be afraid by myself."

"It's not that far," Mary said, then hated herself for saying that. "Not even a day's journey."

"But Mary, I am just me."

"Indeed you are," Mary said, remembering Sally's fraught little life, even though her own had been harder. There were times in the Cooper family when no one ate much, but no one had ever pinched her arms and back until the cruelty turned into bruises, or grabbed her wrists in meanness. And now Sally's own father was too busy to see her to Plymouth. She had thought better of Luke Wainwright; liked him, even. Maybe more than like. *I suppose you are like all the rest*, she thought in sorrow, but not in anger. At least he wouldn't be too hard to forget.

Mary knew Plymouth wasn't far and there would be good people on the mail coach. It was all safe and reasonable, and so she told Sally, who looked more mournful by the second.

"I will do this," Mary added, hoping she had enough money. "I'll send an express letter tonight, and your father will have someone there to meet you. Please, my dear, it's the best and quickest way."

"I suppose we must," Sally said. "Oh, Mary, why is life so hard?"

"I wish I knew, dearest."

They continued their slow walk to the shop, Mary mentally adding up the coins remaining in the strongbox after even their modest funeral expenses. She would finish the two landscapes tomorrow, deliver them and collect her fee, then knock on a few doors to collect the remaining fees. Surely that would be enough.

"For what?" she asked out loud, but softly, so Sally wouldn't worry.

To her relief, there was a letter waiting for them in the letter flap. She didn't recognize the handwriting, but the corner address was 152 Palmer Lane, Plymouth. She sat down and pulled Sally onto her lap as she read the letter. She read it through, then decided what to tell Sally. "This is from your father's new housekeeper, Mrs. Caldwell," she said. "It is as I thought, my dear. It seems your father was far too busy to attend the funeral, but he is hoping to see you as soon as ever possible." She kissed the top of Sally's head. "You are to pack everything. Let us have a little dinner, then get busy."

Mary thought she did a fine job, keeping up the chatter and good will, and won't it be nice to see Papa again? Sally went along with it well enough until she folded her favorite muslin dress, then put her hand on Mary's arm. "It's not fair," she said, sounding so much older than she was. "Papa will not get home until I am asleep, and probably leave before I wake up."

"Oh my dear," was all Mary could think to say. It wouldn't

do to tell Sally that even though her own father was overworked and never paid enough, he had time for her in the evenings after Mama died, time to sit close together and listen to Mary read from Mama's book, her pride and joy. Mama loved Shakespeare's sonnets. *Oh please, please, God, let there be a kind governess soon,* Mary prayed in silence. *Or let the housekeeper be kind and teach her things.*

She probably could have carried it off, this farce of good cheer when neither of them were happy, and probably both of them wondering, in their own way, about Papa. Mary could have managed, if Gargantua hadn't roused himself from his after-dinner stupor and plunked himself down in the middle of Sally's luggage.

"I can't leave him here," Sally said suddenly. "I just can't. And I can't leave you."

If some cosmic hand had just yanked her heart out, Mary knew this was the moment. It was also not the moment to make matters worse for this lovely child by mentioning it. It was time to gather her meager forces around herself and pretend they were great ones. Taken a day at a time, she realized she was adept at not making matters worse.

"Dearest, I will get you to Plymouth and your father," she said evenly. "That is where you belong. Yes, take along Gargantua, by all means. I can't imagine what I was thinking, to make you travel alone."

The monster cat fit well in a market basket. Cheerful now, Sally lined the basket with a towel, and added his favorite treats, except Mary drew the line at trapping a mouse. But first things first. Calmly, she sat Sally with Gargantua overflowing her lap, and sketched them. *You'll be with me forever now,* she thought.

The mail coach had other Christmas travelers, but no one took exception to a large cat, who fit quite well in the crowded space on their two laps. He purred when a little boy across the aisle petted him, and when an older lady did the same, her eyes shining with probable cat memories of her own tucked in her heart.

"Here we are," Mary said when they reached Plymouth. The

older lady obligingly gave directions when Mary held out the address. "That's a posh part of town, dearie," she said. "You must know the right sort of people."

Mary returned some vague answer, but with a smile. It didn't look too far to walk, if they took turns carrying the basket of cat, and Sally's possessions. They passed through the Barbican, noting people carrying presents. A fellow outside a pub invited one and all the come inside for the best Yuletide eggnog ever, but Mary and Sally hurried along.

And there it was, 152 Palmer Lane. "My, this is a grand house," Mary exclaimed. And thank goodness there was a Christmas wreath already. She knew Luke Wainwright well enough to suspect that it hadn't been his idea. Poor, forgetful soul! If any man needed a wife…

"I don't like it," Sally said, rubbing her arms where, thankfully, the bruises were gone.

"Your father said he installed new domestics," Mary reminded her. "And look, there is a wreath. Up we go."

A knock summoned a kind-looking maid, to Mary's relief, who summoned the housekeeper. "This is Sally Wainwright," Mary said simply. "And Gargantua."

The housekeeper's eyes softened. "They are welcome. The master is so sorry, but war demands his attention and he regrets he was unable to attend the funeral of his aunt. And you are…"

"Mary Cooper," Mary said. "He…he sent us a letter, and Sally is here. I'll leave you now."

"You can stay, too," the housekeeper said. "I doubt the master will be home before dark, but …"

"No worries," Mary said. "If I hurry, I can catch another mail coach home to Liddiard. I believe it runs regularly." Whether that was true or not, she had no idea, but it wouldn't do to stand here and make it even harder to leave Sally.

Before the child could protest, Mary gave her a kiss on the cheek, and a hug to remember. "Write to me, Sally," she said, then turned and fled down the street before her emotions betrayed her and troubled Sally more.

She didn't go far, but waited until Sally and Gargantua were ushered inside by what she hoped were good people. It was only a little after noon. When the door closed, she walked back to Palmer Street and took out her sketchbook and pencil. A tear she didn't wipe away fast enough smudged some of her rapid artwork, but never mind. She planned to copy the whole thing and add colors when she returned home, and mail it here to 162 Palmer Lane.

There was another coach heading north in an hour, which gave her time to work up her courage to go into a nearby public house for something to eat. She had enough for tea and toast with a dab of marmalade, which tasted better than she thought it would, since all she wanted to do was curl up somewhere and die of loneliness. Another cup of tea, that wonderful British elixir of glad tidings, convinced her that life would go on. Whether it would without Luke Wainwright, she wasn't so certain. No, no, it would. After all, she told herself, even the Mary Coopers of the world deserved one fellow to moon about and imagine being far better than he was, most likely.

She lingered a moment in front of a stationery shop, wanting more crayons, because hers were getting short. She cast caution to the wind and bought two, a green the color of ivy, and a bright red for berries. That preliminary sketch of the Wainwright house, firmly in her memory, occupied her until the mail coach arrived.

Mary sat between a farmwife on one side of her and an old gentleman on the return trip. Two stops from Liddiard, a frowsy-looking woman and a sailor squeezed in. Thank goodness she wouldn't have to make this trip again. Looking on the bright side was easier than she thought. There wouldn't be anguish in saying farewell again to someone she had grown attached to, and glory be, she had seen the ocean, two blessings for the price of one.

Or was it three? No, no. She hadn't grown attached to Luke Wainwright. Not at all.

She hurried the short distance to Notions. Her mental inventory included a cup of tea and at least shortbread and raisins. She came up behind a group of carolers, singing with more enthusiasm than expertise, which suited her, even if several of the singers were Sally's age, and broke her heart a little, but only a little, she assured herself.

When she turned the corner, she took out her key, then put it back in her reticule, stunned. She couldn't overlook a large padlock securing the front door. She felt her face drain of color, so she leaned against the wall until she saw a sign next to the lock. It was still light enough to read. *Attention all and sundry. Until and unless a new owner is secured, the premises of Notions on the High Street belong to Mallard Counting House.*

Mary wasted a brief moment cursing the law, the day, the phases of the moon up to and including God, Himself. She apologized to God, then took inventory of her choices, which were few but sufficient unto the day thereof.

Looking around to make sure no one was about and eager to tattle to the constable, Mary walked to the rear of the shop, the yard all weedy and overgrown. She wouldn't know until she got closer.

Ah, there. Only two months ago, she had cut out part of the door and installed a flap for Gargantua to come and go as he pleased. She had soon added an inside brace against the flap when she knew Gargantua was indoors, which discouraged the occasional arrival of mice.

To Mary's memory, the brace hadn't been in place since before Aunt Luella's death. Mary sat down by the door and patted the flap. To her relief, it swung to the side. It was wide enough for her to stick in her whole arm and reach up inside to make sure the key was in the lock. It was. She turned it, and sighed with relief when the door opened.

In a short while, she had three things working in her favor: The last of the eggs boiling on the range, water heating for tea, and a plan. Granted, it was a feeble one, but it was better than no plan at all.

Chapter Eight

When she woke up, Mary decided she deserved a fine Christmas. Granted, things were in tatters around her, but when had that not been the case? She had two things in her favor, determination and a skill.

The strongbox held four shillings, which was four shillings more than she had when she took that placard out of Miss Wainwright's dusty window. They went into her pocket right away, in case some nosy person saw her through the display window and alerted the constable. The morning light was better in the shop, but that was too risky. She preferred drawing at the kitchen table, anyway.

She wiped away breakfast toast crumbs and assembled her puny arsenal of crayons and thick paper. Drawing always calmed her. Soon she was humming and sketching more of the landscapes and then miniature houses with Christmas wreaths. She liked them so well that she decided to call them homes, imagining a home of her own someday with a wreath. The notion was farfetched, but she felt the pull of the season and it warmed her.

As the shadows of afternoon changed the lighting, she lit the lamp in the kitchen and finished the last landscape. Except for a scrap or two of paper, she was done. A dozen miniature masterpieces lined the kitchen counter. She scrutinized them with a critical eye, pleased with the idea of outlining in permanent ink, then filling in with crayons. "I'm no Rembrandt," she announced, "but Mary Cooper, these are as clever and resourceful as he was."

All she had for dinner was tea, but there was plenty of sugar, so her stomach didn't protest too much. She thought about going across the street to the public house for something to eat, but that would alert everyone that Mary Cooper was back and living in a padlocked house. Tomorrow was soon enough to spring herself on Liddiard. Besides, she never knew money to last that was spent.

She set the final two pieces of paper on the table, pieces she hadn't cut. One would be a modest-sized wreath, the better to save her crayons, and the other Mr. Wainwright's house in Plymouth.

Even considering that she slept in a padlocked, off-limits shop, Mary woke up optimistic. After breakfast of more sugar and tea, she began. She did the wreath first, giving it her full attention because this was the gift going across the street to the public house, and it was truly a gift. If Edwin and Winnie Gower liked it well enough, maybe they would let her set up a small table to sell the dozen miniatures. The Gowers were reasonable folk.

If, if, if. If they were truly feeling jolly enough, perhaps the Gowers would give her work in the public house. It was hardly grandiose, but life was made of small things.

The wreath made her smile. Each little holly berry seemed to have a sheen. Bending over the drawing made her back ache, but wreaths were for once a year and she had eleven months to recover before she tried another. Or so she reasoned.

She took particular care with her other drawing – Mr. Wainwright's Plymouth house, from the handsome greenery, to the brass doorknocker, to a wreath of holly berries only, because she had mostly used up her green crayon on the Gowers' wreath.

Gargantua found his way into the drawing, too, although it took some careful thought to draw him on the front step. She didn't draw in Sally, because she knew that would make her cry. Hopefully, the new housekeeper in Plymouth was kind.

She looked at that empty space in the area behind the lace curtains of what she assumed was the sitting room, with its two windows. Impulsively – never a good thing for an artist – she tried to draw a man and woman in the space. It didn't work. She took a cloth from the sink and ended up smudging the whole thing into a mess that made ghostly images instead. "Bother it," she muttered, and drew lacy curtains to partially hide her misdemeanor.

Mary rummaged through her dwindling stack of pasteboard until she found the right pieces to pack the Wainwright house in. She inserted a note in her best handwriting, consisting only of "Happy Christmas, from your friend Mary Cooper." She addressed the package and went to gather up her few possessions, which still fit compactly in Papa's seed bag.

She made sure both bedchambers were tidy, and that was it, except not quite.

She had never drawn a self-portrait, but she drew one now, looking into her scrap of a mirror and using the last of her miniature paper. She knew she needed to work more on smiles, so she drew herself serious. Since ink was unforgiving, and she was well-acquainted with her skill level, she drew it in pencil. She signed her name on the back and slipped it in the package to the Wainwright house before sealing it. The wreath intended across the street went into a sleeve of brown paper.

Seed bag on her shoulder, package in hand, Mary stood a moment more, reliving the brief pleasure of life here with Aunt Luella and Sally. Soon someone else might own the shop. She lingered a moment more, hopeful that all would be well with Sally and her father. *Luke Wainwright, perhaps I could have known you better, had things been different,* she thought.

She went out the way she came in, careful to lock the door behind her. "I had hoped to spend more time here," she said out loud. "It was a good place, Aunt Luella."

She went first to the posting house where the agent weighed her small gift to the Wainwrights, and asked for six pence, half a shilling. Goodness. No wonder it was hard for an ordinary person to get ahead in England. She was down to a bare shilling, so she cast caution to the wind and bought a few more crayons from what she called the all-purpose shop next to the tearoom. Her change was two pence. She would have hung onto it, except there was a beggar a block beyond.

Next stop was the public house, owned by Edward Gower,

which could be success or failure, or more bluntly, a job or the poorhouse. She squared her shoulders, straightened the seed bag, wished for a bonnet, and opened the door. Mrs. Gower stood behind the counter, drying glasses. Mary looked around, glad to see the room otherwise empty. She handed her paper wreath to Winnie Gower. "I wanted you to have this, Mrs. Gower."

"Thank you, child," Winnie replied. She leaned across the counter. "I wondered where you had gone, and then that nasty constable put a lock on the door. I didn't know what to think."

"I took Sally and Gargantua to Plymouth and her father's house. I was surprised when I saw the lock, too, but I have no claims on anything or anyone, I suppose." That seemed enough, but Mrs. Gower was watching her out of thoughtful eyes. "I don't have much, but I needed my other dress and apron, and all these landscapes." Mary took them from the seed bag, spread them on the counter, and whispered, "I went in through the cat door, or near as. This is yours."

The innkeeper's wife laughed, the hearty sound giving Mary's heart a lift. "You do have a knack." Mrs. Gower admired her larger wreath. "I hope you will let me pay you for this."

"Oh, no. You were kind to us," Mary said simply. She took a deep breath and committed herself. "I was wondering – Would you let me put these on a table here and sell them?"

Nothing changed in Mrs. Gower's eyes, to Mary's relief. If she could sell enough, she might be able to buy more paper. "I only need a small space."

"You can have that and more," Mrs. Gower said. "Where will you stay?"

"I don't know." All she could do was tell the truth. "Could you possibly use some help here? I don't take up much space and I'm diligent."

Winnie Gower lowered her eyes. "What with war, times are tough. I can give you a place to sleep and your meals, but can't promise anything else."

"That's still the offer I'd like," Mary said. "I know times are tough. Believe me, I know."

Done and done.

Chapter Nine

Luke Wainwright sank into his easy chair, full of chicken fricassee, and with hot buttered rum at his elbow. He closed his eyes, reviewing the day-long, exhausting meeting with Artemis Biddle of Biddle & Bancroft, the lending agency for the proposed new drydock. Biddle had been accompanied by his senior accountant, a man dry as toast and humorless, who pored over the proposal, M&W's assets and debits, and the plans for the new construction.

"We will let you know soon, sir," had been the final remark, again delivered with vast solemnity. But that was Biddle and Bancroft, two birds of a feather who squawked and chittered about spending a pence. He knew M&W could – and would – succeed.

After dinner, Luke took the matter to his father-in-law, laid up at home with that toothache which had grown worse overnight, it seemed. What he received was bad news, delivered by a man with his jaw wrapped.

"After your meeting with Biddle, I received a visit from Bancroft," Magleby said, or tried to say. "B&B want a drawing of the proposal. Now that's a fine how-de-do."

"*What?*"

His father-in-law winced. "Talk softer! Something about competition for the loan from Hedges in Chatham." He sighed, and touched his jaw tenderly. "Dunno why Biddle didn't tell you. Hedges submitted a drawing." A sigh ended in a moan. "We need a drawing, too. Damn that Hedges."

"They've never asked for anything like that," Luke protested, even as another part of his brain started hopping about, turning somersaults. *An artist, eh?*

"Find an artist," Mr. Magleby said. Luke thought that was what he said, what with his swollen jaw and tooth so painful that even the heavy tread of Mrs. Magleby from the hall to the sitting room, and her cheerful greeting to Luke made the old fellow wince. "Now!" Or that might have been "Ow!"

He had an artist in mind, but how to finesse this? Another sip of rum helped. Luke opened the slim package from M. Cooper, brought to him by his housekeeper, who, from all appearances, wanted to know what it contained. "I could barely keep Sally from opening it on the spot," the woman said. "I promised her you would show it to her in the morning over breakfast."

"Thank you, Mrs. Gooch," he said. When the housekeeper hovered, he added firmly, "And you will see it in the morning, too."

This was his moment, his piece of quiet. Biddle and Bancroft could damned well wait. He slit open the package and a scrap of a portrait fell out. It was Mary, and it made him smile, even though it was a serious drawing. "Was this the end of your paper?" he asked her.

He turned it over, hoping for more, and was not disappointed. She had written in equally small printing. "I wish I could draw me smiling, but I haven't had any practice with smiles. This will do…" He squinted at the tiny words on the edge of the fragment. "…for now."

He thought about her prosaic words, something an artist would write, and gave it another meaning, this one for himself. "I haven't had any practice with smiles lately, either, dear lady," he whispered to the image. He set the portrait on the table next to the rum.

He took out the large picture, marveling at an artist's rendering, largely in ink, of his house. He had watched Mary work her little landscapes, sometimes making basic outlines, to be filled in later. It was obviously his house, but some of the details were missing. She must have been in a hurry that day she left Sally here, getting just enough of the basic outline before dashing to catch another conveyance back to Liddiard.

He laughed to see Gargantua on the front step of the drawing, looking lazy and overfed as usual. Too bad Sally wasn't there with him. He held off the drawing, and noticed what looked like ghostly figures in his sitting room. Mary had tried something, but working in ink wasn't her forte yet, and she had tried to erase it. Still, what were they?

He squinted, then sucked in his breath. The smoky-looking smudge must be two people, one shorter than the other, a man and woman.

He could have slapped his head at his stupidity and wondered why anyone allowed Luke Wainwright, a certifiable idiot, to wander the streets, much less be a partner in a major business in Devonport. "Is it that simple, Mary?" he asked the portrait. "Were you trying to draw…us?"

He was probably over-thinking it, this smudge partly disguised with a curtain. He held off the picture of 152 Palmer Lane. From an arm's-length distance, he saw only a house. He sat back, because he knew what was missing, having had it once before in his home. It was no smudge or his imagination. Love was missing.

That night, he tossed about in bed only briefly, because the matter resolved itself in pleasing fashion. In the morning, he would compose a letter to Mary Cooper, care of Notions, Liddiard, England, asking her to drop everything and come to 152 Palmer Lane. He would send it express, persuasively writing that M&W Shipbuilders needed her to draw the completed drydock to compete for the contract. He would offer her a hefty fee, state the urgency of the request, and include funds for a post chaise. Make it a business deal. That would get her here, and once she was here, he might remember how to court a woman. Surely he hadn't forgotten everything. Perfect. He slept.

Breakfast with Sally proved even more of a delight. Luke propped up the picture on the empty chair in the breakfast room and couldn't help his huge smile as his daughter roared into the room in her usual lively fashion, saw the drawing, let out a whoop!, then capered around the room. "It's Mary's drawing! I know it!"

"It is indeed, right down to Gargantua on the front steps."

She nodded and sat down to breakfast. He watched her as she ate, her eyes on the drawing. "Papa, it's wonderful, but it lacks something," she said finally.

"What is that, dearest?"

"Mary."

"I plan to remedy that," he told her. "I'm sending her an express delivery letter this morning, asking for her assistance, which we do need, and not just in this house. It's a business matter. I predict she will be here tomorrow."

Sally kissed his cheek and returned to her omelet while he wiped the egg off his face, blew her a kiss and started for the office, even hailing a hackney to speed him along. He smiled, grateful to the dratted Hedges for a drydock rendition that necessitated a response in kind. *Thank you, Mr. Hedges*, he thought.

Content, with that letter already composed in his head and needing only pen to make it real, Luke picked up his usual stack of mail and took it to his office. From habit he scanned the various letters, in case there was something more important to deal with immediately.

Good God, there was. He dropped the other correspondence on his desk and stared at an official-looking letter from Mallard Counting House, Aunt Luella's bank. He silently cursed his own thoughtlessness, knowing he should have sent Mallard a letter after her passing, telling them he would be in touch when he had more time. Hopefully it was nothing he couldn't solve with a letter of his own.

He opened it, swore as impressively as those navy men he worked with daily, and sank into his chair. "God help me," he whispered. "God help me."

There it was, laid out simply, his own orders come back to haunt him. "'Sir, you told me three years ago that when Luella Wainwright passed from this life, I was to padlock the shop, to prevent trespassing. I have done that. Rest assured that the contents of Notions, and her other possessions are safe. Let me know when we can meet and finalize her affairs. Yrs. Sincerely, Jedediah Mallard, Esq."

Luke closed his eyes in utter misery. It was as though a cosmic hand had suddenly thrown a bucket of cold water on him. He shivered as he thought of Mary trying to get into Notions, and finding no way. She was too poor to lodge in a rooming house, had Liddiard even possessed one. She knew hardly anyone, and was not the sort of person to ask for help, grounded as she was in the reality that people of her station in life expected little.

He rang the bell for his second in command. "Sir?" the young man asked moments later. In terse sentences, Luke told him he was in charge for the next few days. "I have a family emergency in Liddiard and I cannot discharge the duty to anyone else," he explained. "I know you can manage," he said more calmly. "You've been training for this moment for several years now."

"Yes, but..."

"Lad, I only hire the best, you included," Luke said. He spoke precisely and in the doing, felt himself growing in the position. "Do what you have seen me do." He looked at his cluttered desk and handed yesterday's notes to the young man, who, to Luke's relief, looked more serious than frightened now. "Everything you need is here. I hope I will not be long. Certainly no more than a day or two." He smiled, on sure ground. "You know ships."

"Very well, sir," his assistant said calmly. "I hope your business is successful."

God in heaven, so do I, he thought. He sent a note to his father-in-law, explaining the situation briefly. He returned to his house to pack a small bag, and hurry away before Sally was aware.

Sally would have none of it. Her eyes filled with tears when she caught him sneaking down the stairs, bag in hand.

He fumbled about, trying to explain what had happened and why he needed to be in Liddiard as soon as possible. "I am coming, too," she announced.

Luke tried to think of all the reasons that was not a good idea. Try as he might, he couldn't come up with anything except that feeble parental admonition he had used upon occasion – "No, and that is final." He couldn't say it. When had he not been anything but a disappointment to his daughter?

Her bruises had faded, and she didn't cling to him so much. He knew he owed both circumstances to Mary, who had been far more aware of Sally's situation after the briefest of observation. He had been too busy for his daughter. He was still trying to shirk his responsibility. It was time to change.

"Yes, come along, by all means. Get one of the maids to help you back a bag."

She nodded and nudged him. "Papa, their names are Trudy and Jane."

"I'm not too observant, am I?" he asked in all contrition.

"You can change," she told him, wise beyond her years.

Yes, I can, he thought, humbled to the dust. *I had better begin now, if I am not too late.*

Chapter Ten

FREQUENCY GLAD HOLICES

They arrived in Liddiard long after the noon hour, slowed because of rain mixed with snow. As desperately as he wanted to skip luncheon and get there to begin what he hoped wasn't a fruitless search, Sally had insisted they stop.

He was prepared to argue with her, and remind her that his housekeeper had sent along biscuits and fruit for them, but Sally taught him another lesson. "Papa, it's not just for us," she said. "Don't you think the post boy and the wheel boy would like to get in out of the rain?"

"You are absolutely right," he said, and stuck his head out of the window in the door, telling them to stop.

"Thankee, sir," the post boy said. No boy he, but an older man, he called to the wheel boy, who turned out to be his son. "Thankee from both of us."

"Thank my daughter," Luke said. "She has better manners than I do." Soon they were eating in the public house while Luke and Sally had a private room.

"Well done, daughter," he said. "You'll make a kind person of me yet." He slapped the side of his face and she giggled. "And Lord smite me if I haven't even asked what you would like for Christmas. I believe it will be here inevitably on the 25th of December."

"Papa, you're a tease," she replied graciously, and provided him with a generous excuse. "I know you are busy."

This time, Luke decided not to let himself off the hook so easily. "No father should be *that* busy. What would you like?"

She pondered the question, reminding him all over again that she was a pensive child, much like her late mother. "I would like for Mary to come to our house and paint pictures."

"Why that?" he asked in surprise. "Isn't there something *you* want, in particular?"

"Papa, your house doesn't have any paintings on the walls. We need them to help make it a home."

Damned if you aren't entirely right, he thought. "So that will make it a home?"

"It's a start," she replied, and dabbed her lips. "I'm certain there is more. We'll know when we see it."

The sleet let up before they reached Liddiard, much to Luke's relief, because Sally kept staring out the window and worrying about the postboys. *What if I cannot find Mary*, kept running through his mind until he had a headache. She was the only illustrator he knew who could turn a drydock into something that would stifle the competition.

He directed the post boy to the Gowers' public house, then took Sally's hand and walked down the street to Notions. He sighed to see the heavy lock on the door, a "tribute" to his own instructions a few years earlier, and Mr. Mallard's efficiency.

"Sally, I have no idea where she is," he said. "Let's go see Mr. Mallard."

They walking to the counting house, a modest affair, compared to Carter and Brustein, where he kept his money in Plymouth. Mr. Mallard offered tea and sympathy, which went down in lumps, but Luke was getting used to lumps. "Put the property up for sale," he told the counting man. "I'll entertain any offers."

"Aye, sir, I will do that." Mr. Mallard leaned back in his chair. "That little woman who worked here – she set it to rights and turned it into something profitable. We should have no trouble selling it."

"Do you have any idea where...where Mary Cooper went?"

"No idea, sir. She disappeared." Mr. Mallard gave him a sympathetic look. "Disadvantaged people like Mary Cooper have a way of vanishing."

Speak of disappearing...Luke looked around for Sally. Nowhere in sight. Did people simply vanish in Liddiard? It was a small village, one Sally knew better than he did, because she had stayed here with Mary. Luke spent a few more minutes fidgeting, as Mr. Mallard wrote down instructions on how to handle his late aunt's affairs.

"It's all in her will, which you have notarized and filed here," he reminded Mr. Mallard. "We can talk again after the holidays. I expect you will have papers for me to sign."

"Yes, indeed, sir, in triplicate," Mr. Mallard said. From the way he rubbed his hands together, Luke knew how much the old fellow enjoyed bean counting.

This was getting him no closer to finding Mary, and now, Sally. He stood a moment, enjoying the watery sunlight like old Gargantua, then started toward Gowers' Public House.

As he passed Notions, he heard someone tapping on glass. He glanced over, and there was Sally, sitting in the display window, going into whoops of laughter as she teased him from inside the shop. How in the world... He watched, open-mouthed, as she made a wide, sweeping gesture and pointed behind her.

Luke was no slouch. The winter grass was slick, so he walked carefully down the incline behind the bank of houses. There it was, Aunt Luella's back door. As he approached, it opened and Sally stood there.

He came closer. "How did you know about this?" he asked, then he couldn't help smiling. "I can tell I will have to get firm with you when you are of age to elope with a worthless man and slide down the ivy at 152 Palmer Lane."

"Oh, Papa," she said, sounding generously willing to overlook such nonsense. "I am only six years old."

"Nearly seven! How did you know about this?"

"Mary made Gargantua an oversized cat door. He used it all the time. I suppose Mary knelt down and reached up to open the door. I'm small. I crawled through." She giggled.

"Obviously Mr. Mallard had no idea of this," Luke said. "I wonder...."

"I think Mary was here," Sally told him. "Every bit of drawing paper is gone, and her whole stash of crayons, even the ones worn to stubs."

She wasn't here now. Luke leaned against the open door, defeated. Mary could be anywhere. He knew she was likely to land on her feet, if she was resourceful enough to remember Gargantua's entryway, but she remained a woman with no one to turn to, not that she would have.

They left the way they came in, after Sally found another of Gargantua's little yarn balls and tucked it away. "We don't know where to look for Mary, do we?" she asked as they walked up the slope to the street.

"Haven't a clue," Luke admitted. "I suppose we could hire Bow Street Runners and…"

"Papa, look," Sally said, her voice strangely soft. She pointed.

Same ragged cloak around her, Mary Cooper swept the walkway in front of the Gowers' public house, where he had sent the post boys to eat and dry off. She swept with her usual vigor, intent, concentrating on getting every scrap relocated to the gutter, doing a good job whether it was a window clean and sparkling with ammonia water, a landscape of rolling hills, or a hurry-up drawing of his own house. She worked for food and a place to sleep, nothing more. One thing more occurred to him, and made him wonder at his own obliviousness: Mary Cooper was kind.

"Mary," he said. He didn't think he said it loud, but she looked up, alert, even wary. She gasped to see Sally, dropped her broom, and knelt as his daughter threw herself into outstretched arms. They clung together, Sally in tears and Mary nearly so. Or maybe that was his own clouded view, except that he wasn't prone to unmanly tears.

He joined them. "We didn't know where to look," Sally said as she sobbed, holding tight.

"I'm glad you looked across the street," Mary joked, not letting go, either. She kissed Sally and held her off a little. "Let me finish here, then we'll go inside." She turned sweet eyes on him. "Mr. Wainwright, are you a little frazzled?"

"I *am*! I need you." Good God, he really did. "I mean, well, it's like this…"

Again those sweet eyes: Mary Cooper, who had nothing and no one and somehow managed. She gave him a little push. "Go inside, Mr. Wainwright. It looks like Sally and I will finish up here."

Meekly, he did as she directed, truth to tell enjoying someone ordering him about. Mrs. Gower must have watched the whole thing from the front window, which, Luke noticed, sparkled as bright now as Aunt Luella's front window had sparkled…was it two months ago? She sat him down in the pub, considered the matter, and placed hot buttered rum in front of him.

He took a sip, not knowing what to say. Mrs. Gower was never one to hang back, to his relief. She filled the conversational space. "Mary came here after your aunt's funeral. You know how forthright she is, but calm-like. She said she didn't have a place to stay, and did we have work for her?"

"Thank God you did."

Mrs. Gower did hang back then. "Times aren't easy right now, and I couldn't promise her wages. Right now it's food and a pallet in the kitchen. She's been selling her little Christmas fancies." She looked at the wall, where three of them hung. "Those are the remainders."

"I think I'm going to make her a better offer," Luke said apologetically.

"Oh?" Mrs. Gower perked up.

"Yes. As you know, I'm a partner to my former father-in-law in the shipbuilding trade. We're in competition for a sizeable loan to add onto the business, but the loaning house wants a true drawing of our proposed drydock. I want to hire Mary to draw it."

For some reason, Mrs. Gower gave him that look he had seen her give others, particularly those who tried to cheat her or Mr. Gower. It was the look Clarissa used to refer to as the you-don't-measure-up stare.

"That's it?" she asked.

"I intend to pay her quite well," he assured the innkeeper's wife.

"And?"

He was spared further inquisition when Mary and Sally came in, looking windblown and rosy themselves. Sally fit well next to Mary's side. A fleeting thought passed through his overworked, frazzled brain. *I wonder how Mary would fit next to me?* It was a brief thought. He had a business deal for this person; that was the only guarantee. Another fleeting thought: *I wonder how old Mary is?*

It scarcely mattered. She could draw and he needed an artist. A few words to Mrs. Gower, and there was hot buttered rum for Mary, too. Sally started to pout. He was going to give her The Father look, but Mary beat him to it with a smile and "Hot cider?" which erased the pout. *I'll have to remember that,* he thought.

It wasn't his particular choice, but Mrs. Gower sat in on his proposal to Mary for work. As he spoke, he realized that the innkeeper's wife was looking out for Mary, too.

"That's it. We need that loan from Biddle and Bancroft, who have requested an actual illustration. What do you think, Mary?"

"Do you have blueprints?" she asked. "I could...No. Could you take me to those...those..."

"...South Yard Docks..."

"...South Yard Docks and let me draw what is there, with the new modifications, against a fitting background?"

He considered the matter, and suspected that the competitor's drawing was probably the structure only. The mechanic in him said that was sufficient unto the day. The man who had seen what Mary could do wanted to take a chance on more.

"I like your idea, Mary," he said. "I would agree to it on one condition."

"Which is..."

"You call me Luke instead of Mr. Wainwright. He's a stodgy fellow. I am not."

Chapter Eleven

The nice thing about owning nothing was that it took no time to pack. Mary sent Sally in search of the rest of Gargantua's yarn balls to give herself time to think about Luke's conversation in the public house.

Mr. Wain...Luke...was going to pay her a princely sum to draw a drydocks, but she only had a few days to do it. "According to Mr. Magleby, Biddle and Bancroft want it before Christmas," he had told her. "I'll take you to the South Yard first thing tomorrow morning. You can stay in my house. There's a room right next to Sally's."

"And when she is done? What then?" Mrs. Gower had asked. When Luke didn't reply immediately, she turned to Mary. "There is always and ever a place for you here." It was nice to know, and a relief, in fact. There may not have been any room in that obviously mismanaged inn in Bethlehem, but then, Mrs. Gower wasn't running that one. There was room in Liddiard.

Mary agreed. After Luke rounded up the post boy and his son, they returned to Plymouth, arriving after dark. She embarrassed herself by falling asleep, leaning against Luke. At some point his arm went around her. When she woke up in Plymouth, she saw that Sally slept with his other arm around her. Poor man. His arms were probably both numb.

What a lovely house. And here was a smiling housekeeper, and Gargantua twining around them until Mr. Wainwright put his hand on her waist and escorted her away from the cat's determination to give all his affection away. She wondered for the first time how old Luke Wainwright was. She told herself it had never matter before. Why should it matter now?

The hurried, late supper was followed by a charming bedchamber that brought tears to her eyes. She had never seen a room so lovely, much less set foot in one. Sleep came fast and easy.

She must have left her door open. At some point during the night, Gargantua decided to plop down his big self next to her and start purring as he kneaded her hip. Groggily, she heard "Here kitty kitty" in a nice baritone, followed by someone picking up said cat, who hissed, then growled low in his throat. "Silence, you misbegotten feline," she thought she heard, then the door closed.

Her dress looked no better in the morning than it had for years, but Luke had told her to leave her muddy shoes in the hall. Now they shone to a fare-thee-well, which warmed Mary's heart. Breakfast began with oatmeal, continued with eggs and bacon, and ended with a sweet roll. Mary knew she ate too much, but when a girl doesn't always know when or where the next meal is coming from, she considered it wise to indulge. A glance at the platter showed more bacon. She was too full, but it was so nice to see food no one needed.

When she saw Luke watching her, she blushed, because she knew what he must be thinking. Might as well not mince words. After all, he was going to pay her for a rendering and that was that. "I like to see food," she said simply.

He amazed her then. "So do I, Mary Cooper. I'm a Wainwright, which means that some generations back – not too many – my people made wagons. And do you know, if times ever get tough in this shipbuilding business which is currently driving me to distraction, I could make a wagon again. I understand you."

If her heart stopped beating then, Mary wouldn't have minded. Someone she cared about understood her. "Then let us get about business," she said.

Sally objected to being left behind, but her father was firm. "Mary's right. This is business, my dear. We will see you later."

They walked in near silence to Devonport, a town already awake and in motion. She heard hammering from another dock, and the creak of a mast being stepped, and stopped to watch. All around was the chaos of construction. "It's almost a living thing," she said.

"I never thought of it that way."

"You don't have an artist's eye," she said, willing to be generous. She wondered where she got the courage to say that much, considering that her life had been one of want and disappointment.

"I'm a builder," he said. "You are, too, in your own way."

M&W Ship Builders was a modest-enough structure. "These are the South Yards," Luke told her. He stopped her with a hand on her arm this time. "Those monsters are the M&W dry docks. See that empty space? That will be the third dock, provided we get the loan."

"You will," she said. "I can draw this." She couldn't have told a jury of twelve men where that courage came from, but she felt it in her bones.

Luke's desk was a jumble of paper and blueprints, for which he offered no apology. He held up a blueprint. "Here it is. I gave Biddle and Bancroft our specs and requirements, but Mr. Magleby said our competitor included an actual drawing. We need one, too."

She looked at the blueprint, understanding it, and also understanding competition. Nothing came free in the world. She returned her attention to the rough drawing, willing herself to see the finished product. "Do you have pencil and sketchbook? Oh, and crayons."

"Not yet. I told Mr. Magleby I would wait until I had you in hand to tell me what you need."

You have me in hand, she thought, liking that turn of phrase. It was one she had heard before, but now it seemed personal, almost intimate: To be had in hand by someone concerned about her welfare to the exclusion of all others. Mary spent a tiny moment imagining how nice it would be, to not worry about every meal or a bed. To be had in hand felt like so much more. She decided that somehow, some way, she wanted more.

A tiny moment to contemplate such wealth was all she allowed herself. She had not a single illusion left. "I will need a sketchbook and good drawing paper, six sheets. Make them fairly large. And crayons and pencils. I'll probably outline in pencil first. Oh, a sharp penknife."

It was too much to someone used to scrounging for the barest necessities. "Am I asking out of turn?" She couldn't help herself.

Apparently not. Luke scribbled it down without a blink. "I'll have this here at once," he said, "once my clerk rubs sleep from his eyes."

She smiled at that. "I have another big demand."

"Say on, missy," he said cheerfully, which warmed her deep inside.

"I…I'd like to see the front of the drydocks from the water. Is there a little boat around here?"

He laughed at that, and took her arm, steering her toward the door. "Miss Cooper, boats are our specialty." To her surprise, he touched his head to hers. "And didn't you send me a bathtub drawing of a boat? We have all shapes and sizes."

In no time she found herself being handed into a small craft with one sail. Luke stepped in as carefully as she did, and nodded to the man at the tiller.

She clutched Luke's arm as the sailboat heeled into the wind and began its silent approach to the South Yards. Without a word, he put his arm around her, which she thought quite kind of him.

"Here, right here," Mary said, after a quick tour of the harbor. She took a sheet of paper from her reticule and unfolded it, well aware that this was her last sheet. Out came her stubby pencil. The sailboat bobbed about, taking her stomach with it. Was that last piece of breakfast toast a mistake? Never mind. She had an idea. "Can we sort of stay here for a few minutes?" she asked.

"I think we can." Luke gave that order to the man at the tiller, and he grinned.

She sketched quickly, superimposing that third unbuilt drydock next to the two docks, and showed it to Luke, who seemed to be fixated on that empty space. For all she knew, he was seeing that drydock, too. "Is this what it will look like?"

"Very like. Mary, you're good at this." He scrutinized her drawing. "There will be a larger crane, in fact, two, here and here. Can you do it?"

Mary raised her eyes to his. They were seated close because it was a small craft. "You will have it, Luke Wainwright."

Chapter Twelve

At M&W, Mary began work seated at a clever desk with an easel she could raise or lower. There was another stand for her preliminary sketches on the water.

"I'm right next door," Luke said. "I'll be in and out all afternoon, but here are those art supplies you needed." He looked around. "Is the light good enough?"

"Another lamp or two would be good," she said.

"You're going to stay here all night?" he teased, then must have noticed her serious expression. "I believe you are."

"I like to work when it is quiet. You said you need this composition soon."

"Sooner the better," he admitted. "I'll get a cot for you. And sandwiches. Beef? Chicken?"

"Both," she told him, not shy this time. Maybe she wouldn't eat two sandwiches, but just the idea of two? That was luxury.

She drew the new drydock in pencil, and set it aside. By the time the office building began to empty out, she had roughed in the South Yard, using pencil and eraser liberally. Luke was as good as his word. A cot appeared, and three sandwiches, which made her smile. *You have me in hand*, she thought.

He dropped by after seven o'clock. "I'd stay and keep you company," he said. "You don't need company, do you?"

"You'd be a distraction," she told him, which made him blush.

He recovered quickly. "Just as well," he said cheerfully. "I have promised Sally that I will join her caroling party from St. Michaels. God knows I cannot carry a tune, but I'm not sure that matters."

She thought he would leave, but he stood there a moment more. She watched several expressions cross his open face, from sadness to something that looked hopeful. "I have never taken the time to celebrate Christmas in a long while," he admitted. "I figure there is room for improvement."

She drew rapidly and handed him two attached musical notes, one with "eyes" looking heavenward and mouth in a perfect O. The other note looked horrified.

"Sally will love this. The vicar, not so much!" Luke gave her a chaste kiss on the cheek and left. She turned back to her work, pleased.

Mary knew she had a sure touch, and this was fine paper from the stationer's, the best she had ever used. She picked up the smaller sheet containing the roughed-in setting and studied her sketch of the drydock to come. She took a big breath and dipped the pen in the inkwell.

The third drydock quickly materialized next to the two permanent ones. After long thought, she outlined it in blue, to differentiate between the current drydocks and the imagined one. The effect was simple and obvious: This was the place for a third drydock. To celebrate, she ate the roast beef sandwich and drank water. The other two sandwiches could wait, but she lifted up the bread on the chicken sandwich, just to look at the white meat. *My goodness, but a body could get used to this*, she thought.

She sat a long moment with her eyes closed, imagining it, then continued. She began tentatively enough, filling in with color the small brick buildings and larger ones she had roughed in, plus a long building that Luke said was a ropewalk.

The result was precisely what she hoped for – the absolute sense of that third drydock completing the already busy South Yard. The buildings suggested workers, and the houses where they lived with their families, as they all did their part to defeat Napoleon. Maybe she was reading more into the picture than anyone needed, or just trying to stay awake. In the upper right corner, she drew a portion of England's flag of St. George and St. Andrew, flapping in a stiff wind.

Her vision started to blur as midnight approached, but there was time to add another row of houses above the Yards and fill them with crayon color. Oh, why not? On the nearer street of houses, she inked in a little gathering of carolers.

She would have slept then, but the chicken sandwich revived her. Another roast beef sandwich remained. To her surprise, consternation, tears, and then a smile of triumph, she realized she didn't need any more food. She was full. The notion pleased her heart and soul.

Mary's back ached abominably. She got off the stool, stretched, and felt every vertebra complain. She rubbed the small of her back, and wondered how nice it would feel to have someone with strong fingers do that for her.

She gave her rendition of the third dry dock another critical scrutiny and added a little more white chop to the reasonably well-mannered waves. It was beyond her skill level to add some ships on the water. And glory be, but crayons blended well together to suggest a brilliant blue sky. She stood back, satisfied. That was Devonport – bustling docks, ships under construction, commerce she could almost hear as she gazed. The houses and shops added the right amount of softness, and a certain vulnerability, as if the ships that firms like Magleby & Wainwright built were there to keep homes and shops safe all over England.

Mary glanced at the clock. There was another project, a Christmas present. She took out another sheet of that beautiful paper and with a sure hand, drew the house at 152 Palmer Lane again, adding more details. Sally now sat beside Gargantua on the front steps.

How to make the house more inviting, more a home? She drew the front door slightly open. She spent a long time staring at the windows on the main floor, then her heart told her what to add, something she could do with crayons and a lighter touch than a drydocks. She had learned from her earlier attempt that maybe she could hope.

Mary took a long look at her creation, happy with it. She tucked it under the unused paper, hoping Luke wouldn't mind if she kept

212 • CARLA KELLY

it, along with the pencils. She could tidy up in here tomorrow. No, that Palmer House rendering was for her alone, considering what she had drawn into the sitting room. She doubted Luke expected a Christmas present from her.

She carried the artwork that M&W Shipbuilders had commissioned to Luke's office. Luckily, the door wasn't locked. She smiled at the clutter and wondered if he even knew where the key was. After moving around some paper, she squared away the drawing in the middle of his desk.

At the last moment, she put her initials in the lower righthand corner, just a small MC riding on one of the waves. She stifled any doubt that this wasn't what they really wanted, because something in her artist's heart told her that no one could have done better. Luke had promised her that she would be paid, no matter what.

Besides, there was that third roast beef sandwich. She returned to what she wanted to always call "her" office and lay down on the cot. The sandwich was close at hand, so she took a bite out of it. That was all. She was full.

Chapter Thirteen

Luke lay awake for hours, wondering if Mary would actually spend the night working on this commission. He had been careful to tell her that the building was always patrolled and that he had specifically told the guard to see her safely home, if she finished.

He got up several times and went downstairs to look out the window and pace the sitting room, chastising himself for leaving her there to draw and color alone, even if she felt she needed solitude. He reminded himself that his guard was a trusty fellow with a wife and daughters, who would never countenance Mary walking back to Palmer Lane alone. That knowledge was the only thing that allowed him to sleep, only to be wakened an hour later by his housekeeper's morning knock on his door.

After he dressed, he knocked on Mary's door, dithered about, then opened it a tiny crack to see for himself. No, her room was tidy, bed made, and no clutter. Then again, what clutter did Mary Cooper possess? She was a woman with absolutely nothing.

He leaned against the wall in the corridor, knowing that wasn't true. With a jolt that nearly felt like a cosmic slap to his head, he knew that Mary possessed a fierce resolve to survive, and if humanly possible, make the world around her a better place. She had turned Aunt Luella's wretched Notions into a tidy, sparkling, even cozy place for ladies who did fine sewing to shop. He chuckled. Complete with a fat cat in the yarn bin. That was Mary.

That same little nobody that the world had no use for had also alerted him to the fact that his only child was being abused by those who should have cared for her welfare. For that alone, he owed her a debt he could never repay. That was also Mary.

"Papa, where *is* she?" Sally asked over their shared breakfast.

There was no overlooking his child's distress. He placated her as best he could, explaining that Mary wanted to finish that commission for Magleby & Wainwright, and all was well. Sally was not happy, but Luke had to smile inwardly. She gave him that same one-eyebrow-arched look that her departed mother used to give *him*, when he wasn't measuring up.

He walked to work, reflecting on his reaction to Sally's expression. Only a few years ago, that reminder of Clarissa's funny quirk, gone for good now, would have left him to mope for days. Now it was a gentle, funny memory that touched his heart, but didn't wound him. He owed it to Mary Cooper. He stopped short of the drydocks, captured by the knowledge that he was ready to move on. He knew Clarissa would always remain in his heart as his first love and a wife to treasure. Without a doubt, he also knew he wanted Mary Cooper. How did all that work? He had no idea, but he wanted to – needed to – find out.

His first stop was the small room next to his office, just to reassure himself that Mary was there. He tapped. No answer. He opened the door a crack and there she was, sleeping deep, her breathing rhythmic and steady. He had to swallow once or twice and compose himself. She held that third sandwich, half-eaten. He closed the door quietly.

She had put the drawing of the drydock on his desk. He stared at it in amazement, he, who was only proficient with stick figures. She had outlined the proposed drydock in blue, so there was no mistaking it, and no mistaking how much a part of South Yards it would become. He smiled to see how she had rough-sketched in other maritime business, and trees and greenery. He admired the two rows of houses, nodding to see tiny wreaths on doors, and laughed at what had to be Christmas carolers.

Luke decided that Biddle and Bancroft would be hard cases, indeed, if they could resist all the charm of Mary's landscape, plus her skillful blending of prosaic drydocks into what made

Devonport and Plymouth so essential to Britain's seagoing commerce and national safety.

Luke took the artwork, for such it was, to Mr. Magleby's office, hoping he was at work and not languishing at home with the dread toothache. His father-in-law's cheerful "Come in, come in," suggested that the tooth crisis was over.

"Dear boy, did you know that some dentists are kind enough to use a little laudanum to keep a man from leaping off a tall building?" he said. "He told me I will live to fight another day. And what have we here?"

Luke put Mary's art on Mr. Magleby's desk. He stepped back, relieved and pleased, to see his father-in-law's reaction. "Amazing, amazing," he said over and over. "Oh, and look, carolers!" Another look. "Is that a dog treeing a cat? Well bless my soul."

"I hadn't noticed," Luke said, wondering what else the picture might reveal. "Well, sir? Will this suit those persnickety fellows at B&B?"

"Without a doubt," Mr. Magleby said. "On your way out, tell my secretary to summon me a hackney. I'm going to Biddle and Bancroft without a moment's delay. Good day to you, sir, and my best to Mary Cooper!"

Mary was up and folding the bedding on the cot when he returned to his side of the hall. He noticed that the sandwich was gone. He also noticed the dark circles under her eyes.

"Mary, you've exceeded all possible expectations," he said as he leaned against the doorframe. "Mr. Magleby is positive that the loan will be ours."

She nodded, her satisfaction evident, even if her eyes were tired. "Then you'll have what you want and a happy Christmas, too."

I want more, he yearned to tell her, but settled for, "Yes, indeed. And now, Miss Cooper, I am going to escort you downstairs where there should be a hackney ready to take you back to 152 Palmer Lane. Sally promised me she will keep everyone quiet so you can sleep a little longer."

He thought she might object. She even opened her mouth to speak, but he held up his hand. "No argument, dear Mary," he told her, keeping his tone light. "You have earned a solid day's sleep."

"Aye, sir, I have," was her quiet reply. "Thank you for the work. I enjoyed it."

It was simply said and effective, polite permission for him to go back to work, which he did. Or at least he stared at the year-end facts and figures, thinking at a tiny thing she had said that probably gave him way too much hope.

When he handed her into the hackney – she had protested about a hackney, but he was firm – Mary said, "You need to be home for dinner. Sally wants to sing some Christmas carols to you. None of this late-night work, she told me and she was adamant about it. Home, sir."

They had both laughed over that, and he promised. What kept him on edge and hopeful all day was what she said: You need to be *home*. Home.

Good Lord but he was a hopeless case, sure of his own mind now, but wondering to what extent Mary cared. You would have thought he was twenty again, and full of piss and vinegar, contemplating kissing some pretty miss under mistletoe, and not thirty-two and tired and worried and so uncertain. What an idiot.

He knew he was prone to over-thinking. Clarissa had called it a hiss and a byword. "You know you needn't do that, my love," she told him once. "Trust yourself."

She was right then and right now. Here he was, imagining something hopeful about a future with another wife, and he was partner in a firm with his former father-in-law. What would Mr. Magleby *think* about this whole matter?

"Shut up, Luke," he muttered to himself. "You're getting tiresome."

And he was. He almost didn't want to go home and over-think some more. He wanted to remain until his father-in-law returned with news, good or bad, from the counting house. Mr. Magleby had already sent the ship builders home, such being company practice on the remaining days before Christmas. Others might keep their lads working long hours as the 25th approached, but

M&W reaped the benefit of time off, when time occasionally became of more value than money, when families yearned to gather together.

He could at least tidy up his desk, and then the little room Mary had occupied. His desktop was easy. He opened a drawer and swept everything into it. He knew the office Mary had used would be simple, too. It was due to be painted, and nearly everything had already been moved.

The cot and bedding were already gone. He smiled. And the sandwich. The desk next to her drawing board was littered with the remains of her work, the crayons almost waxy lumps. There were a few large sheets of paper remaining, so he stacked those.

He noticed that the last piece of stiff paper was colored. It was her second rendition of his house. Intrigued, he took the drawing into his office and sat down to study it. Since she had been here a few days, she had taken more time to observe the front of his house. She had drawn the entrance arch correctly this time, with four windows across the front instead of three, two on each side of the door.

The Christmas wreath, a vibrant splash of red berries and green ivy, mirrored the one already in place. There on the front steps was Gargantua again, but with Sally holding him. The effect was charming, but that wasn't what caught and held his attention.

There was nothing of interest beyond the lacey curtains that he knew graced the dining room windows. When he glanced at the sitting room windows on the other side of the door, he knew he was looking at quiet Mary's own way of stating her intentions.

He took the drawing to his window, where the light was better. No, he wasn't indulging in wishful thinking over that first smudgy outline in her earlier sketch. A man and a woman stood close together, their arms around each other. Her face in profile was raised, his was lowered. They were on the verge of kissing. It was stunning in its simplicity.

No, Mary hadn't drawn a random house. Plainly over the front door was 152 Palmer Lane in the same lovely script actually painted there. This was his house, no, their home. And this was his Mary.

Chapter Fourteen

Luke would have left right then for home, but reason prevailed, reminding him to wait until Mr. Magleby returned from Biddle & Bancroft with the verdict on whether drydock number three would begin with the new year, or wait a while. "Come on, come on, sir," he muttered as time passed.

Ah, yes, he finally heard voices on the stairs, and then Mr. Magleby opening the door to his grander office across the corridor. Luke almost managed a leisurely stroll to his father-in-law's office. He knocked.

"Come in, laddie." Amused, Luke wondered if he would always be twenty-two years old and a talented and ambitious laddie in the older man's eyes.

"Good news for us, sir?" Luke asked, as Mr. Magleby waved him in and pointed to a chair.

"Aye, and aye again," Luke heard. "They couldn't say yes fast enough." Mr. Magleby chuckled. "Merry Christmas to us! I swore I almost heard Mr. Bancroft say, 'Take our money, please. All of it!'"

Luke smiled. "I'm not really surprised. Mary's sketch was bound to charm the stockings off two old gents like B and B. When do we begin?"

"With the new year," Magleby said. "Are you going home now?"

"I am, sir, but I'll be back tomorrow. I plan to…" Luke stopped. Out of the corner of his eye, he noticed something familiar wedged partly behind the bookcase. It couldn't be. He looked closer. It was Mary's beautiful drawing of the drydocks, the work that was supposed to make the difference between aye or nay on that loan. "Wait a moment."

Was he seeing things? Luke pulled out the very landscape that had sent him into raptures this morning, when he took it to his father-in-law. He stared down at it, then up at Mr. Magleby, who was starting to look like a boy with his hand in a cookie jar.

"You didn't take this to any meeting," he accused.

A long pause, then Mr. Magleby cleared his throat, his guilty look replaced by a genuine smile of affection. "Sit down, dear boy," he said. "I have a confession."

Luke sat, unable to think of anything to say.

Magleby sat next to him, and not behind his desk, his hands in his lap. He wore a momentary look of real contrition on his face, but it didn't last. His eyes soon glowed with their usual good humor. "Was it two weeks ago that your aunt passed away? Maybe three?"

Luke nodded, unsure of himself and badly out of his league.

"You were so anxious to go to Liddiard and see how Mary was doing. I went past your office a few times, and I swear you were pacing a trench from window to window."

"I knew I should be there. I have to say I resented you insisting that I remain here," Luke admitted, unable to hide his anger. "Mary needed me! Well, I hoped she did. Dash it all, I wasn't sure. Why did you do that?"

"I knew you were still getting acquainted with Mary, and I know you are a cautious man." He sighed. "I also knew you were lonely. My wife knew it, too."

Luke looked down at his hands. "I was. There was something about Mary, and I wanted to…Oh, I don't want you to ever think I am being disloyal to your only daughter."

Mr. Magleby reached over and put his hand on Luke's. "Son – you will always be a son to me – I miss Clarissa, too, but it has been nearly seven years, and life goes on." He strengthened his grip on Luke's hand, then released it. "Mary Cooper was the first woman you seemed to be interested in. I thought if I manufactured a good reason for her to come *here* and paint, you might be able to decide yea or nay." He chuckled. "And so I schemed. Was I wrong, lad?"

"Not at all, sir," Luke said, but cautiously. "I'm not sure when or how it happened, but I did want to know Mary better. You've seen her. She's lovely and quiet and never seeks attention. And she's so smart! I may have decided she was the wife for me, but I didn't know how she felt."

"Just a moment, sir." He hurried to his office, retrieved the landscape of his house and set it in his father-in-law's lap. "I thought she left this here by mistake this morning, but now I think it was Mary's way of letting me know how she feels. What do you think?"

He pointed to the silhouettes of the two lovers – what else could they be? – in his sitting room. Mr. Magleby laughed, then wiped his forehead, which had sprouted perspiration.

"I'm relieved," Mr. Magleby said. "You won't call me out for a duel then? Or sever our partnership? Or cut me off from ever seeing Sally?"

"No, no, and no!" Luke assured him. He steeled himself to look his father-in-law, a sympathetic man but a man of business. "You have been good to me, even when I think I am floundering."

"You're not floundering," Mr. Magleby said kindly. He stood up, went to the window, and seemed to make up his mind. *What now?* Luke thought. *There can't be more to this. I'm already in his debt.*

"I must confess all and not add another layer to my misdemeanor."

"There's more?" Luke asked, interested because this Mr. Magleby was more complex than he had suspected. "What else could there be? You just said they never asked for an illustration, and believe me, I appreciate that now."

Mr. Magleby's smile stretched across his face. "Here is the whole truth, I promise: There was never a rival for our proposal in the first place. B&B promised me weeks ago that they didn't even need your presentation to give us the funds. It was already settled."

Luke stared at his father-in-law. Generally a careful man, he forced himself now to think through the whole business. *I wonder*, he thought, *would I have gone to Mary for a drawing? Or would I have dithered about and ruined a perfectly good opportunity to find a wife?* He tried to be stern, tried to hide his smile, but he couldn't. It wouldn't do to let the old boy off too easy, now would it?

"You, Mr. Magleby, are a meddler and a scheming scoundrel," he settled on, ruining the effect because he had to smile. Damned if the man wasn't precisely right.

"Yes, I know," Mr. Magleby said, with a certain complaisance that made Luke laugh out loud. "Would you have reached out to Mary if I hadn't forced your hand?"

Luke considered the question. "I suppose I will never know." A worse thought made him look away. "She could so easily have vanished and I might never have found her." *Mary, thank God you turned to the Gowers as a place to sell your landscapes*, he thought. Still, he didn't want to let his father-in-law off the hook so easily.

"Tell me, sir, did you really have the worst toothache since the invention of toothaches?" he asked, all innocence.

"Let us say, it was not quite as serious as I let on," Mr. Magleby said, with no shame and a bigger smile.

"Then I thank you," Luke said simply. "I might have dithered away a great event, which, of course, remains to be seen." He patted his heart. "I don't know what she will say when I go home."

"Let me offer you some advice, oh cautious partner! Fling open your front door, haul her close and kiss her."

The partners regarded each other. Luke took Mr. Magleby's hand this time and kissed it. "In a perfect world, I would be going home to Clarissa, but this is not a perfect world." He saw the struggle on the old man's face, this grandfather to Sally. "I trust I have your blessing, you old schemer."

Mr. Magleby chuckled, his good humor restored, the sorrow gone from his eyes. "You do. It's time. Sally needs a mother and you need a wife." He wagged his finger at Luke. "If there are more children, I fully intend to claim them as mine."

"And so you may," Luke said. He picked up Mary's drawing of his house. "I believe I'll frame this and put it where I can see it every day of my life." He nodded to Mr. Magleby and went to the door. "I'm going home."

"Good luck, lad. I trust you haven't forgotten how to propose."

"Indeed I have not. Good afternoon, sir."

"On thing more, lad," his father-in-law said. "Let's you and I keep this little secret about the drawing of the drydock to ourselves." He cleared his throat. "I wouldn't want your mother-in-law to know what a schemer I am. And certainly not B&B!"

"Fair enough, sir, even though I think women are generally smarter than we are. And I intend to assure Mary that her work made all the difference to Biddle and Bancroft."

"Our little secret."

He took a hackney home. *Home.* What a grand word. That pile of stone and wood and handsome furniture had been a house for too long. He checked his timepiece. He had promised Mary that morning that he would be home for dinner – imagine that – and to hear Sally singing Christmas carols in the sitting room. It was only four o'clock. He wondered if Mary was even out of bed yet, considering her sleepless night.

Sally met him at the door, her eyes wide with surprise. "Papa! It is you!" she exclaimed, which made him resolve to never, ever work past their usual dinnertime of six again.

"It certainly is me. Where is Mary? Is she asleep?"

"I couldn't sleep," he heard from the doorway of the dining room. She dropped the knife she must have been polishing, because Mary never gave herself an idle moment. He decided that was going to change, probably as soon as he could get a special license and marry this woman.

She gasped when she saw her rendition of 152 Palmer Lane in his hand. To his glee, Luke saw her blush all the way across the foyer. "I...I didn't think you would find it! I was hoping to keep it for myself. If I was forward..."

"Mary." Like *home*, it was one word that said everything. "Mary." He set down the drawing, flung off his hat, grabbed her around the waist and pull her close. His lips were almost on hers when he said, "Let's recreate the couple in the drawing. Aye or nay?"

"Aye," she said promptly and quietly, as was her nature.

"Should we go into the sitting room for a true reenactment?" he teased.

"It's too far," she said, as if his sitting room was in Tibet and not mere steps away. She kissed him first, her arms under his, her hands on his back, pulling him close. Before he closed his eyes to completely appreciate this stunning moment in his foyer, he noticed the housekeeper gaping, Sally jumping up and down, and...and was that the greengrocer's delivery boy? Oh, God, the vicar.

"You're right, it was too far, Mary my love," he said when they came up for air. He winced when their audience applauded, and wondered how fast this news would travel throughout Devonport and Plymouth.

"Perhaps they'll go away if we keep kissing," Mary suggested.

"We can try."

"Let's go to the sitting room," she added. "It has a door."

"And it locks, Papa."

Luke hadn't reckoned on Sally, the other little lady in his life. She hurried into the sitting room with them. Calmly, she turned the key in the lock and stated most formally. "Papa, a week ago, you asked me what I wanted for Christmas."

"I did. Your present is upstairs in my room." Thank goodness for a most useful housekeeper, who had hesitated not at all, buying a handsome hunk of fabric and assuring him she could find a seamstress.

But Sally was looking at Mary. "I really would rather have Mary close by forever. What do you want, Papa?"

He had to swallow down a lump in his throat as large as a boulder, but he managed. "My goodness, the very same thing." He pulled Mary close. "What would you like for Christmas, Miss Mary Cooper?"

"Such a dull bunch we are," she said. "I want exactly the same thing."

And that was that. Luke held Mary tight, with Sally squashed between them.

To his amusement, Sally separated them in a formal way, which was somehow so touching in a six-year-old. "Papa, I believe you have something to ask Mary before anything else can happen."

He copied her serious demeanor. "I do indeed, dearest." He turned to Mary and took her hand. She gave his hand a gentle squeeze, then looked upon him in her benevolent way that made his knees wobble a bit. If that was what a simple look did, he was a no-hoping goner.

In his lifetime so far, Luke knew he had made two wise decisions. He had married Clarissa Magleby, as charming a wife as a man could hope for. He also accepted Roger Magleby's offer to become a ship builder and eventual partner, something he was truly fit for. Time and tide had changed things, but he understood now that those equally fine decisions had brought him to this moment.

He moved close to Mary, realizing that this would be the third wise decision, provided she agreed (and he thought she would).

He put it to the test. "Miss Cooper, it has finally come to this blockhead's attention that he is in love again," he began, which earned a chuckle from Miss Cooper.

"You're no blockhead," Mary said in his defense. "You're tired, and torn so many ways. Napoleon is not helping, either. When have you had a moment's time for yourself?"

When she paused, her eyes merry, he kissed her, no little peck, because he was more experienced than that. It was a bonfire of a kiss, the sort of kiss that might have shocked any number of prudes.

Sally was obviously no prude. She applauded. "Jolly good, Papa."

Luke bowed to his daughter. "Thank you," he said, and returned his attention to his rosy, smiling lady, for so she was. "And you, Miss Cooper. What say we marry, since I know I am in love, and greatly suspect that you are, too. Is it wise? Are we being smart? I don't care. Please marry me."

"Aye, sir, I will," Mary replied. "You will have all my love and devotion, and Sally will, too."

She spoke with such conviction that it humbled him. He

took her in his arms gently this time, calmly, and with his own conviction. "And you will have mine," he said quietly. He touched his head to hers, then, "Plus all the drawing paper and crayons you could possibly want."

"And brothers and sisters for Sally?" Mary asked.

"You can depend upon it."

She held herself off a little, looking deep into his eyes. "In all my life, I have never been able to count on anything. It may take me a little time to get used to the notion."

Luke laughed then. "Dear Mary, it was notions that brought us together!"

"Aunt Luella Wainwright's Notions," she said. He heard the wonder in her voice. "I was so desperate that day." She clapped her hands. "I kept that help wanted placard because I want to remember the scene I drew on the back of it."

"We'll frame it."

"That, my dearest Luke Wainwright, is an excellent notion."

About the Author

USA Today best-selling author Carla Kelly is the author of forty-six novels and three non-fiction works, and numerous short stories. She is the recipient of two RITA Awards from Romance Writers of America for Best Regency of the Year; two Spur Awards from Western Writers of America; three Whitney Awards from Storymakers; and a Career Achievement Award from *Romantic Times*.

Carla's interest in historical fiction is a byproduct of her scholar's study of history. Her variety of jobs include medical public relations work, feature writer and columnist for a North Dakota daily newspaper, and ranger in the National Park Service at Fort Laramie National Historic Site and Fort Union Trading Post National Historic Site. She has done contract research for the North Dakota Historical Society.

Interest in the Napoleonic Wars led to novels about the Royal Navy Channel Fleet, as well as the British Army in Spain. Carla has also written novels set in Wyoming in the late nineteenth and early twentieth centuries. She has also written about World War II on the home front. Her books have been translated into numerous languages.

Printed in the USA
CPSIA information can be obtained
at www.ICGtesting.com
CBHW011911140924
14363CB00016B/423